MURDER
SKY HIGH

*Detectives crack the mystery of
a deadly cargo*

LINDA HAGAN

THE
BOOK
FOLKS

Published by The Book Folks

London, 2021

© Linda Hagan

ISBN 978-1-913516-75-8

www.thebookfolks.com

Murder Sky High is the second novel in a series of standalone murder mysteries set in Belfast and beyond. Details about the other books can be found at the end of this one.

Chapter 1

The note of the twin turbofan engines changed as the plane began its gentle descent into Belfast City Airport. Some of the passengers, first-timers in Northern Ireland, looked out of their windows with varying degrees of interest and excitement as the aircraft followed the line of Belfast Lough snaking its way to the sea. They watched the tapestry of green fields set out below them, the islands peeping out of the distant waters of Strangford Lough, County Down looking its best in the weak February sun before quickly giving way to the urban sprawl of Belfast. Others, the seasoned business travellers, began gathering their belongings together, aware that they would soon be arriving at George Best Airport and wanting to make a quick escape.

In row 24 seat A, there was no movement. The passenger lay back, eyes closed, legs stretched out before him. The middle-aged man, grey of suit and grey of face, had been silent throughout the flight. His nearest neighbour, a lanky twenty-something in jeans and sweatshirt with a beanie hat covering his fair hair, had had his back turned to him for most of the flight. He was busy talking to his girlfriend across the aisle. The two had eyes only for each other. As the seatbelt warning sign pinged and the cabin staff began to gather up rubbish into black plastic bags and ensure overhead lockers were tightly closed for landing, he stood up and knocked against his slumbering neighbour.

'Sorry, mate.'

The man didn't respond. He couldn't. He was dead.

Chapter 2

Chief Inspector Gawn Girvin slowly opened her eyes and took a moment to register where she was. This morning it was her own bed. Since she had got together with Sebastian York they had played what he had dubbed 'bed ping pong'. Unable to decide where and how they would live together, they both still asserted that they wanted to. He was keen that she move in with him. His house was bigger with a spare bedroom he could keep as his study where he did his writing. Her two-bed apartment would never be able to cope with his collection of books. And anyhow, he argued, Ballyhackamore was a livelier spot, only a short glider ride from the city centre or a quick car journey to his work at the university or Police Headquarters. She didn't want to tell him that living there would remind her too much of how they had met and her ordeal with a serial killer.

Instead she made excuses to him but sometimes she wondered if she was really making excuses to herself. After all, if his home reminded her of those experiences, her apartment should do so even more. Instead of making any decision, she kept her apartment in the loughside town of Carrickfergus under the looming grey presence of the medieval castle and he stayed on in Belfast. It was satisfactory, most of the time, but sometimes Gawn wondered if their inability to decide on a home together signalled a deeper issue about commitment and about the prospects for their long-term relationship.

She looked across at this man who had come so quickly to mean so much to her. A strand of his hair had fallen over his eye and his mouth was slightly open. He looked like a toddler exhausted after a day of mayhem at the nursery and sometimes she felt that was like his life. She loved him. No one could have been more surprised than she was to realise that very soon after they had first met. But he was unpredictable. She sometimes felt like a responsible adult trying to keep an errant child in line. Her job demanded she be serious and steady, not capricious and impulsive. Sometimes his surprises were wonderful like the romantic trip to New York he had arranged for them just before Christmas. But he didn't seem to really understand her commitment to her work and its demands.

They had had their first serious argument when she had forgotten to call and let him know she was busy and would not be able to get to dinner at his house after he had spent all afternoon creating a very special meal for them. She had been apologetic the next morning when she remembered to phone him after working eighteen hours straight. She thought she'd done well taking the time to ring rather than simply collapsing into bed exhausted, but he didn't seem to appreciate that and only responded like a petulant teenager. Of course, she didn't realise he had intended to ask her to marry him that night and had had the ring ready to produce. She still didn't know.

She glanced at her watch and slipped out of bed, not wanting to wake him. She had barely made it across the room when her mobile started ringing and she darted back to snatch it off the bedside table.

'Sorry to bother you at home, ma'am, on your day off.' It was the voice of her new sergeant, Michael Harris.

'What is it?' Her voice was serious, unwelcoming. She didn't want to encourage him to think he could phone her at home all the time. He needed to show initiative.

'There's been a body found on a plane at City Airport. The Super wants us to take over from Uniform.'

She didn't hesitate. It was not that she was jumping to an order from her superior. Rather, she was excited to be involved in a new case. That flutter of not knowing what lay ahead, the thrill of the chase was her drug of choice nowadays.

'I'll be in the office, in…' She glanced down at her watch and made a quick calculation. 'Give me an hour. Be ready to leave with me.'

'Yes, ma'am.'

She practically ran into the shower. An hour was going to be an ask. No time to waste.

'Gawn?' Seb's sleepy voice sounded plaintively from the bedroom.

'Go back to sleep. I've had a call-out. I'll see you later.'

He would have to be content with that. No time to go into explanations or discussions or for another row. They seemed to be arguing more frequently lately but she couldn't take time to think about that now.

He didn't respond and she could imagine what he had been planning for their day together and how disappointed he would be. But, for her, duty would always come first. He needed to get used to that or this relationship just wasn't going anywhere.

Chapter 3

The officers on the Serious Crime Squad team that Gawn led were surprised to see her when she appeared at the door. That much was obvious. Harris hadn't told them she was coming. Billy Logan, a veteran detective who was heading towards retirement, was lounging over his computer screen and hastily shut the page when she approached, but not before she had seen what he was looking at – the latest football news. Jamie Grant, the baby of the squad, was sitting with his feet up on the desk and almost fell off his seat in his haste to get them down onto the floor. Gawn was not impressed if this was how her new sergeant, Michael Harris, ran things while she was away.

'OK, you lot. Listen up.' Harris barked out the words as he entered the room behind her. Suddenly realising she was there, he hastily came to a halt and, looking extremely flustered, managed to say, 'Sorry, ma'am, I wasn't expecting you so soon.'

'That much is obvious, Sergeant.' She had made better time than she had expected. The traffic hadn't been too heavy and she was ahead of schedule.

His face flushed an even brighter red. He had been so delighted to be given the opportunity to work with Serious Crimes and become a real detective, as he had told his friends. He had waited for quite a long time since passing his sergeants' exams but he felt it was worth waiting for. Her team, and especially the chief inspector herself, had quite a reputation in the PSNI. He knew she wasn't popular with all her colleagues but that didn't seem to worry her. Now, for her to find some of her team – there was no other word for it – seemingly skiving off under his command was devastating for the young man.

'I take it not a lot has been happening.' She raised her eyebrow in query as her look swept the room.

Everyone else's head was down. They were hunched over their desks, clearly trying not to catch her eye. Harris had no such luxury. The question had been directed to him.

'Well, ma'am, not too much. Not until now. We were just ticking over, finishing off odds and ends. Jack's away giving evidence in the Bingham case today and Erin's working with the tech boys to see if we can retrieve

Montgomery's emails. Everybody else has just been finishing up work. But we've just had that call now about the body at City Airport. The coroner's requested an investigation and the Super wants us for it.' His words came out in a rush, an indication of his nervousness around his new boss.

'That'll make us popular with someone.' She didn't really care if she was popular or not. She never did. A case was a case, the more challenging the better. 'Right, Sergeant, you and I had better head down to the airport and see what's what.' She raised her voice enough to be heard throughout the room. 'The rest of you, get your "finishing off" finished. You'll be busy soon enough.'

* * *

Two police cars parked in a chevron formation blocked entry to the dual carriageway at the beginning of the Sydenham Bypass and two bored-looking officers were directing traffic, sending cars round onto other roads. As Gawn drove slowly up to one of the officers, she could see him preparing himself to respond to yet another silly woman asking what was wrong or demanding to be let through to get to her flight. He moved closer signalling to her to wind the window down.

'Sorry, I'm afraid you can't use the bypass this morning, madam. You'll have to take the Newtownards Road instead.'

Gawn lowered her car window a little further and held up her warrant card without speaking. She didn't need to. His response was immediate.

'Sorry, ma'am.' He quickly turned away and signalled for one of the police cars to be moved so she could drive through.

She waved in thanks to the officer manoeuvring his car out of her way. Harris hadn't travelled with his new boss before. One thing he had found a little disconcerting about their journey was that she didn't seem to go in for very much casual conversation. It seemed she wasn't one for small talk. He wondered if she was still annoyed at finding the office not exactly a hive of activity and angry with him for not cracking the whip and getting the others working flat out.

She pulled her car into the taxi waiting area directly in front of the main doors. Another uniformed officer, sub-machine gun slung across his body, was just about to tell them to move on when Gawn got out of the car and it was obvious that he recognised her. He merely nodded his head in acknowledgement and moved back to where he had been standing guard.

She walked through the automatic doors with Harris following closely behind her. Inside was thronged with travellers, most of them with luggage. This would normally be a busy time of day – first flights in and out of the airport; the business travellers clutching briefcases and newspapers heading into the city for meetings, the little family groups and couples excitedly waiting for their early holidays to begin. Those who had been lucky enough to arrive before the discovery of the body would be safely away, perhaps even unaware that anything had happened. But those wanting to get away were now sitting disgruntled waiting for news. There would be all kinds of rumours circulating and the sight of uniformed police officers would add to the speculation.

It was obvious the discovery of the body had caused major headaches for the airport staff. The two help desks had long queues; the check-in desks were unmanned. Overhead signs indicated indefinite delays to every flight leaving although one flight from Tenerife had just landed. Prospective passengers with their luggage gathered all around them were filling what few seats there were. A large group of excited primary school pupils identified by their school-logoed sweatshirts, accompanied by a trio of stressed-looking teachers, was sitting on the floor right in the centre of the concourse. Other hopeful travellers were perched uncomfortably on top of their suitcases or standing around them in huddles like groups at a campfire. The little café area, never designed to deal with such numbers, was packed and two harassed baristas were working hard to keep up with demand. There was a buzz of noise and some angry voices raised in complaint. Gawn caught the eye of someone she knew on the far side of the concourse and strode across to him.

'I wondered who they would send to take over.'

'Good morning, Paul.' Gawn smiled in greeting. She knew Inspector Paul Maxwell only too well. He had been her sergeant until just a few months ago but had moved to the local station and back into uniform when he got his promotion. Their paths had not crossed again professionally until today.

'Good morning, Chief Inspector.' He smiled too. He wasn't exactly glad that someone was taking over but if it had to happen then he was glad it was Gawn.

'Paul, this is Michael Harris, my new sergeant.' Her eyes twinkled as she continued, 'And this is Inspector Paul Maxwell, my former sergeant.'

The two men shook hands, sizing each other up. Harris was a few inches shorter than Maxwell but he had a rugby forward's build – short and stocky with wide shoulders. His bulging biceps filled the arms of his suit jacket. Maxwell's slim build and open friendly face were a contrast and he couldn't help wondering how this new man would get on with Gawn and, more interestingly, how she would get on with him.

'We'll have to get together and compare notes sometime, Sergeant,' Maxwell suggested.

'Like hell you will. Now, Inspector, bring us up to speed.'

'Right, ma'am. The 9am KLM arrival from Amsterdam landed on time and when the passengers started to disembark, the cabin crew found what they initially thought was an unconscious passenger. They assumed he had simply taken ill but then they quickly realised they had a corpse on their hands and no indication of how he'd died. They immediately notified the control tower and kept the rest of the passengers on board until they could verify what had happened.'

Succinct. She had taught him well.

'So all the passengers are still on board?'

'No. They were getting a bit obstreperous by the time I got here and forensics and the pathologist needed space to work, so we disembarked them and they're being held in a separate area. My men have started interviewing them and checking their details.'

'OK. Good work, Paul. Who is our corpse then? I presume identification would have been straightforward between the passenger list and his passport,' Gawn asked.

'His name is Willem de Bek. He's a Dutch businessman. He was booked on a return flight this evening to Heathrow. He had his ticket in his pocket. So he was obviously over for just a short visit, a business meeting most likely, but there's no indication where or with whom.'

'Can we take a look at the scene?'

'Of course, boss.' The words were out of his mouth without thinking.

'Old habits die hard, eh, Paul?'

'Sorry, ma'am.' He was embarrassed to have reverted to the role of Gawn's sidekick in front of Harris.

He led them through security, with the civilian searchers and baggage handlers standing around, hands in pockets, looking unsure what they should be doing. The three were aware that they were being watched as they walked past. Rather than taking the passenger route to the plane, Maxwell led them through a set of doors marked 'Airport Personnel Only'. This was obviously a working area, no oversized tourist posters and trendy decor here, just scuffed plain white walls and utilitarian flooring to take the heavy baggage traffic of a busy airport. After a short walk down a corridor they found themselves heading outside. The plane was on its stand.

The three climbed the steps, Maxwell leading the way.

Gawn immediately got that claustrophobic feeling from the inside of the plane. It was smaller than she liked to travel in, preferring something more the size of a transatlantic Airbus. Here, two seats either side of a narrow aisle left her feeling hemmed in. Two burly SOCOs filled the back of the plane, meaning the three officers could only reach part of the way to the corpse. Another white-suited figure was leaning over the body blocking out their view. When it turned, Gawn saw a face she didn't recognise.

Maxwell whispered to her, 'The new locum pathologist, Dr Jennifer Norris. Munroe's on a sabbatical and she's the duty pathologist today.' Al Munroe was the Chief State Pathologist and their paths had crossed a few times.

'Good morning there, folks. How y'all doing?' Norris' cheery welcome sounded out of place.

Dr Norris was, Gawn judged, about mid-forties although well-preserved for her age. A wisp of blond hair had escaped from her coverall and she hastily pushed it back. She was slightly built with a thin waistline, a tanned complexion from what Gawn could see of her face, and those big baby blue eyes so beloved of men of a certain age. Her voice had a faint American twang.

'Good morning, doctor. I'm DCI Gawn Girvin and this is my sergeant. Do we have something to investigate here or is this just natural causes?'

'It's a sudden unexplained death, Chief Inspector, and I need to have a closer look before I can go certifying the cause. I don't know this guy's medical history so he could have had high blood pressure or a heart condition. Any number of things could have caused his death. From what I can see here, there's no obvious trauma, no wounds, no bleeding. But I'm a little suspicious of a slight split, I guess you'd call it, on the arm of his jacket which could have been caused by a needle or stiletto or some other very fine object. Maybe he just caught his jacket on something, but it doesn't look exactly like a tear. Until I get him back onto my table and out of his clothes where I can examine him properly, I don't know what caused it.'

'You think someone stabbed him?' Harris' voice was sceptical. He didn't see the smartly dressed, middle-aged man slumped in the aircraft seat as a typical target for a murder, especially a dramatic murder on a plane. It reminded him of something Agatha Christie might have written.

'I'm not suggesting anything. That's your job, not mine. But there's no blood externally on the clothes, so probably not.'

'But you're not prepared to call this natural causes?' Gawn asked.

'No, I can't. Not yet. I need to take a closer look and run tox screens.'

Gawn thought the new doctor might simply be being overcautious, not wanting to miss something, but her thoroughness and her willingness to pursue answers to her concerns was something Gawn could relate to. Better to take the time and get it right.

'If I can get his medical details and it turns out he had an ongoing serious health condition that he was being treated for and I can examine any marks on the body and rule them out then I'll certify natural causes. Otherwise you just need to let me do my job.'

'Of course, doctor. We'll get details from all the other passengers and we'll join you at the PM to see if we need to follow up.'

'Fine. My schedule's clear tomorrow – so far anyway,' she added. 'I'll talk to his doctor, if I can, and, if not, or he didn't have any health issues, then I'll do the autopsy tomorrow afternoon. But the tox screens will take a few days. Is 3pm OK for you?'

'Yes.' Gawn noted the doctor's use of the American term 'autopsy' and wondered what other different attitudes and approaches she might bring to her work. Munroe was a good pathologist, careful and meticulous in every detail but sometimes infuriatingly slow and pedantic.

Gawn swung round, surprising her sergeant who was standing tightly behind her in the narrow aisle. He seemed to be unsure whether he should turn and walk out in front of her or step aside into a seat and let her pass. He did the latter. When they reached the fresh air again and Harris had gone to get a passenger list from the airline desk, Maxwell turned to his former boss.

'You have him terrified.'

Her face furrowed.

'Do I?'

'You know you do. The same way you had me at first. Give him a break, Gawn. He'll be doing his best, you know. It's not easy getting up to speed, especially your speed.' He smiled, that little boy smile he had tried to employ with her in the past. Sometimes successfully, mostly not.

Maxwell's advice drew a smile onto Gawn's face. Before they could say anything more, the sergeant was back.

'Have we got a seating plan?' Gawn directed this question to both men.

'Yes. My men put one together. Here.'

Maxwell produced an A4 sheet of paper from the leather folder he had been carrying. Gawn smiled at the sight of it. She had bought him the folder on his promotion to inspector and had it engraved with his initials. The paper he was holding out to her was a photocopy of a seating plan with the names of the passengers neatly marked beside each seat in pencil.

'Here's where de Bek was sitting.' He indicated a window seat near the back of the plane. 'The passenger next to him was David Smith. Then in the two seats behind them were Paul Vanhoeven and William Andrews. Lots of individual travellers on the flight. It's too early for much holiday traffic so they're mostly businessmen. Except Smith. He and his girlfriend, she was sitting here.' Maxwell indicated a seat across the aisle. 'They're here on holiday.'

'Nobody in the two seats in front of him?'

'No. The flight wasn't full today.'

As Maxwell finished speaking, a voice from behind chirped in.

'Excuse me, folks.' Dr Norris passed between them carrying her heavy leather bag. 'See you at three tomorrow, Chief Inspector.'

She smiled a friendly smile at them as she passed. She took half a dozen steps then paused and the three watched as the white-garbed doctor released her hair from the hood of the forensics suit and shook her head to free it. Then she walked briskly across the tarmac to the main building where she disappeared from their view. Gawn had the distinct impression the new woman had known she was being watched and had enjoyed it.

'Have you come across her before, Paul?'

'Yes. I have. Just last week actually. Munroe brought her to the station to introduce her. They were doing some kind of tour, some sort of induction programme they've developed to improve communication between us and them.' He held up his hands and mimicked speech marks, smirking at the idea of communicating with the pathologists.

'What did you think of her?' Gawn was trying to form her own first impressions of their new colleague. There had been quite a few changes recently and she was trying to come to terms with them all.

'She seemed fine. She seems a bit more approachable than the others, I think. Bit more normal. And friendly enough.'

'Where'd she come from?'

'Ah, now that's interesting.' Maxwell's voice became more animated. 'She was with the Medical Examiner's Office in Boston.'

Gawn was pleased that her ear had picked up the flat Bostonian vowels.

'But her accent's mostly from here.'

'Yes. Originally. She's a bit like yourself, she was in London for a couple of years and then the US but she's from Northern Ireland.'

Gawn always liked to know who she was working with. It might seem that she didn't know much about her colleagues – she didn't spend time chatting with them about their families for instance – but in fact she knew a lot. She knew that her new sergeant still lived at home with his parents and that his mother had MS. She thought the fact that he wasn't married and didn't have the responsibility of children would mean he could commit more time to his work without problems. Kerri, Maxwell's wife, had always nagged him about the time commitment Gawn expected of him.

'Right, let's go and speak to these people and get them on their way. We don't want to waste any more of their time.'

Her voice made it clear, she felt she was wasting her time here.

Chapter 4

They walked back into the building and made their way to the room where the passengers had been sequestered. There were about twenty people still there. Some were sitting in bored-looking or agitated clumps around the wall. A few were seated at tables facing police constables.

As each conversation finished, the passengers were escorted out of the room to collect their luggage.

Maxwell pointed to three men and a young woman seated along the wall in the far corner of the room. Two of the men were older. One was sitting looking over papers as if he couldn't take time away from his work. The other sat looking around the room, watching what was going on, his eyes darting from group to group. She thought he looked a little furtive but then decided that was probably only her imagination. While Gawn watched, his hand went to his coat pocket and brought out a small white paper bag. After careful examination of its contents, he extracted something and popped it into his mouth. She noticed he didn't offer to share with anyone.

The two others who had been separated out were both in their early twenties. The man was tall and slim. Even though he was sitting down, the length of his legs in his skin-tight jeans showed he would be well over six feet tall. His companion was short, not just in comparison. Gawn reckoned she wouldn't be much over five feet tall. Her feet barely touched the floor from her sitting position. She could pass for a schoolgirl, Gawn thought. Her slim waist and heavy bosom reminded her of a character from the *Carry On* films that her father had loved so much. She had always found it strange that such a straight-laced almost puritanical man could revel in such ribald comedy.

'That's the three men who were closest to de Bek and one girlfriend who wouldn't be separated.'

'OK. We'll have a word with them then.'

Maxwell held back while Gawn walked across the room aware of eyes watching her. She could read degrees of annoyance and unease among the people still waiting to be interviewed.

'Shall we make it ladies first?' she asked the group.

'Lady' might be stretching it a bit. 'Girl' for a start. And the way she was poured into her jeans and threatening to burst out of her blouse suggested anything but lady. Gawn felt old, not for the first time. Recently it was happening more often as she realised how out of fashion and out of touch she was becoming. She didn't really know why she had said 'ladies first'. As a rule, she didn't think women deserved any special favours. She had only ever sought equality for herself, not preferential treatment.

A deeply tanned man of about fifty with a goatee beard and a receding hairline of wispy fair hair, dressed rather as de Bek had been in the businessman's uniform of suit and tie, stood up. The light glinted off his blue-tinted spectacles, momentarily hiding his eyes. Gawn thought his skin looked leathery but he didn't have the appearance of a man used to working outside.

'Look, we've all been held up. I had an important meeting this morning in Belfast. I want to cooperate with the police, of course I do, but I need to get to my meeting.'

It was on the tip of Gawn's tongue to tell him to sit down and wait when the female passenger spoke up.

'I'm only here because of Dave – my boyfriend.' She inclined her head towards the youngest of the three men and flashed him a smile. 'I wasn't anywhere near your dead man. I don't mind waiting.'

'Thank you, Miss?' Gawn waited for an answer.

'Robson. Mandy Robson.'

'Miss Robson. Thank you. I'll speak to you first then, sir.' She turned to the belligerent little man. 'Shall we go over here?'

Gawn realised that although she was thinking of him as a little man, in fact he was not that much shorter than she was. Rather, it was more to do with the way he held his body, his shoulders hunched up, his stooped stance with his stomach overflowing the waistband of his trousers and his agitated demeanour, that made him seem smaller. She led the way to a table set well away from everyone else. Harris joined her and the two sat down on one side facing the passenger.

It was Harris who started the questioning. He already had his notebook at the ready.

'Name, please?'

'Paul Vanhoeven. They've already asked me that.' Annoyance sounded in his answer.

'May we see your passport, please, Mr Vanhoeven?' Gawn asked and held out her hand.

Her eyes displayed some surprise when he handed her a green passport which she immediately recognised as South African. The leathery skin made sense to her now. The hot African sun. Of course. She scanned the pages, then handed the document to Harris so he could record the man's details.

'And what brings you to Northern Ireland, sir?'

'I have a meeting at the university. My company sponsors certain research activities and I visit twice a year for updates.'

'So it's not your first time here then, sir?' Harris inquired, handing the passport back to its owner.

'No. Not at all. I've been here four or five times.' His impatience to get away was clear. Understandable if he was missing his meeting but not endearing when a man had lost his life.

'You don't have a South African accent.' It was a statement but really a question Gawn was posing.

'I'm a South African citizen but I was born in the Netherlands and still have family there. That's why I was flying from Amsterdam. I'd been visiting my brother and his wife for a few days. But I've lived all over the world so I don't have much of an accent, I guess. Look, is all this really relevant? I was sitting behind your dead man. And I wasn't even directly behind him. I didn't speak to him. I didn't see anything. I can't tell you anything.'

He seemed very definite and, until they were sure they had a crime to investigate, Gawn didn't want to push too hard.

'Are you staying in Belfast, sir?' she asked.

'I'll be here until Thursday. If you need to contact me, I'm staying at the Europa Hotel.'

'Yes, we know where that is.'

Vanhoeven stood up and so did Gawn. She seemed to tower over him.

'Thank you.'

They shook hands. Her immediate impression was of flabby hands that had never done any manual work. Pen-pusher's hands as her father had called them. As Harris escorted Vanhoeven to the door, Gawn turned her attention to the other two men. She decided to leave Smith until last. He had been beside de Bek. He was the one who was most likely to be able to provide some information to help them work out what had happened. When Harris returned she sent him to bring their other witness across.

'This is Bill Andrews, ma'am.'

Andrews was a ruddy-faced man with dark wavy hair which was just showing its first signs of greying at the temples. He had the look of someone used to spending his time outdoors. Dressed today in a suit, he looked uncomfortable in it and his tie was loosened at the neck as if it had been choking him. And perhaps it had been. His neck was huge. It immediately made her think of the Russian weightlifters she had seen at the Olympics on television. He dragged a small overnight bag on wheels behind him and, draped over it, was a heavy gabardine coat from which he had extracted the bag of sweets earlier. His expression was friendly but nervous, which could just be an indication that he was not used to dealing with the police.

'Mr Andrews. I'm DCI Girvin. Thank you for waiting.'

'Didn't think I had any choice.' It was said more in good humour than anger. He was not being aggressive. 'Poor man, dying like that. Doesn't bear thinking about.' He seemed genuinely upset. Perhaps it had something to do with being approximately the same age as the deceased.

'I see from the passenger list you're British.'

'Yes. Born and bred in County Down. I live outside Banbridge.'

'And you were in the Netherlands for…' She left the sentence hanging for him to finish.

'Business. I'm a farmer. I was visiting a farm there and looking at some cattle.'

'What can you tell us about Mr de Bek?'

'Is that his name? I only passed the time of day with him when we first got on the plane. He was already in his seat. I was getting myself comfortable behind him. I lent on the back of his seat to get past my neighbour. There's not a lot of room in these wee planes for a man my size, you know.' He patted his stomach. 'I excused myself and tried to make a bit of conversation about the weather and the flight. Something about hoping it wouldn't be too bumpy with the wind but he didn't really answer me back. He seemed to be half asleep. He just nodded at me. And that's it really. I didn't speak to him again.'

Gawn thought the farmer a little garrulous. She didn't think he could add too much to their knowledge of what had led to the man's death, if indeed anything other than high cholesterol or a dicky heart had caused it. She was becoming more sure they were wasting their time.

'Thank you, Mr Andrews. Leave your contact details with my sergeant just in case we need to get in touch.'

Once again, they shook hands and Harris escorted him out. Just David Smith left to talk to, and his girlfriend of course. It wasn't looking like there would be much of a case to investigate. The poor man had just died, probably of a heart attack. Without being asked to, Harris brought both the lanky young man who had been seated beside de Bek and his girlfriend across to her. He pulled up an extra chair for the girl. When they were all seated and Smith had stowed his heavy backpack under the table, Gawn began to question the Australian, as she saw from his passport.

'Mr Smith, what, if anything, can you tell me about Mr de Bek?'

She sat back in her chair, not really expecting that he would have too much to add to their meagre information.

'He was already in his seat when we got there.' He glanced across nervously at the girl to include her in his response and she nodded in agreement. Gawn noticed his habit of pulling his sleeves down over his hands so that they were ripped at the cuffs and only the tips of his fingers peeked out from the sweatshirt material. 'It was a real bummer. We hadn't been able to book seats together and we'd hoped that whoever was in that seat would swap with Mandy but he was already out of it when I tried to ask him. Then the guy beside Mandy wouldn't swap either and the cabin crew wouldn't let us move to another row although there were plenty of empty seats. We spent most of the flight talking across the aisle so I had my back to him. Most of the time.'

'What do you mean he was out of it?' Gawn jumped on the comment.

'He was asleep when you first saw him?' Harris spoke at almost the same time. He glanced across, fearful that she would be annoyed at his interjection.

'Yeah. Sort of. Not one hundred percent maybe, but he wasn't gonna talk to me anyway.'

'Did you speak to him again at any time during the flight, sir?'

Smith smiled across at his girlfriend. 'I was otherwise engaged most of the time, if you know what I mean.' He looked directly at Harris not quite with a wink but near to it.

'You did speak to him once, Dave, remember? You said he sort of moaned or something.'

'Oh yeah, that's right. Maybe about ten minutes before we landed I wanted to put something away into my bag in the overhead locker and I knocked against him when I was reaching up. I said sorry but he only kind of moaned at me. I noticed that he seemed to be sweating a lot and drooling. It was hot so I didn't think too much about it and like, old guys like that do sweat and drool, don't they?'

Both Harris and Gawn wondered what age Smith would regard as 'old'. To anyone his age, twenty-two according to his passport, anything over fifty would be ancient.

'And there's nothing else you noticed?' She looked closely at the Australian as he shook his head. 'Well, we may need to speak to you again, Mr Smith. How long are you staying in Northern Ireland?'

It was Mandy Robson who replied to Gawn's question.

'We'll be here for at least three months. Dave's goin' to meet my family and see a bit of the country.' Her accent was Derry moderated by Melbourne, Gawn reckoned.

'Thank you for your help. Both of you. Leave your contact details with the sergeant here. Enjoy your stay.'

While Harris walked them out, Maxwell walked across to his former boss.

'Anything useful, ma'am?'

'No joy. Unless you count the fact that the man was asleep and was sweating which might suggest he was ill, but we don't have anything definite and won't until Dr Norris is finished. It's probably all been a total waste of our time. Just down to our newbie pathologist being overly careful but it was good to see you, Paul.' She smiled broadly at him.

'You too, ma'am.'

He watched her walk away with her new sergeant following in her wake. He couldn't help thinking how Kerri had said he followed Gawn like a puppy. It wasn't true but for ten seconds he allowed himself to remember when that would have been him. He loved his new job and Kerri loved the extra money which was allowing them to move house and the fact that his hours were more predictable, but he couldn't totally ignore a little pang of regret not to be in the thick of investigations again alongside Gawn.

Chapter 5

The last time Gawn had visited the Regional Forensic Mortuary it had been to question the State Pathologist as a suspect in her serial killer investigation. She could remember the nerves in her stomach that day, the enormity of what was happening and how it could mean the end of his career, or hers even if he wasn't guilty. Today was very different. Harris was by her side this time, not Maxwell. She considered Maxwell's suggestion that she go easy on the new man and give him a chance. He should have known her well enough to realise that wasn't her way. Harris needed to understand what she expected of him and, if he didn't measure up, he needed to know that too. It wouldn't be doing him any favours to let him get used to being sloppy.

As they approached the examination room they were surprised to hear music. Gawn immediately recognised it. Billy Joel belting out *We Didn't Start the Fire*. They suited up before entering the room. The music increased in volume when they opened the door. Dr Norris seemed to have already started even though they were on time, one of Gawn's character quirks. She hated being late for anything.

Dressed in a long green gown and white boots, the pathologist was standing, back to the door, over the body which was partially uncovered and lying on a cold steel slab, the middle of three in the room. The others were empty. Bright light flooded down onto the body. The pathologist hadn't heard them coming in over the noise of the music and only became aware of their presence when they entered her peripheral vision. She immediately switched the music off looking guilty.

'Sorry. I don't know what the protocol is here but I always had music when I worked in Boston. The medical examiner didn't mind but I guess Dr Munroe might. But he's not here.' She smiled conspiratorially as she added the last phrase.

How the pathologist chose to do her work didn't really concern Gawn although she expected Munroe would have apoplexy when he found out. All she was worried about was that the work was accurate and preferably speedy.

'I didn't think we were late.'

'You aren't. I started a bit early. I undressed Mr de B and bagged his clothing for your forensics people. I'm just about to start the external examination now. I waited for you. You'll be pleased to know I kill the music at this point so I can record my findings. Judges don't tend to like a rock 'n' roll background when they listen to my evidence.' She smiled at them.

Gawn remembered Maxwell always complaining that the mortuary staff had a weird sense of humour. She had never thought they had any sense of humour at all but this one seemed like a lively sort. She would certainly bring some fresh thinking to the job. She speculated how Norris would get on with Munroe when he got back from his sabbatical and guessed there might be fireworks ahead.

'And I was right,' she continued. 'There's some indication of a mark on the upper right arm corresponding to the mark on his jacket. Not a knife. Too fine for that. Even for a stiletto. Probably a syringe. I could have missed it if I hadn't noticed his jacket.'

'You mean he was a junkie?' asked Harris.

'You guys must have really funny junkies here if they shoot up through their jackets.'

Harris blushed and Gawn interrupted, displeased with the doctor's sarcasm towards her officer. 'If not a junkie, what are you suggesting, doctor?' And she thought of the woman's comment from yesterday about not speculating.

'He may have been injected with something recently. But obviously not at your local doctor's surgery when it was through his coat. We'll have to wait for the tox report to know exactly what was injected. And even then, depending what it was and how long ago it happened, there may not be any traces left in the body.' The doctor sounded disappointed. Perhaps she was bored already with her move from Boston to much more parochial Belfast and was seeing mysteries where there were none.

'But I'm sending his clothing to forensics,' she added. 'There's a chance there may be some residue of whatever it was on his sleeve.'

Gawn wondered how Munroe and McDowell, her boss, would feel about financing speculative tests like this. She suspected it would never have happened if Munroe had been here though she liked to think he would have picked up on the mark on de Bek's arm. But she wasn't sure. She was beginning to think Norris was the kind of pathologist she could work with.

Dr Norris pulled back the covering on the body, fully revealing the corpse. Gawn was aware of a slight movement to her right. She glanced quickly across at Harris but he seemed OK. Meanwhile, Norris had been hunched over the body. She called on her assistant to help her turn the corpse over and then on his back again before she spoke.

'Other than that, the body is of a well-nourished fifty-five-year-old man. There are no distinguishing marks and no indication of any other external trauma. Inspector Maxwell was quick off the mark and got me de Bek's medical details from the Netherlands. He hadn't seen a doctor in the last six months and there was no indication of heart problems or high blood pressure or anything like that in his medical history or his family history either. He seemed to have been remarkably healthy, until he wasn't.

However, at his age, if he had a stressful job, it could have crept up on him or come out of the blue. But an examination of the heart and brain will tell us that. Our answers all lie inside the body.'

Gawn was pleased to hear about Maxwell's good work. She had been sure he would do well and wouldn't be surprised to see him make chief inspector before very long. Maybe someday she would be answering to him.

Dr Norris turned and addressed the two detectives.

'There are no other external marks on the body but with even just a quick look I've seen some damage to the rectal area. I'll need to examine the rectum and bowel more closely to know what might have caused it.'

'You think he was gay, doctor?' Harris asked.

'How would I know what his sexual proclivities were?' came the sharp reply.

Gawn was still enjoying the thought that Maxwell's career move seemed to be working out well for him when she noticed that Harris was beginning to look slightly green. His voice when he had been speaking to the doctor was slightly higher pitched than usual and now she watched as his eyes scanned the room trying to focus but avoiding to take in the equipment sitting ready for use – the saw, the electric drill, the metal dishes, the specimen jars. The pathologist was poised with her scalpel over the chest cavity ready to make the Y incision to give her access to the internal organs. Gawn didn't relish the prospect of having to try to catch her sergeant if he fainted or worse still accompany him to A&E if he injured himself.

'I think we'll leave you to it then, doctor. If anything shows up in the body, let me know. Otherwise we'll wait until you have all the test results back.' Gawn turned as she spoke, signalling Harris to follow her, which he seemed only too glad to do.

Once outside in the fresh air, the sergeant stood still, hands on hips, bent slightly forward and took several deep breaths. He looked abashed. A normal colour was beginning to return to his face. Gawn had walked ahead to her car ignoring him, and was sitting inside waiting, engine running. He ran across and jumped in beside her.

'Sorry, ma'am.'

She looked across at him. Her expression was not unkind. 'First time?'

He didn't speak, just nodded.

'It happens to the best of us. Next time you'll be better prepared.'

It had never happened to her. She had seen worse than a body sliced open neatly and respectfully by a pathologist. Her mind went to twisted and bloodied bodies, missing limbs, even missing heads. Men, women and small children, blown apart. Some of them, her friends. One of them, her lover.

Chapter 6

Seb had phoned several times over the previous three days. Each time she had rejected the call. She wasn't ready to speak to him; wasn't sure exactly what she was feeling and what they might end up saying to each other if they did speak. Better to put it off. Keep some space between them.

Eventually, by Thursday, when they were still waiting for de Bek's post-mortem results to come through, and she was trying to find any excuse to ignore the pile of reports which had been accumulating on her desk, Gawn decided she would follow up on finding out what the man had been doing coming to Northern Ireland. Then, if it did turn out that it was not a natural death, they would have a head start on the investigation. She was sitting at her desk waiting to hear back from the Politie with background on the dead businessman. The Dutch had notified de Bek's next-of-kin, his son. He was arriving in Belfast this morning to identify the body. Gawn had dispatched Harris to meet him and escort him to the mortuary. Not that there could be much doubt about the identification. All that would be left to do then was for the coroner to release the body to the family and he could be repatriated to the Netherlands for burial.

When her desk phone rang she expected an internal call but instead it was the switchboard.

'There's a Dr York on the phone for you, ma'am.'

Her thoughts had been elsewhere and she took a minute to react.

'Tell Dr York I'm busy at the minute and I'll call him back. I have his number,' she added.

She had no sooner put the receiver down, than it rang again.

'Chief Inspector.'

Gawn recognised the warm tones of Dr Norris, the pathologist. She wondered how the woman managed to sound so cheery doing what she did every day. Perhaps being around the dead all the time gave you a deeper appreciation of the joys of being alive, she thought.

'Dr Norris, I hope you have some good news for me.'

'It depends what you call good news, I guess. I'll email my full report as soon as I get off this call but I wanted to give you the dummy's guide first.'

Gawn drew her breath in sharply.

'Sorry, that sounded patronising.' Now the pathologist seemed a bit ruffled. 'I've been working with the same people in Boston for a while and they know me and they know my wacky sense of humour. I guess you don't and that could have come across as very rude. Apologies, Chief Inspector.'

'Apology accepted.'

'Bottom line, if you'll excuse the pun, Mr de B died of natural causes.'

Gawn wondered why the doctor seemed so upbeat if they had all just been wasting their time. She relaxed back into her chair feeling a bit deflated. She was dealing with no major cases at the minute. She had been hoping that de Bek's death would provide a bit of a challenge, something out of the ordinary.

'I was going to say, are you sure, but that would be rude to you. You know what you're doing.'

'Thanks for the vote of confidence.'

'What was the actual cause of death?'

'Myocardial infarction,' came the prompt reply.

'Heart attack? Wouldn't he have been feeling pretty ropey? He would have called for help, surely? Said something to somebody? The cabin crew or one of the passengers nearby? I've always imagined people collapsing and clutching their chest and all that sort of stuff.'

'You'd be amazed at the number of people who wait. They convince themselves it's something else. They've got bad indigestion. It was something they ate. Remember he was on a plane, heading to a foreign country. Maybe he couldn't speak English well.'

Gawn interrupted her.

'He could, I'm sure. Most Dutch are very competent English speakers and he was travelling for business.'

'OK, well maybe by the time he realised how bad it was it was too late but what I'm going to suggest might explain why he didn't want to cause a fuss and draw any attention to himself.'

Gawn sat up in her chair again and waited. Norris' timing was perfect. The pause was not too long but just enough to build a sense of expectancy.

'I examined his rectum and there were clear indications of damage.'

There was silence on the end of the line. The pathologist was obviously waiting for Gawn to pose a question.

'Do I want to know how? We're not talking about sexual assault, are we?'

'I think in this particular instance it's much more likely we're talking about smuggling.'

'Smuggling? Smuggling what?'

'It's impossible to say without at least some trace evidence and there wasn't any.' She sounded disappointed. 'But there was damage to the mucus membrane and when I've come across that before it was caused by drug smuggling.'

Gawn remembered hearing some of the Drugs Squad boys talking about catching smugglers at Heathrow who had inserted huge amounts of cocaine inside their body cavities.

'There's no other indication de Bek was involved with drugs?' Gawn questioned.

'No. No evidence of any drug-taking current or historic. He wasn't a user but he could have been a mule. I just offer the thought. And…' The doctor paused. 'I also asked forensics to have a look at his jacket. Remember I mentioned there was a tear or kinda rip in it?'

'Yes.'

'They found traces of propofol on the material,' she finished with a flourish.

'I'm afraid that doesn't mean a lot to me.'

'It's a short acting drug used in anaesthetics. Depending how much was injected it would have knocked him out very quickly and he wouldn't have remembered too much about it afterwards. Anaesthesiologists refer to it as milk of amnesia. It didn't turn up in his tox screen. I wouldn't expect it to unless he'd been injected just before his death. A single dose wears off within a couple of minutes and it would have been eliminated from the body within anywhere from two to twenty-four hours.'

Gawn wasn't sure exactly what all this meant.

'You're suggesting he was knocked out and then what?'

'Who knows? That's your domain, not mine. I give you the facts. It's your job to join the dots.'

'Could he have been injected on the plane and that caused his heart attack or prevented him trying to get help when he felt ill?'

'Probably not. I think there would still have been some traces in that case. More likely it was done sometime before then. Did you find a syringe on the plane?'

Gawn wasn't sure how hard they had looked. Reading the reports, she had seen no mention of finding anything like that. But then the passengers had never been searched. Someone could still have had the syringe on them even when she had been questioning them. Maybe they had all, herself included, being going through the motions assuming at the back of their minds they were wasting their time and the man had died of natural causes.

Being injected, possibly smuggling. She had no idea what it all meant. It all sounded crazy like a plot from a spy thriller. But she wasn't going to jump to any conclusions. On the plane, de Bek had looked like a very insignificant middle-aged businessman. Nothing to suggest anything criminal. They needed to hear back from the Dutch police urgently. De Bek may not have been murdered but if he was involved in smuggling then they needed to know what he was bringing into the country, or planning to bring in if this was a practice run, and who else was involved. If she couldn't find something definite quickly, McDowell would close the investigation down.

'Thank you, Dr Norris. You've certainly given me plenty to think about.'

'You're welcome. I just hope you appreciate that I had to put a rocket under your lab guys. If I hadn't kept at them, we probably wouldn't have had the results until next week.'

'Thank you again then.' Gawn meant it. With at least one of her prime witnesses leaving the country today and the victim's son arriving, these results were good timing.

'Is everyone around here so formal all the time?'

'I suppose we are a bit.' She hesitated and then added, 'I'm Gawn.'

'Jenny.'

'Yes, I know. Thank you, Jenny.'

Gawn wasn't used to pathologists who speculated about their victims or followed their hunches to prove a point. She hoped this new woman didn't see herself as some sort of Quincy. But her comments did open some interesting lines of enquiry for them. Had de Bek been smuggling? And if so, what? Drugs was the likely answer but she could imagine there might be other possibilities. They needed to get a full background on this man and find what he might have been involved with. Now it was becoming urgent. Three days had passed. Evidence would have been lost and witnesses could be dispersing to the four corners of the globe. Hell!

Gawn rang off quickly thanking Jenny again before she cut off the call. She needed to contact Harris urgently. With any luck he would still be at the mortuary with de Bek's son. They needed to speak to him straightaway.

After five rings, which saw Gawn's impatience rising, she heard Harris' voice on the line.

'Boss?'

'Sergeant. Are you still with Mr de Bek?'

'Yes, we're just waiting for him to identify his father's body.'

'When you're finished there, bring him straight here please. We need to speak to him.' She offered no further explanation.

Chapter 7

Nico de Bek was a younger version of his father; what his father might have been like about twenty years ago. Except his dress sense was very different. He was wearing a pair of tight jeans with their designer tears, a cowl-neck sweater in garish colours which didn't seem particularly appropriate attire for a death in the family and what Gawn thought was called a reefer jacket. The word reefer immediately reminded her of marijuana and Seb's silly T-shirt he wore around the house calling for it to be legalised. He thought it was amusing with her being a police officer – another sign of his schoolboy sense of humour. The Dutchman's dirty fair hair was tied back in a ponytail exposing an earlobe holding three colourful earrings adding to the gold stud she had already noticed in his eyebrow. As they shook hands she glanced down and noted the nicotine stains on the fingers of his right hand.

'Mr de Bek. Thank you for coming in to speak to us. Sorry for your loss. I know this is a difficult time for you.'

They were talking, not in an interview room but in a space normally reserved for victims of sexual assault or children involved in a crime. The chairs were leatherette-covered easy chairs rather than hard grey plastic but they had seen better days. One had a slash across the seat allowing grey stuffing to peek out. The centre of the room was dominated by a scratched wooden coffee table which bore the ring marks of teacups and glasses of juice accumulated over the years. The walls were painted in a pale green and there were floral curtains on the windows trying to inject a homely touch. Not exactly interior decor at its highest but better than a sparse, bleak interview room when you had just identified your father's dead body.

'Is there a problem? When can we get our father home?' He was holding his emotions in but it was clear he was in a distressed state. He couldn't keep his hands still. He rubbed his right thumb over the knuckles of his left hand in a nervous gesture. Gawn noticed a piercing in his tongue which gave his speech a slight lisp.

'Mr de Bek, I'm sorry to have to tell you but we believe your father may have been involved in criminal activity or the subject of some sort of assault.'

Gawn left it at that and watched carefully to judge the young Dutchman's reaction. She knew she was taking a bit of a stab in the dark here. If Nico de Bek denied absolutely that his father was involved in anything criminal she would be against a brick wall. She had no evidence, only supposition. An instant look of disbelief passed across his face. He opened his mouth to speak but no sound came out.

'Can I get you some water or a cup of tea, sir?' Harris asked. Because he hadn't had a chance to talk to his boss before the interview, the news that de Bek had been up to no good was new to him too.

'Can you think of anything your father might have been involved in? Any shady business deals?'

'Involved? What...' he started and then stopped, unable to get the words out.

'He had evidence of drugs on his body.' She didn't explain what kind, allowing him to jump to his own conclusions.

'My God, it all sounds like something out of a movie. My father wasn't a junkie. He loathed drugs. He would have had drug-pushers put away for life.'

De Bek reached into his jacket pocket and drew out a packet of cigarettes.

'I'm sorry, you can't smoke here, sir,' Gawn said, not unsympathetically.

Stuffing the packet back again, de Bek spoke. His voice was barely louder than a whisper.

'My father was a bookseller and antiquarian. He wasn't a drug addict or connected to any criminals.' After the briefest of pauses he added, 'Do you think he was murdered?'

It seemed like a big jump to make; a strange question to ask.

'Why do you ask that, Mr de Bek?'

'I don't know. My father was fit and healthy. I just thought when you told me about the drugs that maybe someone had killed him.'

It sounded like a bit of a flimsy reason and Gawn wondered if Nico was as surprised as he had seemed. Did he know more?

The young man looked stunned.

Although he hadn't responded to Harris' offer, when the sergeant came back and proffered some water, de Bek took it. His hand was shaking as he lifted the plastic cup to his mouth and some of the liquid spilled over the rim and fell on his lapel.

'Do you know what your father was doing in Belfast; who he was meeting?'

'I don't know any specifics about his work. I guess he was probably meeting someone to discuss the sale of a book or maybe delivering one to somebody. His boss would know.'

'Who did he work for?' Gawn didn't have this information yet. The Politie had been slow getting back to her.

'Antiquariaat Meyer. His boss is... was Gert Meyer.' The young man seemed to gather himself together and looked straight at Gawn. 'I need to phone my mother and my sister to let them know about Papa.'

Gawn would have liked to question the Dutchman further. She needed to try to get an angle on his father and what he might have been up to but she was mindful that the young man was in an emotional condition, maybe even in shock at the news of his father's death and she couldn't push too hard. She would leave it for now but not for too long.

'My sergeant will arrange a car to take you to your hotel but we may need to speak to you again before you leave.'

They all stood and Gawn extended her hand.

'Once again, our sympathies, Mr de Bek.'

He didn't reply, just acknowledged her comment with a nod of his head. Harris led him out of the room. And Gawn watched them go, thoughtfully. What had seemed like a straightforward case of natural causes and a jittery or overenthusiastic newbie pathologist could be something very different. De Bek may not have been murdered but there was something strange and, she added to herself, something criminal going on. She was getting more and more sure of it. She would need to speak to the Drugs Squad and see if they had any knowledge of the man or any whispers about drugs coming into the country from the Netherlands. But she didn't want to approach them directly. She knew what would happen then. They would sweep in and take over. She felt that familiar sense of expectancy at the start of a new case, the rush of adrenaline that she always got. Someone had once accused her of being an adrenaline junkie – she smiled at the thought.

Chapter 8

Gawn was in her office going over the forensics report from the plane when Harris returned.

'I just hope these boys did a thorough job.' She didn't usually criticise colleagues to others and especially to a new member of the team like Harris. She didn't know him well enough yet to know if she could trust him, if he was a team player.

'I've had a look at that report, ma'am. There was no mention of any drugs.'

'No. If anything had been hidden they would have found it. I'm sure of that. What worries me is that none of the passengers were searched. If de Bek didn't have any drugs on him, then he may have hidden them or passed them on to someone else.'

'We weren't sure we were even dealing with a crime then so there was no probable cause to search anyone,' he tried to reassure her. 'Are we even so sure now, ma'am?'

'Until we get information from the Politie we can't be sure about anything to do with drugs or smuggling. But what we do know, Michael, is that de Bek was meeting someone here. Whether it was about a book or about drugs or something else, we need to find out. Urgently. We've been wasting time.'

'What about de Bek himself? Couldn't we find out more about him ourselves without waiting for the Dutch?'

If they had been busy, she would probably have told him just to let it go, wait and see if the Dutch came up with something. Manpower and budgets were always stretched. But the truth was she had time on her hands. They had cleared their last big case and now she was facing a mound of paperwork and no excuse to ignore it.

They had been sitting on their hands for three days not sure if they had a crime to investigate or not and maybe they still weren't. They had waited for the Dutch authorities to get their finger out instead of putting pressure on them. It was easy to excuse it because it had seemed likely de Bek's death had been due to natural causes, which of course they now knew it was and there was no crime involved in it but something was alerting Gawn's senses. Maybe de Bek wasn't smuggling anything this time, but she felt there was something about the man and his trip to Belfast that meant trouble. Excusing their inaction and accepting it were two different things and Gawn was harder on herself than she was on anyone else. So, she was not going to excuse the fact that they knew no more about their dead man than his name and occupation. She was going to get something done about this as quickly as possible.

'We certainly should. I want you to contact the Dutch police again and hang on until you get some answers. Don't let them fob you off. Make a nuisance of yourself. And set the others on to background checks of our witnesses. We can't just take anything at face value. If de Bek had drugs with him, he didn't have them on him when he died. If it's possible that he passed them on to someone then we need to know more about potentially everyone on that plane but let's start with the ones closest to him. Let's see what we can find out for tomorrow. We'll have a briefing at ten in the morning. You can lead it.'

Harris was both pleased to be given this responsibility but also terrified. It was the first time he would have to do this in front of his new boss and he feared making a mess of it.

'I'm going to speak to Dr Norris again,' Gawn said.

When Harris didn't immediately stand up, she added, 'Well, what are you waiting for, Sergeant?'

Chapter 9

Gawn had phoned Jenny Norris' office only to be told she would be in a meeting until five. Hearing that, she decided to drive across and talk to the pathologist face to face. She was waiting, glancing distractedly through a magazine in reception at five o'clock when the doctor walked out of the corridor into the foyer. Gawn almost didn't recognise her. She was dressed in casual jeans and an Aran sweater. A pair of cowboy boots completed the look. The whole outfit made her look younger.

'Gawn. I didn't expect to see you again so soon. Is it me or are you here to see someone else?' Her surprise showed in her voice but her genuine pleasure showed in the toothy smile which extended across her face.

'You, I'm afraid, Jenny. I hope you don't mind me just showing up like this.' She knew Munroe liked everything done by the book. She would never have just dropped in on him with a query.

'Of course not. What can I do for you?'

'I should have asked you this morning when you phoned but you took me by surprise. Can you give me any indication of when de Bek might have been smuggling? I mean was it something recent, something long term? I suppose I'm asking, could he have had drugs inside him when he got on the plane?'

The woman took only a second to consider her answer.

'I wish I could tell you. The damaged tissue was quite recent but that doesn't mean he hadn't been using this means of smuggling for some time. He might just have been careless and injured himself. On the other hand it doesn't mean he wasn't smuggling on Monday. I suppose you've checked if he used the toilet on the plane.' She paused and waited for Gawn to reply.

'I don't think we asked about that directly. Everyone seemed to suggest he had been out of it, as one of the witnesses called it, more or less right away. But I suppose he could have gone through customs and security and then used the facilities in the airport and put anything he had inside him into his bag.'

'Did you find anything in his bag?'

'No.'

'Maybe he wasn't smuggling on this trip.'

A sudden thought seemed to strike the doctor.

'Look, instead of talking here, I've been promising myself a nice cold drink tonight after a long hard day. Why don't you join me and we could continue our conversation in more pleasant conditions?'

Gawn nearly dismissed the invitation out of hand. She was annoyed with herself. She didn't think she'd be good company. Anyway she hadn't ever really socialised much with colleagues and never with anyone outside her team. But then she asked herself, why not? A casual drink, a chat with a new colleague, it would put in an hour and help her delay phoning Seb, something which she had left so long, she was now dreading.

'OK. Thanks. Where do you suggest?'

'What about the John Hewitt? Do you know it?'

Gawn did.

'Then I'll see you down there.'

They parted and Gawn found herself unexpectedly buoyed up by the idea of a quiet drink with this interesting woman.

* * *

Thirty minutes later, after fighting her way through the evening traffic on the Westlink, Gawn found a parking space in Talbot Street just by the side of the cathedral. Her eye was attracted to the illuminated stainless-steel Spire of Hope on top of the grey Portland stone building, a building she had never been inside. As she approached the John Hewitt bar she could see people standing outside even though it was a chilly evening. She looked into the brightly lit interior and was dismayed to see how busy the bar already was. There would be no quiet chat, no talk about de Bek here. She spotted the doctor sitting near the window, at a table for two with a bottle of wine and two glasses already on the table in front of her.

'Sorry. I got caught up in traffic.'

'No problem. It gave me time to get the wine in. I hope that's alright. You're not a craft beer person or something, are you?'

'God, no.'

Jenny poured out two large helpings of the wine. 'Cheers!'

'Sláinte!' Gawn responded.

'I haven't been in here for years. I wonder what the food's like.'

'Pretty good I think.'

'I only had a fairly mediocre sandwich at lunchtime. You know, soggy tomatoes and limp lettuce.' Gawn noticed she still pronounced tomatoes the American way. 'I think I fancy something to eat. Would you like to join me?'

Weighing up the fact that when she got home she would be faced with an empty flat and an even emptier fridge and the prospect of having to phone Seb or staying here and enjoying a drink and meal with Jenny, there wasn't much of a decision to make.

'Why not? I didn't even manage a sandwich, just a biscuit with my morning coffee.'

They ordered some food and chatted over the hubbub all around them. They were pleasantly surprised when a duo appeared in a corner of the bar and started to sing a string of songs, some traditional ones they recognised and some new to them. The meal had been delivered to their table surprisingly speedily and both had tucked in enthusiastically. They'd finished the bottle of wine and Jenny was debating if they should order another.

'I won't have any more, thanks,' Gawn said. 'I'm driving and I don't want to end up being breathalysed.'

'That would really be something – new assistant medical examiner leads chief inspector astray.' She held up her hands as if she was holding up a newspaper and reading the headline on the front page. She laughed at the idea.

'I'm sure I wouldn't be the first you've led astray.'

Gawn caught a gleam in Jenny's eye and realised their conversation had sounded dangerously like flirting. It was then she suspected Jenny might have the wrong idea about her. If Gawn had got it wrong and was seeing signs that weren't there, then no harm done. She remembered how snappy Norris had been with Harris when he had commented about de Bek being gay. She decided she should make her situation clear so there could be no embarrassing misunderstanding.

'Anyhow, I have to phone my boyfriend when I get home and he wouldn't be too pleased if he thought I'd been out getting drunk with a friend.'

Jenny's expression changed. The sides of her mouth drooped a little. She looked serious.

'Very subtle, Gawn. When did you realise?'

'Just now. Sorry if I did or said anything to give you the wrong impression.' She liked this woman and didn't want to lose the prospect of a new friend.

'No harm done. I wasn't coming on to you. I like you and it doesn't worry me if you're straight so long as it doesn't worry you that I'm not. I was just hoping we could be friends.'

Gawn raised her glass with the dregs of the wine in it in a toast.

'Well, it doesn't. To our friendship then.'

'Friendship. Now tell me all about this man of yours. He must be something.'

Gawn laughed. 'Oh, he's something alright.' And she found herself telling Jenny all about how she and Seb had met and about her doubts about their relationship. It felt good to have someone to talk to and strange to find herself able to unburden her innermost concerns to someone who was still very much a stranger. Maybe that was what made it easier.

'I'm not the best person to be offering advice about relationships. Part of the reason I came back to Northern

Ireland was because I split up with my partner. Suzi and I had been together for five years.'

Gawn was about to commiserate with her, when Jenny continued.

'What I would say is this, Gawn. If you think he's right for you, nothing else should matter. Where to live isn't important. Being together is. If he makes your heart flutter and you feel like something's missing when he's not around, even if it's just his annoying habits that are what is missing, then hang on to him. That's my advice for what it's worth.'

Gawn was to remember that advice many times in the next few days.

Chapter 10

Friday morning and the Dutch police had eventually got back to them. Harris had information on de Bek. His voice gathered confidence as he addressed the group of men and women standing or sitting around the office. As de Bek's son had already told them, he was a bookseller. Although they had been told originally that de Bek had no criminal record, which was true, what they had also been told about him having no known involvement or association with any criminal activity was not. It appeared that the Dutch authorities had had their suspicions about Meyer's book business for some time and, as de Bek travelled all over Europe, suspicion had also fallen on him. It was suspected Meyer and therefore de Bek were part of a Europe-wide smuggling ring which primarily but not exclusively dealt in diamonds. The Dutch authorities had questioned Meyer and been told that de Bek had been in Belfast to meet with the director of the local museum about a possible arrangement to set up an exhibition of medieval Dutch books. He was going to be the go-between with the museum in Belfast and the museum in Amsterdam where they were normally housed. Harris seemed impressed that the books were valued at over a million euros. The Dutch suspected that he may have had other business in Belfast too but they could offer no help with what it was or who he might have been meeting.

'Did he have the books with him?' Gawn questioned her sergeant from her position leaning up against the door frame of her inner office wanting to let him take centre stage.

'No. Definitely not. They're still on display in Amsterdam.'

'So it wasn't a robbery then,' commented Grant, perched on the edge of Logan's desk.

'No. At least not of books. If he was carrying anything else, we don't know about it and neither do the Dutch.'

Gawn was looking thoughtful and Harris had the good sense to stand in silence and wait for her next question.

'Have we got a list of his belongings?'

It was Logan who withdrew a sheet of paper from a file he was holding on his knee.

'In his pockets was all the usual stuff, ma'am – some cash, not a lot, in euros, a fountain pen, a handkerchief, his wallet which contained more cash. This time in sterling. Credit cards and a photograph of a woman whom we assume is his wife. Though I suppose it could be his bit on the side.' Ever since Logan's wife had run off with his best friend, he brought a jaundiced view of life to his work. His comment drew no response from the room. They were all used to him. 'He was carrying his passport, of course, and he had a set of keys. That's all. Nothing out of the ordinary.'

'Car keys?'

'Yes. VW keys by the logo on the ring and also a couple of house keys.'

'What about his baggage?'

'He was booked on a flight out again on Monday evening so he only had carry-on luggage, a briefcase.'

'What was in it?'

'That's a bit curious, ma'am. There was a copy of the *de Volkskrant*.' Logan tripped over the foreign title. 'It's the morning paper in Amsterdam apparently. There were a couple of pens and a block of file paper.'

'Is that all?'

'Yes.'

'Why would you need a briefcase for that? Unless he was going to bring something back in it rather than bringing something to his meeting or he had already passed whatever was in it on to someone else,' she speculated aloud. 'I think our next move is to talk to the director at the museum. See if he can throw some light on this.'

'She, ma'am,' Harris corrected her.

'Right. She. Of course.' Funny that she had fallen into the trap of thinking the director would be a man. Never assume anything, she told herself. She nodded to Harris. 'With me, Sergeant.'

Chapter 11

Harris was told to get on his phone and google the Museum of Free Thought, where de Bek's books were on exhibition, so they had some background information before they talked to the museum director. He had read out various facts about the museum and its collections as Gawn drove along.

Memories flooded back as Gawn drove past the front gate of the museum, past the original neo-classical section of the building and eased her car into a tight space by the side of the busy Stranmillis Road next to the Botanic Gardens.

The two detectives approached the slightly forbidding-looking grey addition to the museum, its Brutalist style complete with cantilevered balconies a sharp contrast to the classical elegance of the original. Up the wide steps and through the glass doors, they entered a huge space, its central atrium rising up three storeys. Voices, especially children's excited voices, echoed through the space. Harris had phoned ahead to make sure the director was available to see them.

After identifying herself to the receptionist, Gawn chose to take the stairs rather than the elevator as she made her way to the director's office on the third floor. It gave her time to take in an overview of some of the exhibits in the galleries as she climbed the open stairway and to get a feel for the place. There was no sign that anything untoward had happened as far as the museum was concerned. It was just business as usual with families and a school group moving around the exhibits. And why shouldn't it be? They were not aware de Bek's death was anything other than an unfortunate incident. If it was, Gawn had to remind herself.

It was years since she'd been inside the building. She had happy memories of visits here when she was young. She wondered if they still had the Egyptian mummy, Takabuti, 'Belfast's Oldest Resident' as Belfast humour had dubbed her, hidden away somewhere. Seeing it had terrified her as a child.

When they reached the top floor, she found a smartly dressed woman of about her own age waiting for them.

'Dr O'Dowd?'

'Chief Inspector. Thank you for taking the time to come and see me in person. We're all still in a state of shock here about Mr de Bek. We've never had anything like this happen before and we've had some major exhibits on loan in the past.'

Anything like what? Gawn wondered. Did Dr O'Dowd know or suspect de Bek's death was not natural causes?

'Yes, I remember you had some Da Vinci cartoons recently.'

'Did you see the exhibition?'

'No. I'm afraid not. I was too busy.'

'Magnificent. Absolutely magnificent and of course a lot more valuable than these books are. Please sit down.'

She had led them into a corner office and signalled to them with a wave of her arm to take a seat. The room was plainly but functionally furnished and Gawn noted with approval the neat and organised workstation and shelves. Her eye fell on a photograph. She thought she recognised the man in it but couldn't think who he was.

'I see you're looking at one of my predecessors.'

'Sorry?'

'John Hewitt, the poet. He was a deputy director here in the 1930s and 40s.'

'How interesting. I had no idea.'

Gawn was struck by the coincidence that she and Jenny had chosen the bar named after this man for their 'quiet drink'. She saw the view over Friar's Bush cemetery from the large windows which let in the weak February sunshine today and thought this would be a pleasant place to work.

'How well did you know Mr de Bek?' Gawn asked.

The director looked at them quizzically. 'Oh, I didn't know him at all. I've never met him.'

Gawn was surprised to hear this. 'But he was coming to see you?'

'Yes. That's right. We'd arranged a preliminary meeting. I'd spoken to him on the phone. Once. But he said he preferred to do business in person and insisted on coming here and I was happy to accommodate that.'

'He insisted? So, it was all his idea and you were expecting him on Monday for that meeting?' Harris wanted to clarify what the arrangements had been. De Bek's insistence seemed to gel with their idea that he was coming to Belfast for some purpose other than just his meeting at the museum.

The director sat back in her chair and nodded.

'Yes. It's always easier to deal with someone directly, to be able to put a face with a voice on the end of a telephone line, but it's not always possible especially if you're dealing with a museum in the States or somewhere. So I was happy to have him come over, especially as it wasn't at our expense.'

'Was that unusual?'

'I think we'd have expected that it would be included in fees somewhere, but he insisted they were happy to pay all expenses.'

'And that was unusual?'

'What do you think, Chief Inspector? In this day and age, to have someone offer a service for nothing? Yes, it was a bit unusual, but I didn't think too much about it. We're just glad to get an interesting exhibit.'

'At what time were you expecting Mr de Bek?' Gawn moved the interview on but she had made a mental note that the meeting was definitely at de Bek's instigation. He had wanted to come to Belfast. They needed to find out why.

'He said his plane was arriving at eleven so we'd scheduled a meeting for twelve o'clock to give him plenty of time to get here from the airport, especially if the plane was delayed or anything, and then I was going to take him to a late lunch before he flew back later in the evening.'

The two detectives exchanged glances and Gawn's expression warned Harris to say nothing.

The mention of lunch had triggered a thought in the director's mind.

'Can I offer you some tea or coffee?' She half rose from her seat ready to arrange refreshments.

'No. Thank you. We're fine. What exactly are these books he was arranging about?'

Dr O'Dowd sat back down. This time she pushed her chair further back from her desk and crossed her legs. Her wraparound dress opened slightly to reveal her shapely tanned calves and part of her thigh, something which was not lost on Harris.

'Of course. It's not my area of expertise. I'm an art historian, but I visited them in Amsterdam when we were negotiating initially with the museum about the loan. They're part of a travelling exhibition from Germany originally. The books deal with mysticism, eroticism and the occult.'

Gawn raised her eyebrows in surprise. 'You didn't meet de Bek when you were there?'

'No. I only spoke with the museum director there. It was he who suggested we use a go-between because there were so many different parties involved.'

'And he suggested de Bek?'

'Not specifically. No. He suggested we use an antiquarian, Gert Meyer, and it was Meyer who put de Bek in touch with me.'

'Is this normal?' Harris asked.

'What's normal? Different museums and different collectors have different requirements. It's a bit like the diva who stipulates bottled water from a specific spring in the Pyrenees for her dressing room, I guess. This was how they wanted to do it and it seemed OK. We could work with it.'

'Is the exhibition still going ahead?' She didn't think it had any connection to the investigation but Gawn thought she should ask anyway.

'To be honest, we haven't done anything more about it yet. I phoned Amsterdam on Monday when Mr de Bek didn't appear. They didn't seem to know anything about it. It was just a mystery. I thought maybe he'd missed the plane or something. They haven't got back to me since and we didn't know what had happened to Mr de Bek until your officer phoned. So it's all up in the air at the minute.'

Dr O'Dowd didn't seem to see any irony in her use of this expression even though the Dutchman had died up in the air, but Harris' sense of humour was tickled by it and he had to struggle to stop himself reacting. Gawn's warning glare dispelled the smile on his face immediately.

Standing up, Gawn extended her hand and said, 'Thank you for your time and help. Hopefully we won't have to bother you again.'

Harris shook hands with the director too and she showed them to the door of her office and stood watching as they walked over to the glass-fronted lift. She was still standing there as the lift doors closed and they began their descent.

On the way down to the ground floor Gawn turned to her sergeant.

'You noticed the discrepancy of course, Michael.'

'You mean the timing, ma'am?'

'Yes. I suppose it's possible that de Bek had originally planned a later flight but then changed it and forgot to tell Dr O'Dowd but I don't think there is more than one direct flight from Amsterdam into Belfast per day.'

'Unless he had planned on coming on a different flight from maybe London if he had other business there. He was due to fly back via Heathrow that evening,' he suggested.

'Or he had another meeting planned in Belfast before the one here at the museum? That seems much more likely now. He was going to meet someone else. But who and where?' Gawn added. 'It couldn't have been anywhere too far away. He was only allowing himself a couple of hours. I wonder where he might have been going. And who else he might have planned to meet.'

Her sergeant turned a furrowed face towards his boss. 'I don't think that type of book would go down too well in this part of the world either, ma'am. Is it possible someone wanted to stop anything to do with the occult or those other things put on display here using public money to pay for it?'

Gawn noticed that Harris had not wanted to talk about erotica to her. She had come to realise that her sergeant was a little naive. He had been brought up an only child of older parents in a small country town. Sometimes a slight innocence showed in his attitude. In one way, she found it endearing, but he would have to toughen up or the others would rib him mercilessly.

'Let's get back. At the minute we have too many questions and very few answers.'

Chapter 12

By Friday evening, Gawn couldn't really postpone phoning Seb any longer. It had been nearly a week. He had given up trying to contact her except for the occasional text of a sad emoji face. And truth be told, she was missing him. She poured a glass of red wine and made herself comfortable on the sofa. The wind was howling outside but inside it was warm and cosy. She called up her contacts and then his name and then waited. She listened as the call connected and started to ring. And ring. And ring. She expected to hear his voice at any second. Instead a recorded female voice told her he was not available and then invited her to leave a message. She hadn't been expecting that. She had presumed he would be waiting for her call. She hadn't prepared a message and before she had got her thoughts together she heard the beep when she should be speaking and her mind just went blank. She hung up. All she could do now was wait. He would notice the missed call from her and ring back. Soon. She hoped.

But he didn't. The evening passed watching a mindless boxset about gangsters in Chicago which featured such an inordinate amount of gratuitous violence that eventually she was forced to abandon it and turn to her book. She finished the first bottle of wine and opened a second. She got halfway through it before she fell asleep on the sofa.

Gawn woke on Saturday morning still on the sofa. She couldn't believe she had slept there all night. She felt stiff all over and her head was throbbing. It was then she thought about inviting Jenny Norris for dinner. She couldn't face the prospect of Saturday night alone in her apartment if Seb didn't contact her. She needed a distraction. For one second the thought went through her head – was de Bek just a distraction too, was she putting all this time and attention into something which was really nothing at all? Was she seeing crimes where there were none?

Then practical considerations overtook her thoughts. She wasn't sure she had anything to cook in the fridge. She wasn't a great cook at the best of times. It was Seb who cooked for them. He seemed able to rustle up something really tasty from just a few miscellaneous ingredients. She went to the fridge and pulled out some milk for her breakfast cereal. She started the coffee filtering and then turned her attention to an inventory of what she had available. Her cleaning lady was very good at keeping her stocked up with basics like bread, cheese and milk. She knew Seb would have supplies of pasta and rice in the cupboard but what else did she have? If she did invite Jenny she would have time today to visit the local farm shop that Seb had dragged her to one weekend. He raved about the quality of its meat and vegetables.

She looked at her one cookery book – the latest offering from one of the trendy TV chefs. Seb had bought it as part of her Christmas present. She flicked through the pages to see if anything caught her eye. The photographs all made the food look delicious but whether anything she might choose to cook would turn out looking anything like that was the question. She thought she had it sussed with a chicken recipe which looked easyish but when she read that she needed to put the ingredients in a food processor she quickly turned the page. She didn't have any fancy equipment. Eventually she settled on steak and salad. Not imaginative but if she bought two really top quality steaks and threw together a salad and bought some fresh breads, she hoped it would be OK. Add a few bottles of good wine and they could have a fun evening chatting.

Unlike Seb, Jenny answered after only two rings. She was delighted that Gawn had phoned and even more delighted to be invited for dinner. Gawn was careful to emphasise what a terrible cook she was but Jenny assured her she was prepared to take the risk.

Gawn spent the afternoon driving into the countryside to get the steaks and fresh ingredients for the salad. She called in to a local bakery on her way back and bought a selection of artisan breads including her own favourite – sourdough – and then to a local coffee house along the Marine Highway facing the Fisherman's Quay which sold a selection of desserts for takeaway. It was when she was standing in the shower that she realised she hadn't given the de Bek case a thought all day. Seb always complained that she could never switch off. If she was working on a case it was always at the back of her mind. Well, this proved she could. And she would in the future with him.

Jenny arrived at 7.30 as they had arranged. Gawn buzzed her in and stood at her door watching for her coming out of the elevator. Jenny emerged carrying a lovely bunch of flowers.

'I hope you like flowers. I love them and I love to give them to others.'

'Thank you so much. You didn't need to bring anything.'

Gawn led the way into the open plan living room and kitchen, and poured wine into two glasses sitting ready on the centre island. 'Cheers. Thanks for coming. I hope you don't live to regret it. Oh, that didn't come out quite right.' She giggled. 'It sounded like a threat. Of course I hope you live… just that you won't regret volunteering for my culinary experiment.'

They laughed and the ice was broken. Any unease disappeared.

'I'm not here for the food. I'm here for the craic.'

And that was exactly what they had. They talked, they laughed almost to the point of crying, they shared funny experiences about past bosses and work colleagues. They were careful at first to avoid talk of lovers. Jenny had been a good listener when they were at the John Hewitt. Tonight she was an engaging and amusing raconteur with lots of anecdotes to share of her work in Boston and her life in America. Gawn was amazed to find that Jenny was estranged from her family just as her own brother had been because of his sexuality. Her parents couldn't accept that she was gay. She had occasional meetings with her younger sister but she hadn't seen either of her parents for over ten years. She had lost touch with most of her old friends too who had known her before she came out when at university in England. They had moved on. Some had moved out of the area altogether, some had simply married and had their own lives and careers and she wasn't a part of their social scene any more. She was trying to rebuild a social life but didn't want to focus down too quickly on just the LGBTQ scene and seem to be on the hunt for partners. In the States she had had a wide circle of friends both gay and straight. Her relationship with Suzi had meant she hadn't been part of the dating scene for years and she wasn't looking forward to that whole experience again. So, having a straight friend like Gawn whom she could just talk to, no strings, no complications, was great. She really appreciated their blossoming friendship.

They had worked their way through the food as they talked. Gawn was actually rather pleased with herself. The steak had turned out well, succulent but not too bloodied. The salad was fine and the artisan breads had been delicious. She had even produced a pineapple dessert with a flourish before she confessed she had bought it at a local bakery.

'Delicious.' Jenny smiled and set her spoon and fork down carefully on her plate. 'My compliments to the chef. And to the bakery.' She raised her glass.

'I'm just glad it turned out to be edible. I'm not a cook. My mother used to say I could burn boiling water. Seb usually cooks for us.'

'Renaissance man, eh? When do I get to meet this superman? Rescues damsels in distress, cooks cordon bleu meals, but the most important question of all: is he good in bed?'

Gawn wasn't exactly shocked. She couldn't be after multiple deployments where she had been in a distinct minority of one among a bunch of men. But she had lived and worked in predominantly male-dominated environments for so long, with an increasing emphasis on what was acceptable especially in terms of the opposite sex, and she hadn't had a close female friend to confide in since her teenage years, so that she had never been asked such a direct question before. She felt her face heat up.

'I'll take it from the colour of your cheeks that he is.' Jenny laughed.

'He's special. In all sorts of ways,' she added. Even as she said the words, Gawn recognised it for herself clearly for the first time. It wasn't just the sex, though that was good. The truth hit her that she didn't want to lose him. He still hadn't phoned and her stupid pride was stopping her from ringing him again.

'Then why aren't you together? Why is it me sitting here tonight with you – not that I mind that, of course. Where is he, this special man of yours?'

'I don't know.'

'Well, you're the bloody detective for goodness sake. Find out.'

Chapter 13

Monday morning, Gawn was determined to get the team moved up a gear. It had all been too slow. She could justify to her bosses that they had had to wait for the PM results to know if they had a crime to investigate, but that didn't satisfy her as an excuse. This time last week, de Bek had been alive, on a plane heading to Belfast. What more did they know now? Not a lot, she thought to herself. Was it just a business trip about dusty old books? Or was there something more? If their preliminary investigations didn't turn up something soon, she would have to accept it was nothing to do with them. If de Bek was smuggling then it was a matter for the Dutch authorities and her team could get onto something else. They should surely have enough local criminals to fill their time.

As soon as everyone had arrived in the office, she called them together. Harris walked across to her holding out a flat red cardboard box featuring the logo of a Canadian café brand which had recently opened a branch in Belfast. She noticed that several of the team were munching on doughnuts and realised she was now being offered one.

'Don't know if you eat doughnuts or not, ma'am, but I went in the drive-thru on my way here this morning. I thought we could do with some sugar to get us all hyped up.' He smiled at her and she was slightly astonished to find it rather disarming. He was like a little boy keen to please.

'Thank you, Michael. Why not?' She was not a great fan of sugary confection but it wouldn't hurt to join in, just once. 'Don't be doing this too often, or we'll all be putting on so much weight the criminals will be able to outrun us.' It was her attempt at a joke and everyone was polite enough to at least smile at it. She took a bite, chewed it, swallowed and then launched into her questions.

'OK. Listen up. We now know from the doctor that de Bek would have been exhibiting effects of his heart attack but for whatever reason chose to ignore them. No one we spoke to reported him looking or acting strangely when he first got on the plane. The cabin crew didn't notice him specifically which they would have if he'd been lurching about or doubled up in pain so I think we can assume it all started after he got to his seat.'

'One of the passengers in row 20 said she saw him standing up and putting his bag into the overhead locker when she was doing the same,' John Dee said.

'That fits. His bag was found there. So it must all have happened while he was in his seat. Has anyone checked if de Bek used the toilets on the plane? He could have stashed something there.'

No one had.

'OK, someone needs to speak to the cabin crew and find out. Erin, can you check that, please?'

'I don't think you're allowed to use the facilities before the plane takes off, are you?' Grant asked. 'And he didn't get up once they had taken off if all our witnesses are correct.'

'Check it anyway. Let's be doubly sure. So, we have three very clear witnesses who can help us establish what exactly happened especially if de Bek had got something on him.'

'You mean rather than *in* him, ma'am?' Logan asked and laughed.

'Don't be an asshole, Billy.' Dee's comment set the whole room laughing.

Gawn let the laughter subside and chose to ignore him. She asked, 'Who was looking at Paul Verhoeven?'

'That would be me, ma'am.' Erin McKeown spoke up.

'And what have you got?'

'Not much to help, I'm afraid. He's a businessman like he said. He works for a multinational pharmaceutical company.'

At this piece of information, Gawn's ears pricked up. 'So he's involved with drugs?'

'Well, yes, but for medical purposes and I think he's more on the business side. He doesn't handle drugs or anything. He's not a scientist.'

'He's not a rep taking samples round to doctors or anything like that?'

'No, ma'am. He's much higher up in the company than that. His designation is Senior Vice-President. He wouldn't be doing any of that sort of stuff.'

'Get back to them, Erin. Check what drugs they manufacture and if they have had any problem with any going missing. Anything else about him?'

'He's a family man. He lives in Pretoria but still has family in Amsterdam like he said. There's no criminal record. He's been in Belfast three times in the last twelve months visiting the university. His company has some kind of reciprocal agreement where they fund research which goes towards the company's drug development programme.'

'Right.'

'What about the university angle, ma'am?' Harris asked.

'What do you mean, Michael?'

'Well, if they're doing research with drugs they would keep supplies in the university. And you know students and drugs.' He left the thought unfinished.

'Has anybody checked if they've any reported losses or thefts?'

Heads nodded all round. No one had.

'Worth checking, Michael.' Gawn was pleased that her sergeant seemed to be gaining in confidence. His human touch with the doughnuts would help him with his colleagues and if he kept asking pertinent questions, it would impress her too.

'I'll leave you to follow up on that,' she said. 'Moving on. What about our farmer? Who was looking at him?'

Dee didn't stand up, just spoke from his desk in the corner. He was normally a man of few words but his work was thorough.

'Andrews is a dairy farmer. He has a large farm on the outskirts of Dromore. He's well-known locally. Well respected. Some sort of bigwig in farming circles. You name it, he's into it. Only thing is no politics. You'd have thought someone like that might be on the local council or something but he isn't.'

'Did you find any connection to de Bek?'

'None, ma'am. He did travel to the Netherlands a couple of times last year but it seemed legit, to do with his farm.'

'No red flags?'

'None.'

'OK. That leaves our Aussie friend. Jamie, you were checking up on him.'

She wheeled round to face the most junior detective on the team. Grant's perpetual grin didn't shift even though he didn't think she was going to like what he had to say.

'Yes, ma'am.' He hesitated.

'Well?'

'He doesn't exist.'

'What? What do you mean he doesn't exist?'

The atmosphere changed instantly like a bolt of static electricity flowing through the room.

'His passport's a forgery, ma'am.' When he saw the look on her face, he hurried on keen to explain why he was only telling her now, keen to avoid her wrath. 'I only found out first thing this morning and I ran his details and sent his photo to Melbourne where his passport was issued. I was hoping that he hadn't changed too many details about himself. Something you taught me, ma'am. They got back to me about ten minutes ago. One of the cops there recognised him. He'd nicked him a few times. The date of birth and other birth details matched. His name is David Clinton and the photo they sent of Clinton is our man OK.'

'And who's this David Clinton?'

'He has a rap sheet as long as your arm.' He was walking across the room holding out a sheet of paper to give her. 'Everything from muggings to burglary and drug dealing. He's served some time. He wouldn't have been allowed to leave the country as Dave Clinton so he's obviously got himself a false passport.'

'What about his girlfriend? Is she who she said she was?' Harris asked.

'Her passport checked out and her parents live at the address she gave us. I haven't had time to follow up much on her yet.'

'We don't know if this has anything to do with our victim. It might just be a coincidence that they were sitting beside him but if Clinton has a track record with drugs it's something to follow up. If it was just a coincidence he will have been cursing his bad luck if he was trying to keep a low profile to get into the country.'

'He must have been shitting himself when he realised his neighbour was dead and we'd be all over it,' Logan stage-whispered to no one in particular.

'We need to pick him up as soon as possible. Can we get the locals to do that and you and Billy can drive up and bring him back here?' Gawn was addressing Harris.

'Do we bring the girl too?' the sergeant asked.

'Yes. I think so. Until we have a better idea of what we're dealing with, we don't know how much she knows or how much she might be involved.'

'What if they don't want to come?'

'We have more than enough to arrest him. He was travelling on a forged passport. But if he's a career criminal he'll know the game's up. He should come quietly.'

Chapter 14

Gawn and Harris stood looking at the monitor on the desk in front of them. It offered a view of a miserable-looking Dave Smith or Clinton, as they now knew him, sitting at a bare table in the interview room. Most of the time his head was down as if he was making a minute examination of the surface in front of him but then he would look up casting a sly glance at the camera mounted high on the wall in the corner of the room. Once, he sneered at it and gave a middle finger gesture towards it, knowing he was being watched.

'Did he give any trouble?' Gawn asked.

'No, the Derry boys caught him with his pants down, literally. He and the girl were in bed as high as kites on something when they arrived and he didn't even try to run.' Harris sounded a little disappointed. He liked a good pursuit, prided himself on his speed and fitness.

'And the girl?'

'She had hysterics. She insisted that she knew nothing about anything. Threw a wobbly and then scratched and kicked one of our men trying to restrain her so they arrested her.'

Gawn wondered how he defined 'a wobbly'.

'OK. I think we've left him to stew long enough.'

She led the way into the room. They sat down on the opposite side of the table.

Clinton had been watching them through lowered eyebrows as they walked towards him. His cheery expression from the previous week had been replaced by a sullen scowl which did not improve his appearance. He now more closely resembled his mugshot sent from Melbourne.

'I don't know if you remember us or not, Mr Clinton.' Gawn stressed his name to show they knew all about him. Before she could go on, he interrupted her.

'I remember you alright, Chief Inspector, and I'm not answering any freakin' questions.'

The man looked more like a stroppy teenager than any bigtime drug baron, she decided. Strictly small time.

'That's your legal right, of course, Mr Clinton, but we have you bang to rights for illegal entry to the UK, using a false passport, so you're going to be deported at the very least. And you were in possession of drugs. We have you for that too.' Harris had jumped in with his comment.

Gawn had only ever heard someone use the phrase 'bang to rights' on TV shows. Even in her days at the Met she'd never heard it used.

'So you could help yourself by helping us.' Gawn finished his statement for him. Tag teaming. She liked it. She was beginning to feel she could work well with this new man.

'How could you help me?' Clinton asked.

'Depends how you could help us.' He was biting. Now all she had to do was reel him in.

'Some old guy croaks it and I happen to be sitting beside him. What fuckin' luck.'

'What makes you think he just died, Mr Clinton?'

Gawn waited to see how long it would take him to work out what she was suggesting. His face changed. He sat up in his chair. Fear showed in his eyes. She hadn't said anything. He had made the jump to assume de Bek had been murdered and it suited her purposes to scare him.

'Hey, what are you trying to put on me? I didn't touch the old bastard.' His eyes moved warily from one to the other. 'I want a lawyer. Now!' he shouted at them.

* * *

They had spent the time waiting for the duty solicitor to arrive drinking coffee and planning what they wanted to ask. Gawn was pleased to learn Harris was a coffee connoisseur like herself. Another point in his favour; Maxwell had preferred tea.

Their main priority was to try to establish who had spoken to de Bek or who he might have spoken to. They also needed to know if anyone had stopped with him on the way past, when de Bek might have been able to pass on what he was carrying, if he was carrying anything. Gawn knew there were an awful lot of maybes, buts and ifs in what she was thinking. She was sticking her neck out on this one and she wasn't sure exactly why. She suspected that it might have something to do with Seb not being in touch and the need to fill her time.

'The duty solicitor's arrived, ma'am.' Logan put his head round the door of Gawn's office and informed them.

When they made their way back into the interview room, Gawn recognised the new arrival – sharp suit and suitably bulging briefcase conveying an air of a busy and successful man. She thought his name was Conway but wasn't sure. She'd seen him in the courts but never spoken to him before.

'Jackson Conway. I'll be representing Mr Clinton's interests.' The man extended his hand, supremely confident in his own abilities.

'Mr Conway, your client was caught with drugs in his possession, having arrived in the country using a fake passport. The facts are not in doubt. What is in doubt is how quickly and how strenuously we pursue the possession charges and his deportation back to Australia.'

The solicitor leaned in and whispered something in Clinton's ear.

'What are you offering, Chief Inspector?' Conway asked.

'Mr Clinton was seated beside Willem de Bek, a person of interest in a potential smuggling case. We want his full cooperation, every detail he can remember. Answers to all our questions. No holding back.'

'And in return?'

'We may be able to forget any drug charges and hand him over to Immigration Enforcement. And we could push for a quick deportation so he isn't held too long in the detention centre.'

Again the solicitor leaned in. Clinton listened and then nodded his head.

'Can you assure me that my client is not a suspect in any smuggling?'

'I can't assure you of anything. Yet. We need to hear his story.'

Conway had obviously expected her response but he'd had to try. He nodded to his client to encourage him to speak.

'What do you want to know?' Clinton asked in a belligerent tone.

Harris pushed the record button and introduced them all for the tape.

'When did you first see Mr de Bek?'

'When we got to our seats. I told you last week, me and Mandy wanted to sit together. We'd been trying to get on board first so we could sit beside each other and tell anyone else to bugger off. But when we got there, he was already there before us.'

'And you spoke to him?' Harris asked.

'Yes. I spoke to him.'

'And he replied?'

'Not exactly. His head was turned away. He was looking out the window and just ignoring me. Well, that's what I thought. I called him a mongrel and he didn't react so I gave up. I turned my back to him.'

'You weren't aware of him moving or making any sound at any time?' Gawn asked.

'Even when you knocked into him and he moaned, which is what you told us last week as well?' Harris added.

'I did knock into him and I thought he moved. I guess it was just me knocking against him. I thought he moaned but maybe he didn't,' he finished lamely.

'So in point of fact, he could have been dead the whole flight?' Gawn asked.

'Yes.' A moment's pause. 'Well, no. That guy behind spoke to him.'

'Which guy would that be?'

'The red-faced man sitting directly behind de Bek.'

Gawn remembered that Bill Andrews had mentioned trying to make conversation with the Dutchman.

'When was this?'

'Right after we'd sat down.'

That fitted in with Andrews' evidence as well.

'Did they have a conversation?'

'I wasn't listening to two old blokes jabbering. I had better things to think about.'

'We're not asking you to remember their conversation and report it verbatim, just to tell us if they spoke to each other.' Gawn was growing impatient. They really weren't learning very much they didn't already know.

Clinton raised his voice. 'I had my back turned. I couldn't see them and I wasn't listening to them.'

'But Miss Robson would have been able to see, wouldn't she, Mr Clinton? If she was looking over at you, she would have seen and maybe heard them too.'

'I guess so. I never asked her. Why should I? We thought the guy had croaked it. We never heard anything about smuggling. None of your people mentioned anything about that.'

'And no one else spoke to de Bek? No one passing by?'

He just nodded and shrugged.

'And de Bek didn't get up and go to the toilet?'

'No. Definitely not.'

'I think my client has been helpful, Chief Inspector.'

'He has, Mr Conway. We need to speak to Miss Robson to corroborate what he's told us. We're going to return Mr Clinton to the holding cells. I don't intend to talk to him again today unless something comes up when we speak to Miss Robson.'

* * *

Mandy was sitting looking sorry for herself. She was obviously well down from whatever high she had been on. If she was feeling as bad as she looked, she wouldn't be too happy. The girl looked up startled when Gawn and Harris walked in. Gawn was pretty sure she didn't have much experience with police. Harris had already told her that she had no criminal record either in the UK or Australia. She came from a well-known and respectable local family and her parents had been distraught when the police had arrived at their door and dragged their daughter kicking and screaming out to the car. They had seemed less surprised or concerned about her boyfriend.

'Miss Robson, we'd like to ask you some questions.' Gawn offered her the opportunity of a solicitor but the girl declined.

Harris went through the protocols for the tape.

'Miss Robson, Mandy, may I call you Mandy?' Gawn had decided they were more likely to get the girl's cooperation if they took a more gentle approach. Scaring her or threatening her would only lead to another request for a solicitor.

'You understand your rights?'

'Yes. But I don't understand why I'm here. Dave and I were doing a bit of weed but we're not dealers. We weren't out in the street pushing anything.'

'Have you ever been arrested before?'

'No.' Her vehement answer came with the implication that of course she hadn't; how could they think that?

'Mandy, you only had a small amount of hash and I presume it was for your own personal use?'

Gawn waited to give her a chance to agree.

'Yes.'

'Then you'll get a warning. That's all. We're not interested in taking you to court or you getting a criminal record.'

'Then can I go?' she asked hopefully. Her face brightened.

'Not yet. We need your help.'

Mandy frowned. 'How can I help?'

'The man who died, the man in the seat next to Dave, we believe he was smuggling something into Northern Ireland.'

From her gasp it was clear this was news to the girl.

'Smuggling what? Drugs?' She was bright enough to realise that their connection with drugs made them suspects if de Bek was smuggling. 'I don't know anything about smuggling.' Her face turned bright red and even a rookie police officer would have realised she was lying and trying to hide something. Not very well.

'I don't think that's completely true, is it, Mandy?'

Harris was surprised at Gawn's gentle tone. If it had been down to him he'd have been banging the table and demanding the truth.

The girl hesitated and Gawn just waited. The seconds ticked by and Harris was itching to ask another question but Gawn's foot pressing against his warned him to keep quiet. Eventually the tears started. Mandy rocked back and forth in her chair and held her hands to her face. Her words came between gulped sobs.

'Dave said it would be OK. No one would ever look at me and it wasn't very much. It was just for our own personal use.' The girl was sly enough to use the detective's words back at her and she looked Gawn straight in the eye as she spoke.

'You smuggled drugs in?'

'Just some hash. Just a wee bit. Honest.'

'How?' Harris asked.

'Down my bra.'

The two detectives exchanged a look and Harris sucked in his cheeks to stifle a laugh.

'What about de Bek?'

'I'd never seen him before.'

'Had Dave?'

'No. I don't think so. No.'

'And no one else came over and talked to de Bek during the flight?'

'No. Definitely. I'm sure. Not during the flight. I think the man behind him said something to him before we took off but anyone else would have had to lean across Dave and they didn't. I'm sure.'

* * *

As soon as the door closed behind them, Harris burst out laughing.

'I didn't think there'd be enough room to stash anything down there.'

'Sergeant!' Gawn feigned righteous indignation.

'Sorry, ma'am. I suppose that's not very PC but she's rather well-endowed. It must have been a bit of a tight squeeze. I guess it gives a whole new meaning to the phrase "you're busted".'

Gawn couldn't help laughing too.

Chapter 15

Jackie Watson slowly licked the Guinness moustache off his upper lip savouring the taste, let out a loud sigh and sat back into the squishy cushions on a sofa in a secluded corner of the bar. He and Gawn were meeting in a large hotel on the outskirts of East Belfast. He was coming off a long surveillance shift and this was on his way home. He was tired but he always had time for a pint and a catch-up with Gawn. They had known each other since childhood. They had started school together and he still referred to her as Lizzie, her name from school. Jackie had stammered then and that plus the fact that his dad was a 'peeler' meant he was a target for bullying in the class. Gawn's dad was a 'peeler' too but even then everyone knew not to mess with her. She stood up for herself and she stood up for Jackie too. Now he was a sergeant in the Drugs Squad and on wife number two, whom Gawn had yet to meet.

'So what's up, Lizzie? Why the phone call?' He took another draw at his pint. 'Not that I mind you taking me out and plying me with strong drink.' He laughed.

'In your dreams. Can I not just want to hear how you're doing? I haven't seen you since you got married.' She didn't add 'again'.

'Sorry you didn't get an invite. Maura wanted a beach wedding in the Maldives. We only had close family there.'

'No problem. So how's it going?' Having started with the fiction that she wanted to catch up on his personal life, she thought she better ask a question or two even though her reason for the meeting was something else altogether.

'OK, I suppose. How do police marriages ever go? She doesn't like the hours I have to keep, the people I have to mix with. But she's expecting so that'll keep her busy for a while.' He smiled, a rueful smile.

'Congratulations.' When she saw his expression she added, 'Or maybe not.'

'What about you, Lizzie? No man in your life? Don't tell me, none of us can keep up with you.'

'That's it, Jackie. It was you or nobody. You broke my heart.' This was their standing joke.

'So what's the real reason for this meeting?'

This time she didn't think there was any point in wasting any more time pretending. She took a sip of her sparkling water and said, 'I wanted to pick your brains.'

'Pick away, what's left of them when I've been up all night.' And he downed another slug of Guinness.

'Drug smuggling.'

'Yes?'

'What's the latest? Anyone new on the scene?'

'It's changing all the time. It's a bit like whack-a-mole. You knock one lowlife down and two others pop up somewhere else. You intercept a lorry on the border coming from the south one day and next week it's a car on the Stranraer ferry.'

Gawn nodded sympathetically.

'The paramilitaries are involved, of course. Then we've got organised groups moving in from south of the border. What are you thinking?'

'I just wondered if you've heard anything about drugs coming in. Maybe from a new source. Maybe smuggled in, inside a body cavity.'

'A drug mule? Have you heard something?'

Gawn wondered how much she should share about her suspicions.

'I have some evidence that something was being smuggled in from Holland. I'm not sure it was drugs. It could have been something else. I just wondered if you'd heard anything about the Netherlands. Any connections there? Any whispers?'

He seemed to take a second or two to consider before he answered.

'Holland's famous for its drug culture but we haven't heard about any big delivery from there. Our pushers haven't been getting their stuff from Holland. Not up to now, anyway. And, as for drug mules, I've heard of it happening of course but not here, not so far as we know but anything's possible. Where there's money – and with drugs it's big money – people'll do anything.'

So maybe it wasn't drugs de Bek had been bringing in or maybe this was a first consignment, a start of a new source of misery. If it wasn't drugs, could it be diamonds?

Or what? She felt as if she was floundering around in a fog and not sure where she should be heading. Was she making something out of nothing? She knew McDowell would say they had enough real crime without going looking for it where there was none.

The two old friends said their goodbyes outside the hotel's revolving door. A quick peck on the cheek, a promise to keep in touch and get together for her to meet Maura, a wave and he headed off down the hill to his car in the lower car park while she walked over to her Audi parked beside the conference centre. Her route took her through Ballyhackamore and past the end of the street where Seb lived. It was the first time she had been in this part of the city for weeks. She gave into the temptation of driving past his house.

She saw it as soon as she made the turn. It might as well have been illuminated in flashing neon lighting. A 'For Sale' sign outside his house. What did it mean? Well, it meant of course that he was moving house but to where? Why? When was he going to tell her? Was he going to tell her? She drove past so slowly that a car horn made her jump. The man in the car behind gesticulated angrily at her. She waved in apology and spun the car wheels as she made a quick getaway.

Chapter 16

Her meeting with Jackie Watson hadn't really helped at all. She was no further forward. If something definite didn't turn up soon, she would have to let it go. And she was now in a foul mood. She knew that if anyone crossed her, she would react badly. She had almost thought of going straight home and leaving it all until tomorrow but, in the end, she couldn't do it.

She didn't have time to reach far into the general office before Logan accosted her.

'The boys in Derry have turned something up, ma'am.'

'What?' She needed to hear some good news.

'Well, first of all, what they didn't find.'

Harris had walked across and joined them eager to hear what had been discovered.

'No riddles, Billy. I'm not in the mood.'

'There was no bag in his room – the bag he had as hand luggage on the plane. It's missing.'

'Right. A bit funny. We'll need to find out what the story is about that. Whether he got rid of it for some reason.'

'Maybe he had de Bek's drugs in it,' Harris suggested.

'We don't even know de Bek had any drugs. But let's just hope he didn't. How stupid would we look interviewing him at the airport with him sitting with drugs in front of us? Mind you, that was what happened.'

'You mean Mandy's bra?'

She nodded. Logan did a double take of his two senior officers. He hadn't heard about the hash smuggled in, concealed in the girl's brassiere.

'Don't even go there, Billy. What else?' Gawn said. 'Something good this time. Please.'

'They found money.'

'How much?'

'Nearly five thousand pounds.'

'Holiday spending money?' Harris chipped in.

'It was four thousand in euros and a thousand in sterling. Used notes, non-sequential numbers. Tied in rubber bands. Where would a wee toerag like that get that sort of cash?'

'A pay-off for something?' Gawn mused.

'Drugs?'

'Get him back up and get his solicitor here. I want to speak to him. Now.' Her face displayed a mixture of anger and excitement. Maybe now they were getting somewhere.

* * *

They had to wait until the solicitor could be contacted and his presence requested before they could interview the Australian again. Jackson Conway, when he arrived, dressed in a tuxedo and black bow tie, was ready to take out his displeasure at his evening being interrupted on the first person he met and that happened to be Harris, but Gawn was there too and he had to moderate what he wanted to say.

'I have a very special dinner this evening. I hope this won't take long. Your officer said it was important but I don't see why it couldn't have waited until the morning.'

'Thank you for coming, sir.' Harris was taking a conciliatory approach, ignoring the solicitor's complaints.

Gawn didn't speak but the look she cast at Conway was withering. He was being paid. He needed to earn his money. She had no sympathy for him.

The three walked together into the interview room where Clinton was already seated in the same chair as earlier. He was scowling. Conway sat down beside his client; Gawn and Harris opposite. Harris started the tape recording.

'I thought we'd finished.'

'We had before we completed the search at your address in Londonderry.'

'May we know what was found?' the solicitor enquired, knowing full well they had to be told, full disclosure.

'Where's your carry-on bag, Dave?' Harris asked.

As the Australian hesitated, Gawn added, 'We know you had one because you had it with you when we were interviewing you at the airport.'

'It was in the bedroom. Your people took it,' he sneered.

'No, they didn't. What did you do with it?'

For the first time the Australian started to look afraid.

'How did you…,' he started and then stopped. At first, it seemed he was going to bluster, deny everything, but then Gawn saw from his eyes that he was going to try to concoct some story to lie his way out of it.

'I dumped it. It was ancient and falling apart. I threw it away.'

'Where?'

'Some rubbish bin. At the railway station when we were waiting for the train to Derry.'

The two detectives suspected he had already prepared the answer knowing eventually that they might get around to asking.

'We'll check the security cameras at the station, you know,' Gawn said.

'Check away. It might have been the one in the station or maybe the one outside or maybe I threw it away as we were walking around to the station from the City Hall. I can't really remember.' He sat back and smirked.

'If need be, we'll track you on CCTV everywhere you went and find where you got rid of it. And if we have to waste a lot of time doing that, we will not be very happy.' She didn't say any more. It was clear from her expression that it would not go well for him.

Conway whispered to his client and then asked, 'Why is this bag so important, Chief Inspector?'

'We believe it contained smuggled items. Anything smuggled into the country wouldn't be covered by our earlier agreement, Mr Conway, especially if it were drugs. Your client could expect us to come down heavily on that. Our courts don't like foreigners coming bringing drugs, Dave.'

'You didn't find any drugs, did you?' the solicitor queried.

'Not yet. Just a small amount of marijuana. But we did find a significant amount of cash.'

'It's not illegal to have cash.'

'Depends how you come by it. How'd you get the money, Dave?' Gawn swivelled in her chair to face Clinton but her voice remained calm and controlled, all the more menacing for its coldness. She smiled at him, a knowing smile, as if she was already aware of the answer and was testing him.

He bit his lip.

'If you've been dealing drugs, you're in the shite up to your neck. We don't like dealers.' Harris slammed his fist down on the table to accompany his words.

Clinton flinched. He hadn't been expecting such an aggressive line of questioning. He thought he was going to get off lightly. Now it seemed he was in big trouble.

It was his turn to lean over to his solicitor and exchange whispered words.

'My client wishes to be as cooperative as possible. There's no need for such aggressive questioning.' Conway directed this comment to Harris. 'In return for some additional information he may be able to provide, we would expect complete immunity from any charges related to any drugs and anything to do with Mr de Bek.'

'I couldn't give that undertaking without knowing how your client was involved.'

The solicitor nodded to Clinton. He looked Gawn straight in the eye.

'I had nothing to do with that man's death. Nothing.' He repeated the word giving the two syllables equal emphasis.

Gawn let him think they suspected him of doing something to de Bek. It would convince him to cooperate.

'Then what was the money for?' There was an urgency to her voice now. She was getting tired playing his little game. She didn't think he was much more than a small-time crook and druggie but he held a key to one part of a bigger puzzle.

'You think I'd bump somebody off for a measly five thousand?'

'How much would you do it for?' Harris baited him.

'Bloody funny. I wouldn't be stupid enough to do it for any money. Do you think I'm some sort of moron killing the guy in the seat next to me?'

'Is my client suspected of a crime against Mr de Bek?'

It was about time the brief had started earning his money, Gawn thought to herself. So far, he hadn't done very much to protect Clinton's interests, obviously more concerned to get to his fancy dinner than doing a decent job.

Neither Gawn nor Harris considered Clinton a serious suspect for drug running but he had been up to something and whether it had to do with whatever de Bek was involved in or not they weren't sure. If it was something unrelated then they didn't want to be wasting any more time chasing up blind alleys.

Ignoring Conway's question, Gawn spoke directly to the Australian.

'Last chance, Dave. I'm losing patience.' Gawn began to gather her papers together as if she was about to leave.

'A guy paid me the money to bring a briefcase onto the plane and swap it with the one de Bek had. They even gave me a backpack to fit it in. I didn't know this de Bek. I'd never seen him before. I was just doing a job. And I didn't do anything to him. I didn't touch him.'

Clinton put his hands up to his face. The sweat was sitting on his forehead.

'What man, Dave?'

'I don't know any names. I never saw him before. We were in a club the night before. The Pussycat. He came up to me and said he had a job for me. He told me what it was. I was to take a bag onto the plane and swap it for one the same. I thought it must be drugs and I wasn't stupid enough to get involved with that. I told him no. Then when we left the club, he and a couple of his mates were waiting for us. They took me up an alley. I've never been so scared. He put a knife to my throat. Look.'

He pulled his sweatshirt down at the neck and the mark of a recent cut showed clearly on his throat. It was not deep but it was there.

'He knew where we were going. He knew all about us. He even had the tickets for the plane for us. He threatened that he'd come after us to Derry if I didn't do it.'

'So you swapped the bags?'

'Yes. I'd looked in the bag they gave me and there was nothing in it. I thought I'd be the one carrying the drugs and gonna take the fall if I was caught but it was just some pens and stuff so I reckoned the drugs must be in the other bag. I was careful not to do the switch until the last minute so I had it for the shortest length of time. Then I put the bag into my backpack.'

They realised he must have been frantic when they were held back and then interviewed. They hadn't noticed he was nervous. He had played his part well, sitting there in front of them, his backpack at his feet.

'What happened to the bag then, Dave?'

Now that he had started talking, it seemed like he couldn't stop. His words came out in a rush.

'They'd told me to take it straight to the Victoria Shopping Centre. Mandy knew where that was so it was no problem. I was to leave it in the last cubicle in the gents toilets on the top floor. That's what I did. They'd hidden the money behind the cistern as they said. I reckoned that was it. I'd done what they asked and they'd paid me. I didn't hang around to see if anybody picked it up. I just hoped that was the end of it. I never want to see them again.'

'Did you look in the bag?'

'No.'

'Really, Dave?' Her disbelief rang through her words. 'You'd just been interviewed. You knew the guy whose bag you were carrying had died which was a bit of a coincidence and you really didn't have a peek to see what it was all about?'

'No. I didn't. I didn't want to know. All I wanted was to get away and never see that guy again. I told you. He was one freakin' scary guy. That's all I know.' He balled his fists in frustration.

As they left the room, Gawn turned to her sergeant.

'First thing tomorrow, Erin gets onto the Victoria Centre. She needs to get all their security footage for last Monday. We know approximately what time Clinton would have been there. She can check and see who went in and out of the top floor. See if any familiar faces show up. And she could run the faces past the Drugs Squad and Organised Crime in case anyone pops out to them. These people are not amateurs or beginners. They're in the Netherlands and they have people here. It's something big. I just know it.'

'Won't there be a lot to identify?'

'Let's just hope there weren't too many men caught short that day. Oh, and ask them if the cleaners found an abandoned bag. They'll probably have taken whatever was inside and left the bag, I would think.'

If they could identify someone on the CCTV footage they could begin to try to make some sense of all of this. As things stood, everything just seemed to be getting murkier and murkier. A seemingly innocent little Dutchman who wasn't so innocent after all, dead albeit of natural causes and his bag stolen. Whoever the people involved in this were, they were well-organised and had everything worked out in advance. De Bek's death may have been a fluke but it hadn't interfered with their plans. Gawn suspected they would not let anyone or anything stand in their way. But their way to what?

Chapter 17

It had been a long day, starting with the stress of leading the briefing, then the drive to Derry and back, and Harris had hoped that it would be over for him when they had finished with Clinton. Instead, after issuing her orders for McKeown and the CCTV footage, Gawn had told him to get his coat, they were going out. As she drove them out towards the M1 motorway, he tried to figure out where they might be going. Wherever it was, they were going to get there quickly because once she had cleared the heavy traffic on the Westlink and got onto the motorway proper, their speed didn't drop below seventy.

The traffic thinned out even more when they had passed the Sprucefield Shopping Centre. This was an area Harris didn't know well. He was impressed with the number of cars in the car park and the length of the queue at the fast food drive-thru which reminded him he hadn't had anything to eat since the morning. They hadn't stopped on the way back from Derry with Clinton and his girlfriend. Then the penny dropped. There was only one person involved with the case he could think of who lived in this direction – Bill Andrews.

'Are we going to see Andrews?'

'Yes. I didn't want to warn him by asking him to come in or phoning and arranging to interview him. Better to surprise him. One way or another, Andrews should be able to throw some light on de Bek's condition; help us with our timeline.'

As if she didn't want to discuss it anymore, Gawn switched on the media centre in the car. A piece of classical music started playing. Harris was going to ask her what it was but decided he wouldn't. He lent his head back into the headrest, let the music flow over him and shut his eyes.

He woke with a jump as the car came to a halt. He had fallen asleep.

'Sorry, ma'am. I must have nodded off.'

She didn't respond. She was already stepping out of the car. As he opened the door and began to follow her across the farmyard, he was aware of the lowing of cattle in the fields around although he couldn't actually make out any cows. It was dusk and the light fell quickly at this time of year. A PIR security light suddenly illuminated the whole concrete yard in a harsh glare as they approached the front door of a red brick two storey square building which looked as if it would sit more comfortably in a suburban estate than in the middle of the countryside. It had the look of a child's drawing of what a house should look like. Two windows either side of a central door and smoke rising from a chimney. Someone inside had noticed the lights coming on for as they approached the front door, it opened. Bill Andrews filled the opening. This time he looked more like the farmer he was. His polo shirt was open at the neck, a dark blue knitted jumper which had seen some hard use was visible under a quilted gilet. Corduroy trousers and a pair of heavy boots completed his outerwear. The boots were covered in what Gawn's grandfather would have called clabber.

Gawn had noticed a look of almost fear in his eyes until he had recognised who it was who was coming to his door. She knew the fear of attack for farmers in isolated areas and put it down to that. When he spoke his tone was friendly but his expression was wary.

'Chief Inspector. This is a surprise.'

'Mr Andrews. We were hoping to have a quick word.'

'Of course, come in.'

He stood back to let them enter. A wide tiled hallway with a central staircase led to what estate agents referred to as a farmhouse kitchen. The units were in a warm honey pine finish, the walls painted sunshine yellow, and a woman wearing a brightly coloured apron was standing at an Aga cooker stirring something which smelt delicious. It was like a scene out of some glossy homes magazine, Gawn thought cynically.

'This is my wife, Margaret. This is the police, dear. They want to ask me some more questions about the man on the plane.'

The woman turned from her task and gave the two officers a warm smile. Gawn noticed a look pass between her and her husband but she was not sure what it signified.

'Hello. Pleased to meet you.' She didn't go to shake her hand, instead showing them an outstretched hand holding a ladle.

'We don't want to interrupt your evening or hold you back, perhaps we could have a quiet word in private?' Gawn suggested to Andrews.

'Yes, of course. We'll go into the front room.' He directed this comment to his wife, as if he was asking her permission.

'This'll be ready in about ten minutes,' Margaret said. 'And don't forget your boots.'

Andrews glanced down at his feet. 'OK, dear.'

He led them back into the hall, pausing to remove his boots and leave them at the kitchen door. He directed them into a room which Gawn knew would have served as 'the good room' used only for visitors and special occasions. Her parents had kept one of those, a room where they never set foot from one year to another except at Christmas or when special visitors came to call. The room where her mother's coffin had lain the night before her funeral when the neighbours had come to pay their respects.

The decor was very traditional, old-fashioned, she thought. A substantial brown moquette-covered three piece suite lined two walls. The fireplace was heavy mahogany with a large mirror hanging over it. The obligatory piano sat against the other wall. Gawn wondered if anyone ever actually played it. It served its purpose, like so many others, as somewhere to display a range of family photographs. She identified some school ones although she didn't recognise the uniform, and one of a young woman in an academic gown at a graduation. Over the piano hung a large, coloured wedding photograph of the same young woman and her new husband. There was something vaguely familiar about the bridegroom. But then he looked like a lot of the young professional men she came across these days. It was probably just her imagination, trying to see connections where there were none.

'I thought I'd told you everything last Monday. I haven't remembered anything else.'

'We're enquiring into Mr de Bek's activities. We have reason to believe he was smuggling something into Northern Ireland. We would really appreciate it if we could go over everything you noticed on the flight.'

'I've been busy all day out in the fields and the shed. I was just about to sit down for the first time. I'm tired and I really don't think I can add anything to what I told you on Monday.'

Andrews had reacted at the mention of smuggling, but for some reason Gawn thought he didn't look as shocked as she might have expected. He sat down heavily on one of the armchairs. She watched his eyes dart around the room. She knew that reaction. Someone wondering what they should say; what they should hide. He ran his tongue over his lips before he spoke again.

'I don't see what more I can say. Nothing happened. It was a perfectly ordinary flight until we landed.'

Harris stepped forward so he was directly in front of the older man and towering over him.

'You told us you spoke to de Bek.'

'I did.'

'You told us he answered you.'

'He did.' The answer came quickly but then his brow furrowed. 'Well, he didn't speak as such.'

'Either he spoke or he didn't,' Harris pressed.

'It wasn't really words. Not a conversation. I told you it was just me making some ordinary comments about the weather and the flight and him kinda humming in reply.'

'Humming or moaning?' Gawn jumped on the word.

'You know, the way you do. Like "uh uh". Like you don't really have anything to say but you try to sound as if you're agreeing. Well that let me know he wasn't interested in any conversation and anyway I wanted to get settled and get my seatbelt on so I just sat down. I think I made some comment to the man beside me about the weather too and then that was it for the flight. I read my paper and the next thing I knew they were telling us to put on our seatbelts for landing.'

'The man sat next to you, Mr Vanhoeven, was he already in his seat when you got to yours?' Gawn asked.

'Yes. I had to get past him which is why I had leaned on the back of de Bek's seat. I didn't want to end up sitting on that man's lap.'

'And that's all you can tell us?' Gawn just knew he was holding something back. Years of experience told her he was not being totally frank with them.

Andrews seemed to consider what he should say. Gawn flashed a look at her sergeant to warn him to keep quiet, just to wait.

'I don't know if this has anything to do with your case but when you'd finished talking to me and I went out to the car park to get my car, someone stole my coat.'

'Stole your coat? How exactly?'

'They rode past on a motorbike, pushed me out of the way and grabbed my coat off the top of my suitcase.'

'Was there anything special about the coat? Was it valuable?'

'Hell no. It was ancient. It was just an old country jacket but it was brilliant for working about the farm. It kept the wind and the rain out. Margaret's been on at me for years to get a new one. I'd taken it with me for when I was walking around the two farms I was visiting in Holland. But I didn't want to pack it in my suitcase so I just had it over my arm as I was walking out. And then I set it down when I went to get my car keys out of my pocket.'

Gawn visualised what he had looked like as he walked over to them in the airport room. Yes. She could remember he had a coat.

'Did you report the mugging, sir?'

'Not at the time. I just wanted to get home. I didn't want to end up having to hang around again. I needed to get back to the farm. Then whenever I got home it seemed as if there was no point. I wasn't hurt. The coat wasn't worth anything much and your people have enough to do without that.' He paused, then added, 'Do you think I should have? Do you think it had anything to do with the smuggling?'

'I don't know, sir.' She was actually thinking that for her it was too much of a coincidence.

The door to the room opened, allowing the delicious aroma of the evening meal to float in.

'Dinner's ready,' Margaret Andrews announced. 'Would you like to join us? There's plenty.'

'No, thank you. That's very kind but we need to get back.'

As they were walking out of the room, Gawn commented on the photograph on the wall.

'Lovely picture. Is that your daughter?'

'Yes. That's our Dawn,' Margaret Andrews said proudly. 'She's a lawyer.'

'Oh, would I have come across her?' Gawn asked innocently.

'No. She and her husband practise down south. In Dublin.'

They said their goodbyes and Gawn explained that she would be sending someone out to get more information about the mugging and a description of the man who grabbed his coat. Andrews said he didn't think there was much point but he agreed to try to help. It was only when they were back in the car and Gawn was doing a three-point turn to get back out onto the main road that she spoke.

'Send someone down tomorrow to interview him about the mugging. See if they can get any kind of a description. Then pull the CCTV footage from the airport car park. We should be able to see what happened.'

'Do you believe him about the coat?'

'I believe it was stolen but I think he might be hiding why. Only thing is, I haven't a clue whether what he's hiding has anything to do with de Bek or not. Oh and get some background on the daughter and son-in-law. Just in case.'

'Just in case of what, ma'am?'

'You never know, that's why it's just in case,' she replied.

As they were approaching Sprucefield and Harris' stomach was reminding him of how hungry he was, he was surprised when Gawn turned to him and asked, 'Fancy a double cheeseburger, Sergeant?'

'With large fries?' he responded smiling across at her.

'I think I can run to that.'

Chapter 18

It was a pleasant morning. Dry and bright. Gawn was looking forward to meeting her Dutch counterparts and making some progress in the case. But she had received an email from the ACC's office telling her she had to be present for the launch of their Anti-Human Trafficking event at lunchtime today. It wasn't that she didn't support the initiative. Of course she did. She just didn't think it was the best use of her time to stand and look suitably serious behind the ACC. Window dressing was what she thought of it. Although to be fair, it wasn't just her, a number of male senior officers were to be present also to demonstrate to the press how important they regarded the issue. She had had experience in the Met of being the token woman at all kinds of events and she didn't like playing that game.

As she walked into reception, the desk sergeant called her over.

'The super wants to see you, ma'am.'

What now? It was never a good sign to be called in to see Superintendent McDowell first thing in the morning. He would have had all the previous night to mull over whatever he had on his mind and be ready to launch into whatever grievance he had managed to concoct.

She didn't even bother heading to her own office first. Best to get it over with, whatever it was.

'Come in.' His voice sounded gruff.

'You wanted to see me, sir?'

She stood not quite at attention but near enough to give that impression. He didn't invite her to sit.

'What the hell are you playing at, Chief Inspector?' He spoke as he rose to his feet to face her.

She couldn't be a hundred percent sure what he was referring to but her guess would be the inquiry into de Bek's death.

'Sir?'

She waited for him to elaborate and she didn't have to wait long.

'Requests for all sorts of forensics tests.' He slammed down onto the desk a sheaf of papers he had been holding in his hand. 'Overtime claims for enquiries to do with the de Bek case. What the hell is the de Bek case? I thought that Dutchman died of natural causes.'

'He did.'

Before she could continue, McDowell interrupted, his voice rising.

'Then how is there a bloody de Bek case?'

'I was concerned that he had been involved in smuggling something into the country, sir, and I felt we should look into it.'

'You were concerned? You felt?' His words rang with sarcasm. 'You are not paid to be concerned or to feel, Chief Inspector. Policemen's gut feelings are just so much bullshit. I would have thought you knew that by now. You are paid to investigate and solve real crimes. Crimes that have taken place. Crimes here not in the Netherlands. I hear you're making a trip to Amsterdam.'

Word had travelled fast. She had only made the booking late last night before she left the office. She wondered if he had spies in the Finance Department.

'I thought we were supposed to try to prevent crime, sir.'

'Don't be clever with me.'

'Well, it's a bit more than a feeling now.'

To give him his due, the superintendent let her continue.

'One of the other passengers on the plane had been threatened and paid to steal de Bek's briefcase and leave it to be picked up here. He's admitted to that. Someone knew de Bek was smuggling something into the country and whatever it was they had arranged to get hold of it. It was worth five thousand pounds to them to get that done so, whatever it was, must be worth a lot more than that.'

McDowell sat back down and beckoned for her to sit too.

'If you're thinking about drugs, it should be the Drugs Squad on this. Not your lot.'

'It may not be drugs, sir. It could be diamonds.' She could see he was digesting what she had said and went on before he could speak. 'I really need to get over to Amsterdam and speak to the people on the ground there. Question his boss, his family and any other contacts he had. Whatever it was, someone's moving something into Belfast and I think we need to know who they are and what they're up to.'

She waited. He considered what she had said.

'A couple of days. That's all. No fishing. You turn up something concrete, we'll act on it. If you don't, that's an end to it. Understood?'

'Understood, sir.'

Chapter 19

'Commissaris Jansen.'

The voice on the phone was deep and rich, like one of those actors who do voice-overs or narrate audiobooks. If voices were foodstuffs, his would be dark chocolate with marshmallows and cream, Gawn thought.

'Good morning, Commissaris. My name is Chief Inspector Girvin of the Police Service of Northern Ireland.'

Before she could get any further, he interrupted her.

'I was expecting your call. I owe you an apology, Chief Inspector. I was supposed to get in touch with you, wasn't I, but it was a bit hectic over the weekend. I had my hands full. How can I help you?'

She could have gone into a list of complaints about how their investigation had been stalling because they couldn't get any information from Amsterdam. But she didn't. She explained about de Bek's death and their suspicions about his activities. She also felt she should speak to the family. She had questioned his son, Nico, but now she wanted to speak with his wife and his employer.

'Of course, we're only too happy to help. When will you be arriving?'

'I'll see what flight I can get. I can text and let you know. But it won't be until later this evening or first thing tomorrow. I have other matters to clear up first.'

'I see. I look forward to meeting you.' And he rang off.

Jansen's was not the only voice she had been pleased to hear this morning. Almost as soon as she had sat down at her desk, her mobile phone had rung and she had seen Seb's name on the screen.

'Hi.' He sounded tentative as if he wasn't sure of his welcome.

'Hello, stranger.'

'Sorry I haven't been in touch. I was in Los Angeles.'

She hadn't been expecting him to say that.

'I got a call from my agent with an invitation to do a crime writers panel at a convention in LA.'

Someone had had to pull out at the last minute. He didn't bother mentioning the name because she didn't read crime fiction and it would probably mean nothing to her even though he was a famous writer and Seb had been delighted to be regarded as a worthy substitute for him. He'd had so many arrangements to make; his health insurance had expired; he had to rearrange lectures and tutorials, calling in favours from colleagues so he could go. Then there'd been the flight arrangements and then it had been so busy while he was there. His agent had lined up some TV and radio interviews and a couple of meetings with film people for him. He had barely had time to sleep rushing from one thing to another.

'My head's still in a spin.'

'Sounds great.' She tried to inject some enthusiasm into her words.

Sensing her mood he added, 'I did try to phone you several times at the beginning of the week.'

'Yes. I was busy too. I have a big case on. And there's a new campaign focusing on human trafficking so today I have to stand in the background and look decorative while the ACC launches an information leaflet. Tune in at teatime and you'll be able to spot me on TV.'

'I was hoping to see you a little more closely than through the TV screen.' He paused and waited for her response.

'Sorry, I'm off to Amsterdam.'

'How long will you be away?'

'A day or maybe two. No more. I'll let you know when I'm back.'

'OK. I'm jet-lagged anyway. I think I'll get some sleep for an hour or two. Then I'll have a lot of work to get caught up on. Take care. Bye.'

He hadn't said he'd missed her. He hadn't mentioned that he had put his house up for sale. He hadn't said he loved her, but then neither had she.

Chapter 20

Harris paused for a moment and watched Gawn through the glass partition dividing her inner office from the rest. He flushed a deep red as he thought back to the conversation he had had the previous night in the pub with some of his former colleagues. They had met up for the first time since he had moved to Serious Crimes. Stuart, the joker in the group, had asked him if he enjoyed being under Gawn and he had started to explain he thought she was a fair boss before another pal had added he had heard that she always liked to be on top and accompanied it with an obscene gesture. He had realised then they were joking at his expense. Before he could tell them to piss off, Stuart had asked whether he'd not been through the sergeant's initiation yet. He'd heard it was very pleasurable. Harris had laughed it off. He watched her for several seconds sitting at her desk, pen in hand, staring straight ahead, lost in thought. When she began writing again, he knocked and waited for her call to enter.

'What is it, Michael?' She sounded a bit distracted but when she had looked up and saw the two cups he was carrying, her face had broken into a smile.

'I noticed you hadn't had a break for lunch, ma'am. I thought a cup of coffee wouldn't go amiss.'

'I could certainly do with something to get my brain working.'

She had been sitting over this piece of paper ever since she had got back from the press launch. She was still thinking about her encounter with McDowell. He had blustered as he always did but she had weathered the storm and when he calmed down she'd been able to placate him. But she was not happy with the case. If there even was a case. Was she tilting at windmills as he had suggested? Then she thought to herself how apt an image that was. Her main hope was that her trip to the Netherlands would turn up something useful.

Harris handed her a cup and glanced down at what she was working on.

'Maybe I could help?' He spoke tentatively, still unsure of what his role in the team was. He didn't really know her yet.

'A new viewpoint would be good. Pull up a chair.'

He was about to sit down opposite her.

'Bring your chair round here so you can see properly. I'm just trying to get an overview on what we know or suspect.'

She had written de Bek's name right in the centre of the page and drawn an aeroplane around it.

'Excuse my drawing. I'm no artist. OK, he was on the plane. He felt ill but did nothing about it. Why?'

'Like we thought, he had something to hide.'

'Something worth risking dying for?'

'Maybe he didn't realise he was so seriously ill. Like the doc said, he might have put it down to indigestion or something.'

'Or he had something with him that he was so desperate to get delivered, he was prepared to risk his own life.' The suggestion seemed a bit fanciful even to her own ears.

'But he didn't have anything in his bag.'

'No, because Clinton switched it but de Bek didn't know that.'

She underlined Clinton's name on the diagram and the word 'drugs' with a question mark.

'Are we sure it was drugs?'

'We're not sure of anything very much.' She sighed and added diamonds and a series of question marks. 'If only we'd searched some of the passengers. At least the ones near de Bek.' Regret sounded in her words and exasperation too.

'We couldn't really, could we? Not then.'

'Then Smith became Clinton and we've got this whole smuggling link.'

She pushed back a strand of hair which had escaped from her chignon and fallen over her eyes. 'We need to see footage from Schiphol to see what his bag looked like before he boarded the plane and to check if he used the restroom. That could be crucial. If he was smuggling something inside his body, he could have removed it and moved it to his bag then. When I get to Amsterdam, I'll ask them to check that.'

'What about diamonds rather than drugs? Amsterdam's famous for diamonds too and a few of them could be worth a lot of money.'

'Possibly. We need more information on de Bek. He did quite a bit of travelling all over Europe. Surely this wasn't his first rodeo.'

'Not if what Dr Norris found at the PM is correct... which it is, I'm sure,' he added hastily.

Harris moved slightly and felt his leg touch Gawn's. He quickly pulled back. She didn't seem to have noticed. He didn't want to give her the wrong impression.

'So what do you think, Michael?'

He realised she had been speaking to him and he hadn't heard a word.

'Sorry, ma'am.'

'I asked if you wanted to have another go at Andrews while I'm in The Netherlands. I think he was nervous when we spoke to him last night. I could understand him being a bit nervous at the airport. It was all a bit unsettling and people were speculating but after all this time, in his own home, when he's had time to think about it? There was something not quite right.'

'Yes. Sure.'

Chapter 21

It had taken until late on Tuesday evening before Gawn had managed to get away from the office. She had had to change her flight booking. So, first thing on Wednesday morning she found herself sitting in the dart-like Embraer aeroplane waiting to take off from City Airport. She wondered if it might even be the same plane on which de Bek had flown and was glad she was in row ten and not twenty-four, although there would be no sign of anything to indicate a death had taken place there.

'Ladies and gentlemen, we are now on approach to Schiphol Airport. We hope you have enjoyed your flight with us today and wish you a safe onward journey.'

Gawn had looked out of the window glad to see the airport laid out before her, lots of blue and white KLM planes sitting in neat rows. The flight had been smooth and uneventful but she was eager to meet up with Jansen and start looking for answers to her questions about de Bek and what he'd been doing in Belfast.

On landing she had been able to walk straight off the plane having only brought a carry-on bag with her. She was glad of the five-minute walk through the concourse to get to the railway station with a direct link into central Amsterdam. It was good to get moving after sitting for nearly two hours after there had been a slight delay before take-off. She was also glad she had not arranged to meet Jansen at the airport. He had offered to pick her up but it was better this way. The train was speedy and she'd been able to book her ticket online. She followed the sign to Amsterdam Centraal down the escalator and onto the platform. A double-decker train was sitting across on the other side of the track. She had last seen one of those when she and Seb had taken the Skytrain from Newark into New York. A blue and yellow single-decker sprinter train pulled in alongside her. The double row of twin seats covered in bright blue vinyl looked cramped but Gawn spotted two seats facing each other with a short table between them. That would give her more leg room. Not that that was a major issue as the journey only took fifteen minutes. The airport was close to the city and they had passed houses and office blocks and built-up areas all along the route. It was not the most scenic trip she had ever taken but it meant she found herself arriving in the city centre on time and ready to get started.

Gawn walked along the platform. She couldn't help glancing up at the vast expanse of cast iron roof over her head. She had seen photographs of it in the guidebook she had bought in preparation for her trip. She had glanced through it during the flight. She didn't expect to be doing any sightseeing but she liked to get a feel for where she was going and in particular get an idea of the layout of the city. She stepped out of the station into a square busy with people and vehicles, especially bicycles. She was glad not to be disappointed. She had expected bicycles and she got them, for sure, everywhere. The tracks for the trams ran right across in front of her and she could see water ahead across the expanse of open square. She suspected it was the Amstel.

'Chief Inspector Girvin?'

She did not expect to hear her name and swung round surprised. It was a uniformed police officer.

'Yes.'

'Commissaris Jansen asked us to pick you up and take you to headquarters.' He smiled reassuringly.

'How...' she began and then decided to save her question until she met Jansen.

They escorted her to a marked Mercedes police car and she was aware of people watching as the door was held open for her and she was shepherded into the back. She felt like a felon on the run being arrested and was sure that was how some of the onlookers were interpreting it too.

The two men did not chat either between themselves or to her so she spent the time looking out the window and watching clumps of tourists milling about. She caught glimpses of some of the canals and boats of all sizes where people lived on the water.

* * *

Jansen stood up from behind his desk and moved round to greet her. She was not sure what she had expected him to look like but the man in the flesh lived up to the expectations his voice had raised. His face was tanned even at this time of year. His wavy blond hair sat neatly on his collar. His thin lips suggested a fastidious character but his eyes told a different story. They were stunningly blue and there was a devilish twinkle to them. He had enjoyed surprising her.

'Chief Inspector.' He held out his hand and held hers briefly as she returned his smile, aware of his aftershave, a masculine earthy fragrance, which reminded her of the outdoors and spring.

'That was quite a welcome, Commissaris. How did you know where to pick me up?'

'I'm a policeman. I knew what time your plane landed. We picked you up on security cameras at Schiphol and tracked you onto the train. Then it was just a matter of despatching officers to meet you when the train arrived. You were bound to come out the main entrance and we had your picture.'

'Where on earth did you get my picture?'

'A little bit of research and we found you in a photo from your local paper when you were heading up an investigation into a murder in Belfast last year.'

'Very impressive. Just a pity you weren't more efficient in getting us the information we were asking for last week about our dead traveller.'

A frown clouded the Dutchman's face. Gawn bit her lip. Maybe she had been too harsh or at least rather undiplomatic. She needed his help; not to alienate him.

'I'm sorry. This case has me frustrated. We can't seem to get a handle on it at all. I apologise for suggesting you weren't helpful enough.'

Jansen directed Gawn to a sofa in the corner of his office and sat down opposite her in an easy chair.

'I understand what it's like,' he said graciously. 'And I must admit we could maybe have got back to your man a bit more quickly. I apologise too. So, apologies out of the way, let's start over. Coffee?'

He had a cafetière of coffee and two cups and saucers sitting ready on a side table.

'Thank you.'

'How do you take it?'

'As it comes.'

He poured a cup for her and reached it across. She couldn't help glancing at his hand. No wedding ring.

He poured another cup for himself, took a sip and then asked, 'Now, how can we help?'

'I need to speak to de Bek's family. I met his son but it was when he was over to identify his father's body so it wasn't the best time to be asking a lot of questions. And I'd like to speak to Mrs de Bek and also visit where he worked.'

'You think his death is connected to his work?'

'Not his death. No. We know that was natural causes. But there was something else going on with him. If I'm being honest, I have no idea what this is all about. We have reason to believe he was trying to smuggle something into the country but whether that had anything to do with his work, we don't know.'

'We have checked in to de Bek more closely since you phoned. We have had our suspicions about his boss for some time and I should tell you as well, de Bek's daughter has come to our attention in relation to drugs but he was under our radar.'

Gawn's quizzical expression encouraged him to add to his comments. 'Gert Meyer, we have long suspected but never been able to prove, is one of the main fences in Amsterdam. Everything from stolen artwork to black market guns, he'll trade in it. But we've never been able to prove anything. And we'd never suspected he was involved in the smuggling of any of the stuff, just trading in it so we weren't investigating de Bek as a possible smuggler, I'm afraid. Meyer's legitimate business is long-established and well-known in Amsterdam and it has a good reputation among booksellers and collectors. De Bek's reputation was good too.'

'And de Bek's daughter?'

'She has a record for drugs, mostly for possession but a little bit of dealing as well.'

'Then it would be good to talk to her too.'

'All that should be possible. I'll get someone to phone the de Beks and let them know we're coming. I think it will be alright to go straight to Meyer's. They're open for business so there should be no difficulty just dropping by. The de Bek girl might be more of a problem. She doesn't live at home but I have men looking for her. Finish your coffee and then we'll go.'

Chapter 22

Jansen had driven them himself. She'd been surprised, when they left police headquarters, to have him lead her to a little red Fiat 500 car. It wasn't quite the type of car she would have associated with him. If she'd thought about it, she would have expected him to drive something big and powerful, perhaps a sports car. Any of the senior officers she knew selected cars which reflected their position and their idea of themselves. Even her. He had noticed her reaction.

'This is my faithful little city runabout. It's brilliant for our narrow streets and our busy traffic. Of course, it would be absolutely useless for car chases but then I don't get involved in too many of those nowadays. Promotions always bring more paperwork and more time behind my desk.'

'You miss being out on the street?'

'Yes.' He didn't elaborate but she could tell he was enjoying guiding her through the busy streets, skilfully avoiding bicycles which seemed to expect right of way in every situation and often appeared out of nowhere risking their rider's life. He pointed out some of the places of interest they were passing, but not too many. He didn't want to imply they turned the investigation into a tourist trip.

Eventually they entered a narrow street bordered on one side by a canal and on the other by tall buildings. Some were four and five storeys high, others only two, so that the overall impression was of irregularity as if the buildings had developed organically some growing taller while others had remained stunted. All seemed impossibly narrow. Some seemed to be private homes, a few with net curtains offering some privacy from the passers-by just inches from their front doors. Their balconies were festooned with plants bringing some colour and life to the scene. Some were shops but there were few shop signs. These were more discreet premises. The people who would be shopping here would know where they were going and what they were looking for. They would not be casual window shoppers.

Jansen drew the little car into an almost impossible space pointing diagonally outwards over the canal. Gawn noticed that the houses opposite fronted right down to the edge of the water. Some had boats moored outside their windows. It was a pretty scene.

'Here we are.'

Gawn looked around. There was no clue as to which building was their destination until they had got out of the car and walked across the roadway. She was amused to note a 'no bicycles' sign painted on the cobbles with two bicycles chained to a pole within inches of it. Jansen led her to a plain dark brown front door. There was a knocker and to the side of the door a brass nameplate identifying this as Meyer Antiquariat. Jansen knocked and they waited. They didn't have to wait long. Gawn was surprised when the door was opened by a young woman. She had expected a man, probably a fairly elderly man, to be the keeper of the door in such an establishment. Instead, this woman was barely out of her teens. Her long blond hair was tied back neatly in a single plait reminiscent of a schoolgirl. Her eyes sparkled in welcome. Gawn had expected to step back in time with ancient books all around but she did not expect to be transported back to the 1960s. Yet this girl was dressed as Gawn had seen pictures of her mother in her pseudo-hippy days. Denim dungarees over a tie-dyed T-shirt looked so incongruous in this setting. Her youth and vitality were a stark contrast to the rows and piles of old books and the pervading musty smell which assailed their nostrils.

Jansen introduced himself and Gawn and explained that they wished to speak with Meneer Meyer. The girl replied in impeccable English with faint traces of an American accent.

'If you'd like to follow me. He's in his office.'

They followed her through the narrow avenue left free between the rows of books. Some were open, heavy tomes with gold-edged pages and illuminated writing. No one else was in the shop. Gawn thought that patrons would make an appointment. There would be no casual dropping-by on a whim here. They reached a dead end. They could go no further without opening a heavy wooden door. The girl asked them to wait and then disappeared through it. Jansen turned round and smiled at his companion. 'Interesting place. Just think of the accumulation of knowledge and experience combined in the pages of these volumes.'

Before Gawn had time to respond, the door opened again and a square man stood in front of them. At least that was her immediate impression. Gert Meyer, if indeed this was he, was as wide as he was tall. A small, cheery-looking individual with a gloriously bald head which shone in the light coming through the window behind him giving an almost halo effect. He was dressed as Gawn had anticipated for such an occupation. His Dickensian appearance complete with waistcoat and cravat was so over-the-top that her first reaction was to wonder if this was a costume and he was playing a role.

'Good day, good day.' His hearty welcome took them both in, his hooded eyes flicking from one to the other. 'Please come into my office.' His English was good. He stood back and chivvied them into a surprisingly modern and well-organised office. A heavy antique dark wood desk with detailed carvings on its legs took up a large proportion of the space. The walls were lined with shelves holding not the expected books but bulging lever arch files and piles of folders. Business must be good. Behind the desk, against the back wall was a row of steel grey filing cabinets all neatly labelled. A selection of indoor plants in various stages of wilting sat along the top trying to bring a lively touch but failing miserably. A dark painting of Madonna and Child hung on the other wall.

'Please sit. How can I help you?' Before they could answer he continued, 'I take it this is about poor Willem.' Meyer levered himself into a leather revolving chair, his ample body overflowing the arms and bulging out in flabby mounds. He did not look comfortable.

'How long had de Bek worked for you? Jansen asked.

'Nearly ten years,' came the quick response.

'And his work was satisfactory?'

'More than satisfactory. Willem was a trusted employee. He handled most of our more important or delicate transactions.' Meyer did not elaborate and Gawn found herself wondering what sort of delicate transactions he meant.

'Was there a particular reason why you chose to send de Bek to Belfast?' Gawn queried, keen to get to the point of her visit.

'No. I don't travel myself anymore. I find it too much of a strain these days. It's really only Willem or Piet – that's Piet Meulenbelt – but Piet's a junior. He doesn't have the same experience as Willem. He hasn't been with me long so Willem did most of the business when travel was required.'

'And why did you want to deal in person?'

Meyer looked puzzled. 'That wasn't our decision, Chief Inspector.'

'But the Ulster Museum didn't request it.'

'No? I presume the museum here did then. I think that's what Willem told me.'

'Do you know why?' asked Jansen.

'I'm afraid you would have to ask them, Commissaris. We always try to accommodate our customers. After all they are paying us.' He smiled and folded his hands across his ample stomach. His hands were tiny, out of proportion to his body, and white, the hands of a woman, thought Gawn.

'You're not aware of Mr de Bek having any enemies?' Gawn felt they hadn't learnt anything to help her yet. She wanted to move on. There had to be something in this man's life or background that had brought him to the attention of criminals.

'Enemies? No. Willem was a quiet, inoffensive man. I couldn't think of him doing anything to anyone that would make him enemies.'

'And there's been no change in his behaviour over the last few weeks?' added Jansen.

Meyer didn't respond right away. He stroked his chin with his hand as he considered his answer. He hesitated before saying, 'I think he might have had something on his mind. I don't interfere in other people's lives. He didn't confide in me but I had the impression, nothing stronger than that, Commissaris, that he was troubled. Something had happened.' He cocked his head to one side, like a wise old owl, and waited for a reaction.

Gawn jumped in quickly. 'If he didn't confide in you, is there anyone else he would have talked to if he was in trouble?'

'You mean apart from his family?'

She nodded.

'I don't think he would have told Piet anything. Piet's a good boy, a hard worker, but he's just that, a boy. If Willem had problems at home or with money or something, I don't think he would have turned to Piet.'

'Anyone else? What about Miss...?' Gawn didn't know the girl's name but she nodded towards the door to indicate who she meant.

'Kiki? I don't think so. She's hardly more than a girl, not much older than Piet. But please ask her if you wish.'

Jansen stood up and Gawn took her cue from him.

'We'll have a word with Kiki on our way out and Piet too if that's alright?'

'Of course, Commissaris. Anything to help.'

Meyer remained seated behind his desk. He did not try to stand or offer to see them out but that suited them fine. They would rather talk to the other two without Meyer hovering in the background anyway.

They found Kiki and a young man whom they took to be Piet standing in the shop examining a pile of invoices.

'Kiki,' began Jansen. 'We were wondering if you and Piet could answer a few questions.'

Piet looked mildly concerned but the girl turned an inquisitive look towards them.

'Ask away.'

'Did Mr de Bek say or do anything that you thought was strange recently?'

'You mean stranger than usual?' The comment came from Piet and was accompanied by a laugh.

The two detectives didn't speak. They just waited sure, from experience, that the boy would not be able to resist adding to his response.

'He was a control freak. He had to do everything himself. Had to know what everyone else was doing all the time. He used to watch me, couldn't trust me to do anything myself. Had to check up on me. It must have driven his family mad. That was probably why his daughter ran off.'

So that was why she had left home.

'When was this, Piet?'

'Last year. She ran off with her boyfriend last summer. According to him, the guy was not good enough for his daughter. He had a whole rant about it. Went on and on. Always complaining about his children. He must have been murder to live with.'

This was a new side to their victim. They were glad that they had arranged to visit the family as soon as they left the shop. It would be interesting to see the family dynamic in action. In Belfast, Nico had given the impression of a dutiful and grief-stricken son but Piet was suggesting that all was not well with the family.

'What about you, Kiki? How did you get on with him?' Gawn asked.

'Alright. He was a bit formal but he wasn't handsy like some of the old men I've worked with. He was always respectful.' Her eyes had flicked towards the office door as she answered and Gawn wondered if she found Meyer 'handsy'.

'And you didn't notice anything strange or he didn't confide anything in you?'

'I don't think he would have confided in anyone here.' Her eyes strayed towards the office door again. 'He was very private but there was one thing.'

They waited.

'He was getting some funny phone calls.'

'By funny, you mean what?' Jansen asked.

'I don't really know. I just know someone would phone him on his mobile and he'd rush off so I couldn't hear what was being said. One time, he turned as white as a sheet at whatever it was they said, and once he rushed out afterwards. I assumed to go home but I don't know.'

They were learning something new, a new side to de Bek, a side which might indicate he was in some sort of trouble or mixed up with dangerous people.

'When was this? Recently?'

'Over the last two or three weeks.'

'Thank you. Both of you. If you think of anything else, please let me know.' Jansen handed the girl his card.

Once outside, the Dutch detective turned to Gawn.

'Do you have his phone?'

'There was no mobile among his belongings on the plane.'

'Perhaps he left it at home. If we could get hold of it, we could trace his calls and see who was contacting him and find out why.

'And that might lead us to what he might have been smuggling or for whom,' Gawn finished his sentence.

They had reached Jansen's little Fiat and he was just about to reverse out of his parking space when the way was blocked by a limousine.

'A Rolls-Royce. Meyer's having a rich customer.'

But he wasn't. They watched in the rear-view mirror as an expensively dressed woman was helped out of the back seat by an older man. The door beside Meyer's opened and they were greeted by a middle-aged man in a formal suit.

'I wonder what that place is,' Gawn commented.

Jansen pulled his phone out of his pocket, typed in the address and let out a low whistle.

'Van der Meer. I presume you've heard of De Beers.'

'Of course, every woman knows about De Beers.'

'And dreams of getting an engagement ring from them?'

'Of course.' She laughed.

'Van der Meer's is, if anything, even more exclusive and expensive. It is very discreet. Even I didn't know where it was – never having had occasion to buy an engagement ring.' His eyes twinkled at her as he added, 'Not yet anyway.'

Chapter 23

The journey from the bookshop to the de Bek home had only taken a few minutes. Long enough for the two detectives to discuss what they wanted to ask.

'We're dealing with a respectable family, at least outwardly, at the time of the death of the father,' Jansen said. 'It wouldn't be normal practice for us to be too probing in our questions. At least not at this stage until we know more.'

'You mean, go easy on Mrs de Bek?' Gawn paraphrased.

'Yes. We'll take it easy.'

She wasn't about to argue with him. She was on his turf; she had no authority here. She appreciated him taking the time to come with her rather than sending a junior officer. Although she suspected that might be so that he could keep an eye on her and see what she was doing. She would follow his lead.

The de Beks' home was in the middle of a row of what she now recognised as typical Dutch houses again fronting onto a canal. There was nothing outstanding about it. As they approached she saw a movement, a flash of something at an upper window and realised they were being watched.

'Someone's watching us,' she said.

'Yes. I noticed.'

She left it to Jansen to knock on the door. They waited for a minute. Then they heard a lock turn and the door slowly swung open to reveal Nico de Bek. Gawn recognised him even though his appearance had changed radically from his trip to Belfast. The torn jeans had given way to black trousers with razor-sharp creases down the front. They were teamed with a crisp white linen shirt. The earrings were nowhere to be seen. The ponytail was gone, replaced by short slicked-back hair. The young man looked like the height of respectability dressed almost as if he was ready for the funeral right away.

'Mr de Bek, I'm Commissaris Jansen. I phoned earlier.'

'Yes. Mama said. Please come in. You too, Chief Inspector.'

Nico stepped back to leave them space to enter a long dark passageway. The family obviously lived to the back of the house and he led them down to a shadowy room. In spite of the fact there were no curtains at the window, the room was in semi-darkness, even at this time of day. It was lit by a single lamp on a side table, its meagre strength struggling to make much headway against the dark furnishings and the lowering neighbouring houses. A middle-aged woman dressed all in black sat rigidly on a sofa. She looked up as they entered. It was hard to identify what age she might be from her appearance but Gawn knew from reading the background reports on de Bek that his wife, Mathilde, was younger than her husband, not so very much older than Gawn herself. She reminded her of a painting by one of the Old Masters. Her doleful face only needed to be framed by a white ruffle collar for them all to be transported back in time. Gawn realised she was being unnecessarily critical. The woman seemed distraught, and if de Bek was anything like the control freak Kiki and especially Piet had described him as and he had driven her daughter away from the home, Mathilde de Bek had not had an easy life.

'Mama, it's the police.'

The figure didn't speak, just nodded in acknowledgement. A young woman stepped out of the gloom at the back of the room.

'Mama's not in a fit state to answer questions. Whatever you want to know, Nico and I can tell you.'

'I'm sorry. You are?' Jansen asked.

'This is my sister, Lara,' Nico said.

Gawn was surprised. They had been told the girl had run away but obviously she had chosen to come back now her father was gone. She looked surprisingly healthy for a drug user and she obviously took care with her appearance.

'Sorry for your loss,' Jansen said. 'We would really appreciate anything you can tell us about your husband and what he was doing in Belfast.'

At his words, the widow began sobbing into her handkerchief.

'I told you, she's not fit to answer questions,' the girl almost hissed at them.

'Perhaps we could talk outside, Commissaris,' Nico suggested with a gesture inviting them to step out of the room.

'Of course.'

Lara whispered something to her mother and patted her hand. Then she followed Nico as he walked back up the hallway and out the door. The detectives followed behind them. Once outside both Nico and Lara lit up cigarettes.

'It's like a mausoleum in there already. I don't know how we're going to get Mama through the next few days.' The young woman inhaled deeply.

'Perhaps your doctor could prescribe something to help her,' Gawn suggested.

'She's already full of drugs. We just keep her topped up.' Lara laughed bitterly. 'She has been for years.'

'We need to ask you some questions and there's no easy way to do it.'

'Go ahead, Commissaris.' Nico blew a ring of smoke out of his mouth and watched as it slowly dispersed. 'But I can tell you now, we don't know anything about the work my father did. I expect his boss would be able to tell you all that.'

'Were you aware of any difficulties your father might have been having with anyone?'

The pair seemed surprised at the question. It was the girl who answered. 'Neither of us live at home. My parents are... were... Papa was very strict. They didn't understand how we wanted to live our lives. I visited them most weekends for an hour or two but I didn't notice anything out of the ordinary. Papa was just Papa, laying down the law. Complaining that Nico didn't have a proper job, that I hadn't found a nice young man and got married and given them grandchildren to show off to their friends. Complaining that Astrid was a disgrace to the family name.'

'Astrid?'

'Our sister,' Nico explained.

So, this was a different sister. Lara was not the one who had run away.

'Where would we find Astrid?'

'God knows. I haven't seen her for over a year. Have you, Nico?'

'No.'

'And neither of you know of any conflict, any problems your father was having? He wasn't in debt to anyone?'

'Neither a borrower nor a lender be. How often did we hear that?' Lara said bitterly. 'That's why he wouldn't lend me the money to start my own business.'

'And everything was fine between your parents?'

'My God, Commissaris, are you suggesting that my mother somehow drove my father to his death? She put up with everything he did. We were able to walk out, she had to stay.' Lara looked shocked at any criticism of her mother.

'No. Of course not. I just wondered if perhaps your father may have developed other interests.'

Lara laughed out loud. 'You think he was having an affair? Impossible.'

'Nothing is impossible when it comes to human behaviour,' Jansen asserted gently. 'It may be difficult for you to think of your parents in that way but your father was a reasonably young man. It wouldn't be impossible that he met someone.'

'No.' Lara was adamant. Nico put his arm on his sister's shoulder and nodded his head in agreement.

'I would like to arrange a search of your father's belongings. Did he have a mobile phone?'

'Doesn't everyone? He was in business. He needed it especially when he was away travelling.'

'And he had it with him when he went to Belfast? Or could he have left it behind?' Gawn asked.

'He had it with him.'

'How are you so certain?'

'Because he phoned Mama from Schiphol on it just before he was called to board the plane. That was the last time they spoke.'

'I'd like to speak with your mother about that call,' Jansen said.

It was clear from the tone of Nico's response that he was not going to agree to that. 'I don't think she's in a fit state to answer your questions, Commissaris. She told us about the call. It was nothing special. Just that he would be very late home and might stay over at the airport hotel again.'

'Again?'

'Yes. He had stayed there the previous night because he had an early start and he didn't want to disturb her. It was on his way back from Monnickendam.'

'He had been to Monnickendam on Sunday? What was at Monnickendam?' Jansen asked.

'The old family home. Where he was brought up.'

'Who lives there now? Was he visiting someone?'

'No. It's practically derelict. I kept telling him to sell it. He could get good money for the land but he said it had sentimental value. Mama'll be able to sell it now,' said Nico with the insensitivity of youth. He obviously had no sentimental attachment to the home of his ancestors.

Chapter 24

They sat in the car after Nico and Lara had gone back into the house and closed the front door behind them.

'An interesting family,' Gawn said. 'Those two really didn't like their father, did they? And I wonder why they're trying so hard to keep us from questioning their mother.'

'I'm sure you've been a cop long enough to have seen life in all its forms, Chief Inspector. They're not particularly attractive personalities, those two, but at least they're there for their mother. As you say, they obviously didn't get on well with their father which is a pity for us because it means they weren't around to notice if he seemed to be in any trouble.'

'Can you check into all their finances, see if he or any of them was in trouble?'

'You think he might have been in debt to someone or being blackmailed?'

'It's possible, surely?'

'Yes. I'll get someone onto that.'

'And I think we should try to find Astrid de Bek and hear what she has to say about her father. Maybe she can give us another perspective.' Gawn was suddenly aware she was leading as she would do back in Belfast, as if she was in charge and realised she would have to be careful not to be too pushy. She was here as a courtesy. But Jansen didn't seem to notice. He seemed happy to go along with her suggestions.

'She probably doesn't even know her father's dead. But if she's living away from home for over a year, she'll not know what was going on with her father either. She mightn't be a lot of help to us.'

Jansen phoned his office and set one of his junior officers to get him the address of the missing daughter. They had already been looking for her so he hoped they would be able to come up with an address quickly. Another was ordered to begin an examination of de Bek's finances and a third to find the service provider for de Bek's phone.

'What's at Monnickendam? Is there anything special about it?'

'It's a lovely little place. A real tourist spot. I can't imagine it as a centre for crime but who knows? I assume he had a sentimental attachment to the house if he wouldn't sell it. Maybe he stored things there.'

His comment set them both thinking. What could have been stored there? If de Bek was part of a drug gang it could be where they kept their supplies. It seemed as if they had only started their journey back to headquarters when his phone rang. They had tracked down Astrid.

'Good work, Arrens. Give me the address. We'll head straight there.' He finished the call and turned to Gawn. 'Astrid lives on a canal boat. So you'll get the opportunity to see one of our famous canal homes at close quarters.'

They made their way through a maze of narrow streets. Jansen seemed to know exactly where he was going. As he began to swing the little car to make a right turn into one of the canalside streets, he had to pull to a sudden halt. They were facing the scene of what was obviously some kind of serious incident. People were huddled on their front steps. Some of the canal boat owners were standing on deck or sitting, their legs dangling over the waters of the canal, watching the scene. Maybe one of the ubiquitous cyclists had made one too many dangerous moves. Two ambulances sat ready with their back doors open. Gawn could count at least three police cars. Uniformed officers were walking and standing around. It must be something major.

Jansen stopped his car where it was. He wasn't blocking anything because no other vehicle was going to be allowed down this street anyway. That much was obvious. They got out and one of the police officers saluted smartly, recognising the commissaris. They could see a concentration of men dressed in white by the canalside. Jansen made straight for them.

'What's going on?'

The men seemed to stand up just a little straighter as they turned and saw who was speaking.

'Commissaris,' the oldest-looking man in the group responded. 'Double death, sir.'

'Suicide? Murder or murder–suicide? What?'

'We're still assessing the scene.'

'Have you identified the bodies?'

'Yes, sir. They're well known here. The man is Rudy Axler. He was an actor.' The way he pronounced the word left them in no doubt what he thought of the man's acting ability. 'He did a bit of street drama for the tourists. And painted. He was an arty type. He sold pictures to tourists too. He saw himself as a sort of Banksy.'

'And the other?'

'His girlfriend. We haven't got her last name yet but she was called Astrid.'

Jansen and Gawn exchanged looks. This could be no coincidence.

'Can we see the bodies?'

The momentary hesitation showed that the investigating officer wasn't particularly happy either at the possibility of having his crime scene contaminated or at the interference of his senior officer. But, of course, he agreed. He had no choice. Jansen had asked as a matter of courtesy.

They were not going to go into the main body of the barge. It would be enough to get some indication of what might have happened if they looked in from the doorway. Gawn was surprised to see a row of pretty planters and a garden table and two chairs sitting out on the deck. They had tried to make a real home here. Even as they stepped on board, the stench hit them. Gawn had been aware of an unpleasant smell as they'd stood talking, now it became almost overwhelming. She knew this smell of putrid decaying flesh. She had smelt it too often. She was tempted to take her hankie from her pocket and hold it to her mouth and nose for she knew the smell would cling to her nostrils long after she had left the scene but she didn't.

'Who found them?' Jansen called out.

'One of the neighbours. His dog was howling. The doctor thinks they've been dead since last week.'

So sometime around when de Bek had died.

Standing either side of the entrance, they looked down the steps into the narrow room. It took a moment for their eyes to adjust to the darker interior. The configuration immediately took Gawn back to caravan holidays she had spent as a child, the compact layout offering everything needed for living crammed into a tight space. There were colourful paintings on the wall, probably Rudy's own work. Some were askew, disturbed in some sort of struggle. Cushions lay scattered on the floor. But the main impression of the room was of the colour red. Red blood splattered over the walls, over the wooden floor, over the hard steel surfaces of the kitchenette. This had been a frenzied kill. Pots and pans lay where they'd fallen. The man was on the floor face up, his chest slashed open. His shirt looked as if it had passed through a shredder. One of his hands was almost severed at the wrist. He lay in a dark pool of his own blood. The girl was further back. Her half-naked body lay splayed over a pile of cushions. There was a deep gash across her throat. Even from a distance Gawn couldn't help noticing the look of horror caught on the girl's face. She had realised what her fate was to be.

A white-suited forensic investigator emerged from further within the dark recesses of the barge almost below them with a clear plastic bag in his hand. He held it aloft.

'E tabs, cannabis and some cocaine,' he announced triumphantly to no one in particular.

Gawn was glad when Jansen turned and they could step carefully on to the canal path and away from the gory scene. She was glad too that they had not gone inside for then the sickly smell would have clung to her clothes and she hadn't brought another suit with her for the short trip. She found herself wondering what sort of person she had become that her clothes caused her more concern than the brutal killing of these two young people, no matter what crimes they might have been engaged in.

As they stepped off the deck, mortuary staff passed them with two stretchers and body bags ready to move the victims.

'Your officer has just found some drugs,' Jansen told the group of men standing outside.

'Not surprising, sir. They were well-known for it. Rudy had convictions for dealing and the girl was no doubt helping him.'

'A drug deal gone wrong?' Jansen suggested.

'That's what we're thinking, or maybe one of their junkie clients off their head.'

'Keep me informed on your investigation.'

When Jansen saw the expression on the officer's face, he added, 'I'm not doubting your ability to investigate, Frans. It's just that we're looking into the circumstances surrounding the death of the girl's father. He too died last week and while his death was from natural causes there could be some connection. He might have been under some strain because of her.'

They were quiet as they walked back to the car. It was Jansen who broke the silence first.

'I don't think this is a coincidence.'

'No. I agree.'

'What the hell were they all involved in? You think de Bek was smuggling drugs? Could he have been their supplier? Was he even involved in their murder?'

Gawn shook her head slowly. She couldn't imagine a father being there when his daughter was butchered like that. She didn't want to imagine it.

'I honestly have no idea. When we first started looking at de Bek there was absolutely nothing to indicate he was involved in anything shady and you told us he had no police record. But your daughter doesn't get hacked to death at almost the same time as you happen to die, without something major going on. I just can't figure out how it all fits together.'

'Maybe it is just a frenzied killing?' He was trying to convince himself as much as her. 'They would have been mixing with all types of crazies. We might be reading too much into it. The father dying could be just an unfortunate coincidence. This must have been someone off their head. High on drugs. No sane person kills like that.'

'It's debatable if any sane person kills at all but, let's say you were planning something major and you wanted to tidy up any loose ends, anything which could connect you, wouldn't you want this to look like some crazy? To be written off as another victim of the drug scene? Astrid's death makes a nice tidy end. No need to look any further.'

'But, of course, you are going to, aren't you, Chief Inspector?'

'Astrid's murder is not my business. This is your city. She is your victim, but it all just makes me more certain there is something very serious happening or planned in Northern Ireland and that is my business.'

Chapter 25

Jansen had suggested taking her to dinner. They wouldn't be able to go to the de Bek family farm at Monnickendam to look around until the next day. She was alone in a strange city. They had both had a busy day and neither wanted to have too much time on their hands after seeing the bodies on the canal boat. Dining alone in the hotel restaurant or getting room service would be a waste, he had argued. He could show her a little of his city. The good side. The happy places. He knew a quiet little bistro where they could have a good meal and forget about murders for a while. It sounded very reasonable and she let him convince her. Why not? She still had the vision of the two victims in her mind. It would be good to forget for a little while how awful the world could be.

She'd spent a long time under the shower getting ready. The smell of death seemed to cling to her. She knew it was just her imagination. She had used copious amounts of shower gel and especially shampoo to get the smell out of her hair and she had sprayed her favourite perfume more liberally than usual. Perhaps a little too liberally, she thought to herself. She had a change of shirt but had to wear the same trouser suit.

Jansen insisted on coming to the hotel to meet her. She insisted she would meet him in the foyer. So at eight she had emerged from the elevator and found him already waiting. He had changed out of his formal suit and was wearing a pair of jeans and an expensive-looking black leather jacket over a pink, what she took to be, cashmere jumper. He looked relaxed and she admitted to herself, rather attractive.

'Good evening, Chief…' he started and then he stopped. 'I can't spend the whole evening referring to you as Chief Inspector. May I? Gawn.'

'Of course.'

'I'm Hendrik or Dirk to my friends. Have you ever been in Amsterdam before?'

'No. Never, Hendrik.' As soon as she'd spoken she remembered how, on her first dinner – which was not a date – with Seb, she had lied to him about a holiday in Amsterdam. She had wanted to get information about his travels and whether he had been here at the time of a murder. 'What little I saw of it coming in on the train from the airport, it's lovely. You're lucky to live in such a beautiful city but I imagine the tourists must be a bit annoying at times.' She had deliberately called him Hendrik to indicate she didn't regard herself as his friend, just a colleague.

'They can be. In the city centre. In the outskirts, where I live, it's not so much of a problem and, of course, I'm not exactly queuing up to visit the Anne Frank Huis or the Rijksmuseum every day. It can be a pain when you're trying to get somewhere quickly in an emergency but usually I am called in after the event, like yourself.'

She had thought they might be driving or he would hail a taxi but instead he started walking along the street.

'Central Amsterdam is really quite small. You'll see so much more if we walk. You don't mind?'

'No. Of course not.'

She didn't. It was a pleasant evening, quite mild for the time of year. And it was dry. No sign of rain. She was glad of the exercise and he was right, it was a good way to see a bit of the city. Most of the shops were closed, of course, but the lighted windows offered interesting displays. They passed a tourist shop, still open, its ranks of postcards and its invitation to purchase tickets to visit various attractions festooning its frontage. Turning a corner, Gawn recognised the busy Central Station where she had arrived just hours before and to her left a shopfront announcing itself as a Sex Museum. Only in Amsterdam, she thought to herself. They turned off the main square and she realised they were near the Red Light District. She had heard of it but had no desire to visit it and hoped Jansen wasn't crass enough to think she would be entertained by the sight of exploited girls. He wasn't. They quickly turned again into what was little more than an alleyway and Gawn saw a lighted restaurant sign up ahead. He had obviously booked a table and they were escorted to a quiet area towards the back of a small room.

Gawn was glad she had allowed Jansen to convince her to have dinner with him. She was hungry not having eaten anything since her hurried breakfast at the airport. Dinner alone hadn't appealed. He knew Amsterdam well, of course, and the discreet restaurant he had selected, where the music was low enough to let them chat without having to strain to hear each other, was perfect. The menu featured Indonesian food and she allowed her Dutch colleague to select for both of them. They started with a traditional meat soup which Gawn found a little sweet for her taste. Then he had chosen nasi goreng. She didn't have the heart to tell him she had it regularly at her local Asian fusion takeaway.

'Good choice, Hendrik. Absolutely delicious.'

'Thank you.' He smiled back at her delighted that she approved of his selections.

Neither of them wanted to talk about the case. They both had their own thoughts and suspicions. So the talk was more general. Nothing too personal. He had travelled a little in the Far East and shared some stories of his exploits.

When the meal was finished, Jansen hesitated and then with a disarming smile asked, 'It's such a nice evening, how about we walk back to your hotel and we can stop and get coffee on the way? It'll let you see a bit more of the city.'

'Yes. Why not? That would be pleasant.' A stroll in the late evening with the moon over the Amstel would be an enjoyable end to the day which she had found much more useful and productive than she had expected at first, but which had also been more challenging and had given her plenty to think about.

Jansen paid the bill. He assured her that it was on his hospitality expenses otherwise she would not have agreed to let him pay for her meal. They left the restaurant and began walking, strolling really, along the narrow streets. She found herself wondering how they must look to passers-by. Probably like tourists or maybe even a couple.

'I'm taking you to the Brouwersgracht. Everyone goes to Prinsengracht. It's always packed with tourists but Brouwersgracht not so much. There'll still be lots of people about but not so many and you'll get to see the beauty of the canal and the pretty old houses much better, I think. It was named the prettiest street in Amsterdam recently.' He smiled with a boyish grin which she found endearing.

And he was right. Brouwersgracht was delightful. She enjoyed walking along catching glimpses of the lives going on inside the colourful narrow canal boats – ordinary life, a girl cooking dinner in one, a mother nursing her baby in another, a young man hunched over his computer, maybe working or maybe playing a game. Ordinary life but lived on the water. Except she couldn't help being drawn back to the canal boat they had visited that afternoon and the bodies of Rudy and Astrid.

The ubiquitous bicycles were parked up everywhere in huge mounds or chained to the bridges and from time to time they had to practically jump out of the way as a cyclist sped past ringing his bell. There were places to sit and the two detectives did just that. Just sat and took in the atmosphere. Gawn almost felt guilty. On work trips she seldom allowed herself the luxury of any personal time.

'I'm very proud of my home city.' Jansen nodded his head as if he was agreeing with himself.

'As you have every right to be. It's charming,' Gawn assured him. 'How about that coffee now, Hendrik?' It was getting late. Gawn didn't really want to prolong the evening too much. She wanted to get some sleep. She had their journey to Monnickendam in the morning and a flight home booked for early evening.

'Sure. Of course. There's a café just along here.'

He took her by the elbow and helped her up. When she stood he didn't release his hold on her arm but led her along the street to a brightly lit busy-looking corner café. A group of young people were congregating outside laughing and talking. He opened the door for her and placed his hand on her back to guide her inside. It was even busier and noisier now and Gawn thought they would never be able to get a seat, but Jansen pushed his way through to the far corner of the room making a pathway for her to follow. There was a tiny table for two, sitting almost as if it were waiting for them.

'What would you like, Gawn?'

'Just an espresso, please.'

'You'd be up all night with the hit of caffeine. How about a tea or a fruit juice?'

'OK. Tea then. Thanks.'

While her colleague went to the counter, Gawn looked around. She was becoming increasingly uneasy. She had recognised the aroma of marijuana as soon as they'd walked in. She had never considered that the policeman would take her to a coffee shop. She realised that most of the customers were young, mostly male and probably tourists. For a so-called café, no one seemed to be drinking any coffee. She couldn't help being fascinated to watch those around her who were obviously smoking weed or munching on hash-filled muffins. They looked relaxed and happy, having a good time.

'Here we go. Two teas.' He set the two cups down on the table and then held out his hand. 'I got us a gram of weed. I assume you've never tried it… or am I wrong?' He fixed her with a look and smiled, an almost taunting smile.

'No. You're quite right. I never have. It's illegal in Northern Ireland as I'm sure you know.' She was lying. She had tried it in Afghanistan but she wasn't going to get into that with him.

'Of course. But not here, so now is your chance.'

He was still holding the spliff out to her, daring her, it seemed, to take it. She wondered if it was some kind of test. She hesitated. She had never knowingly walked away from a challenge even when it had sometimes got her into trouble or possible danger. She knew that was a weakness with her. And she knew this could get her into trouble, not with the authorities although that was a possibility if word of it got back to Belfast, but more with how it would affect her. She didn't like to feel out of control and for that reason rarely drank more than a single glass of wine or a gin and tonic when she was out. But it was not any sense of fear that prevented her from lifting the cigarette from his hand and allowing him to light it for her. It was the undoubted sense of hypocrisy she would experience. She was here because she suspected someone was trying to smuggle drugs into Belfast. OK, hash was at the low end of the drug scale but it was still a drug and, although she had read the arguments, a way into a world of addiction for many.

The Dutchman set the spliff down on the table in front of her and then sat down himself. The tables were so tightly packed together that their knees were touching. He took a sip of his tea but didn't light the spliff he had bought for himself. He looked around him.

'The secret is not to inhale too deeply. It is not necessary to get the desired effect.'

'Which is what exactly?'

'Don't tell me the PSNI doesn't include drug training for its officers,' he teased.

'Of course it does, but I wondered what you specifically look for?'

'Just to relax. If it's been a stressful day it's good to smoke a little weed and just chill.'

Gawn couldn't believe she was having this conversation with another police officer. She was not so naive that she didn't realise some of her colleagues in the Met, and probably some of her colleagues in the PSNI, took drugs and she had been offered them herself, but this casual open acceptance was something different.

'And has this been a particularly stressful day?'

'Definitely not. On the contrary, Gawn, it has been an interesting day, with company that made it so much more pleasant.'

He leaned forward and set his hand on top of hers. He began to run his thumb up and down the back of her hand.

'You are very good company, Gawn.'

She wondered if it was the effects of inhaling all the weed in the atmosphere that had given him the confidence to hit on her. She could feel her own head slightly fuzzy. But maybe that was just imagination or tiredness. She removed her hand from under his. Until she met Seb it had been several years since she had been involved in a relationship. And their relationship hadn't started off too conventionally either. She decided she was definitely out of practice. And out of practice at reading the signs. She thought of her evening with Jenny Norris and wondered if somehow she had led Jansen on. She didn't think so; hoped not.

'It has been a most pleasant evening. Thank you, Hendrik. But now I need to get back to my hotel.' She spoke very deliberately. She was already standing up.

'I will walk you the rest of the way.'

'That isn't necessary. It's not far. You stay and relax.'

But he was already on his feet. She didn't want to make a scene so she allowed him to guide her out of the café and back towards the hotel. She noted that he lifted the marijuana he had purchased for them and put it in his pocket. Outside she was glad he was with her. She had lost her bearings a little and was not sure exactly how to get back. The air was crisp and clear and she inhaled deeply and then exhaled slowly as if to clear her lungs from the passive drugs she'd been breathing.

More quickly than she had expected, they reached the hotel. He had obviously taken a more direct route back. At the front door she stopped, turned and faced him.

'Good evening, Hendrik. Thank you for your hospitality.'

She didn't wait for his response but turned and hurried inside. She got into her room and collapsed down on top of the bed. It had been a tougher day than she had anticipated. And now she had really misread that situation with Jansen. She had thought it was a purely professional social occasion. She had never anticipated anything else. Her relationship with Seb might be a bit rocky at the minute but she didn't want it to end and she wasn't on the lookout for any casual one-night stand.

She had already started to undress when a knock came to the door. Looking through the spyhole, she saw Jansen standing there. For a second she considered ignoring him, hoping he would go away. Then she thought it must be something important. Hastily rebuttoning her blouse, she opened the door.

'Is something wrong?'

'I've just had a call from HQ. There's a big meeting in the morning.'

He looked around behind him as if he was worried someone would overhear. Then he walked past her into the room and closed the door carefully behind him.

'They've intercepted chatter about a possible terrorist attack or something so everyone's running around chasing their own tails. Panicking.'

'I see. So we have to abandon our trip to Monnickendam?'

She was disappointed. This would have been her last chance to find something useful to help her case. Otherwise she would have to go back to Belfast and depend on the Dutch finding something in de Bek's finances or from his phone, if his service provider gave them the information.

'There's a big council of war in the morning so I won't be able to go out to Monnickendam with you first thing but if you can wait, I'll go as soon as I'm free.'

They were standing only inches apart and she was aware of his aftershave. He had walked past her into the room so now her back was to the door and he was facing her. She had nowhere to go. She realized Jansen was moving even closer to her and noticed the way he was looking at her. Before she had time to react, he reached out and stroked her cheek.

'Beautiful.'

She froze. Part of her wanted to push him away. He leaned in and kissed her, first gently but then with increasing passion. She couldn't help herself. She responded. She felt his hand on her back, skin to skin under her shirt pulling their bodies closer together. It was as if that contact brought her to her senses. Seb loved to trace the line of her spine, to explore her body running his fingers along her scars. She swung around, surprising the Dutchman and pushed him away.

'No.' It sounded like one of those education programmes she had been forced to lead for teenage girls around local schools when she was in the Met. 'Just say no'. Well, she was saying no.

His eyes told her he was not used to being rejected but he didn't seem to be too disappointed. He immediately let her go and stood back, raising his two arms in mock surrender.

'I thought you were OK with this.'

'I'm not. Sorry.' Then she wondered why she was apologising. It was her body, her choice.

'I'll phone when my meeting's finished tomorrow.'

He moved past her, his body brushing against hers, and left closing the door behind him. He didn't slam it but she wondered if she would ever see him again or if he would fob her off with a more junior officer in the morning. Whatever. Her investigation here was almost over. A quick trip out to Monnickendam to tie up any loose ends and she would be able to report back that it was still not clear if de Bek had been involved in anything suspicious. If necessary, she would hire a car and go on her own just for thoroughness.

She had a strong urge to speak to Seb. She wanted to hear his voice; not to talk to him about anything in particular. In fact she didn't want to get into a whole conversation with him at all, just to hear him say 'I miss you' for she was missing him. With only a slight time difference, she knew it would be early enough that he would still be up. He'd probably be sitting at his laptop, glass of wine by his side, hopefully getting some words down on paper. She used speed dial for his mobile number. It rang. And rang. And rang. No reply. He never went anywhere without his phone. Maybe he was simply out of the room and hadn't heard it ringing. She undressed and cleaned her teeth before trying again. She heard the ringing but there was still no reply.

She wasn't one to worry unduly. She decided to text him, tell him she had tried to ring and ask him to phone her in the morning. She had to be content with that. She climbed into bed, turned out the light and tried to get to sleep. After fifteen minutes, she was jokingly thinking to herself she should have tried the spliff to help her sleep. Instead she took one of the sleeping pills her doctor had prescribed. She didn't like using them but she needed to get some sleep. And sleep came. Eventually.

Chapter 26

'Gawn.'

She had expected Jansen would cry off their trip to de Bek's old home, perhaps send someone else with her, so she was surprised to hear his voice. She was sitting over coffee in her hotel room having decided on room service rather than a visit to the hotel restaurant.

'Hendrik, I–' Before she could finish her sentence, he interrupted her.

'Meyer's dead. Kiki found him this morning when she arrived to open the shop.'

'Meyer's dead?' She was aware that she had just repeated what he had told her and that she sounded like a character in a bad B-movie but she couldn't help it. She was stunned. 'Dead or murdered?' she asked, aware too that there was a slight tremor in her voice.

'It's not clear yet how he died. There were no obvious signs of violence but it's strange timing. We question him one day and he dies that night, a week after one of his employees dies too.'

'Someone's cleaning up their mess; getting rid of any loose ends, like I said yesterday.'

'Yes, I think so. It's just too coincidental. My meeting has just finished here. I'll send a car to bring you to Elandsgracht. See you shortly.'

He rang off. He had not mentioned last night. She wouldn't be bringing it up either.

* * *

He looked exactly as he had the first time she had met him. Urbane and sophisticated, his suit well-fitting and his tie perfectly knotted. A senior officer on the rise.

'Good morning, Gawn.' Was there a slight edge to his voice or was she imagining it?

'Hendrik.' She smiled, not too much, just enough to be friendly in a business sort of way. God, this was going to be awkward. She just knew it.

'Coffee?'

He reached a cup towards her as she seated herself in the same armchair as yesterday. Only yesterday. Hard to believe after all that had happened since then. She couldn't help but think about their coffee experience the previous evening. She wondered how often he had sat in this office with the effects of marijuana still in his system. Did he feel guilty as she had done when she was popping her little pills to help her get through? She had Seb to thank for helping her to get over them. But she didn't want to think about him. Not now. And he still hadn't got in touch; hadn't responded to her text.

'They'll still at the scene at Meyer's but there didn't seem to be a break-in or anything stolen, as far as Kiki could tell them, anyway. One of the filing cabinets was open but he may just have been looking through something when he died.'

Astrid, Rudy and now Meyer, all dead and at least two of them murdered.

'Do you think it has anything to do with your case?'

'Probably. Maybe. I don't know.'

'Let me ask you then, Gawn, de Bek may not have been killed but whoever is involved in all this had arranged for your Australian, Smith or Clinton or whatever his name is, to switch bags so that something made its way into Northern Ireland and it was picked up there, wasn't it?'

'Yes.' That made her think of something. 'I haven't checked in with my people yet today. They were going through CCTV footage from the drop. I wonder, would you mind if I phoned my sergeant now?'

'Of course not. I want to check something anyway. I'll leave you for a minute in private.'

'Oh, it's fine. You don't have to.' But he was already making his way out of the room.

Harris answered on the third ring.

'Boss?'

'Any news? And make it good.'

'We got him.' He sounded pleased.

'You've arrested someone?'

'No. I mean we found the man who picked up the bag on the CCTV coverage.'

'He picked it up?' She had expected the bag would have been dumped and only its contents taken.

'Yes. When they checked the toilets first thing, they found the backpack with a briefcase inside but it wasn't the one Clinton had put there. We showed it to him and he identified it was different. Very similar but different. Jamie was really eagle-eyed. We'd been looking for someone going in without a bag but this guy had one and simply swapped the two and Jamie spotted him.'

'Tell him "good work" from me. I take it, it's no one we've been able to identify yet,' she added.

'Not yet. We're running it through facial rec but he was pretty careful to try to cover his face as much as possible.'

'Send me through a still and I'll let them have a look here in case there's another Dutch connection. I should be back later this evening or first thing tomorrow.'

She rang off. With impeccable timing, Jansen walked back into the room. Equally well-timed, her notifications on her phone buzzed to let her know Harris had sent the picture.

'Here's a photo of the man who picked up de Bek's bag.' She held out her phone and Jansen took it, studying the figure.

'Doesn't look familiar.'

'No. We haven't identified him yet either, although' – she paused and took another long look at the screen – 'there's something vaguely familiar about him. It'll come to me.'

Chapter 27

Gawn was surprised that within such a short time of leaving the city they were in the open countryside. The little Fiat sped along the road heading towards Monnickendam. She could have enjoyed seeing all the iconic windmills if she wasn't thinking ahead and wondering what, if anything, they would find at the farm. She didn't know whether she hoped they would find something or there would be nothing.

Jansen's phone rang and he pulled off the main road to take the call.

'And they are sure it was not there anywhere?'

Gawn wondered what was missing and from where.

When he ended the call, he turned to her, a perplexed look on his face.

'Is something missing from Meyer's office?' she asked.

'No. From the canal boat.'

'What?'

'A finger.'

'What!' She hadn't been expecting that.

'Apparently Astrid was missing her index finger. They had assumed it was sliced off in the struggle but they can't find it anywhere on the boat. Then they thought perhaps the killer or killers had taken it away as a sort of trophy but now the doctor has said at the PM that it was cut off anything up to three weeks ago and had partially healed.'

They both stayed silent for a minute mulling over what this might mean. It was Gawn who spoke first.

'You know what this makes me think of?'

'Kidnapping,' Jansen answered.

Gawn nodded. 'Exactly. That's what came into my mind. Someone held for ransom. Proof of life.'

Could Astrid have been abducted to get de Bek to smuggle something? That was what Gawn was thinking but she didn't want to put her idea into words. It seemed like too big a jump. There was no proof yet that the girl had been kidnapped at all and if she had it was just as likely some of their drug-dealing associates were involved, a falling out of some kind.

'Nearly there.'

Jansen had turned the car off the main road onto a much narrower country lane. It was obviously seldom travelled and gradually narrowed until it was little more than a track. Eventually they were faced by a rusty gateway preventing their further progress up to a derelict-looking building.

'I'll open it.'

Gawn hopped out. She was surprised at how easily the gate swung open. Jansen drove through.

Gawn leaned in the car window. 'I'll walk up. No need to get back in the car. See you up at the house.'

He drove on and she walked behind. The path was rutted and deep mud had hardened after days without rain, making it difficult to walk on. She was just grateful that she had worn comfortable flat shoes today for their trip to the countryside in place of her designer heels of last night. It seemed to Gawn, from her days tracking insurgents in Afghanistan, that they were not the first car to have been here. But then of course she remembered de Bek's car would have come this way on the day before he died.

Jansen was waiting for her, leaning back nonchalantly against the car when she reached the old house. Its windows were blackened with age. One of the upper ones was broken and part of a curtain fluttered out of the jagged opening in the light breeze. The front door was closed and wouldn't open to Jansen when he pushed it. Vegetation was growing out of the chimney. Holding his hands up to shade his eyes, the detective looked through one of the downstairs windows.

'The furniture's still here. There's lots of cobwebs. It looks like someone just up and left years ago. No one's lived here for quite a while, I think. Or been here. I don't think de Bek was here.' His voice sounded disappointed.

Gawn wandered round to have a look at the back of the house in case they could get in that way. Her eyes were drawn to a barn across the other side of the farmyard. It looked rundown like the house. Part of the roof seemed to be missing. But what attracted her attention was a large shiny padlock on the door. It was new. Who puts a padlock and chain on a derelict barn at a derelict house? She called Jansen and, when he appeared around the corner, she pointed to the barn.

He realised what she had noticed straightaway. He reached into his coat and withdrew a gun. Gawn recognised the Walther pistol and wished she was armed herself. Unlike many of her fellow officers, she was comfortable around firearms, having served in the army and then the Personal Protection Unit at the Met. She had had to use her weapon a few times but often just having it was enough to deter criminals.

They approached the barn carefully. As the padlock was still in place, the chances were that no one was inside, that it had been locked up when someone left. But there had to be something worth padlocking and they didn't know what it was. They kept well apart not providing an easy double target in case anyone was watching them from inside. There was a window in the side of the barn and Jansen could just reach high enough on tiptoes to see through it. Gawn saw his shoulders relax as he stood down again.

'Clear. No one inside.'

'Pity we can't take a closer look.' Gawn's mind went to search warrants and, although she didn't know much about the law in the Netherlands, she was pretty sure they would need a warrant to be able to gain entry here too.

'We can,' Jansen asserted and pointed to a stain on the ground below the window. 'That's blood, I think. We have reason to believe a crime may have been committed here.' He winked at her.

Gawn wasn't convinced it was blood. It might be. On the other hand, it might not but she was willing to go along with his suggestion. She nodded in response.

Jansen walked briskly back to the car and returned clutching a heavy tyre lever. He applied it to the chain holding the door closed. It had been employed more as a deterrent to discourage casual visitors and snapped easily when he applied pressure. He swung one side of the barn doors open still clutching the pistol in his other hand.

Light was streaming into the huge empty space from the hole in the roof. Dust swirled in the rays of weak sunlight. There was still some hay left over on the floor from the animals that had once been housed here. A pigeon flew up to the rafters, its wings disturbing the air. The two detectives' first reaction was disappointment. It seemed it was just an empty barn. Who knew why anyone would have bothered padlocking it? It was Gawn who noticed first that a ceiling extended halfway across, creating an upper floor towards the back of the barn. It was shrouded in shadows. She signalled to Jansen, pointing him to a set of wooden stairs to their right which led up to this enclosed area. Jansen led the way and they gingerly climbed the stairs alert for any noise from above, any sign that there was anyone else in the barn, waiting for them behind the door at the top. Jansen put his hand to the handle and turned it. It opened easily. He swung it back and they both jumped as it hit against the wall.

'Sorry.' He turned around and smiled in apology. They were both very jumpy.

This room showed all the signs of recent occupation. Someone or more than one had been here. There were two easy chairs, ancient-looking with sagging cushions but probably still quite comfortable. Two camp beds stood against the back wall, bed clothes neatly folded. They reminded Gawn of soldiers' beds ready for inspection. There was the smell of past cooking, rancid fat mixed with testosterone. A soldier's billet. She knew the smell. A camping stove sat on an old Formica-covered kitchen table and above it shelves of canned foods. And some plates and bowls. There was even a small fridge. Using her handkerchief to prevent leaving fingerprints, Gawn opened the door. The light came on inside and they realised there was still power in the building. Only a bottle of milk and two bottles of beer were sitting forlornly on the top shelf. She lifted the milk bottle and sniffed it. The sourness assailed her nostrils, evidence that someone had been here but not for several days at least.

Gawn heard a noise behind her and swung round to see a fat rat scurrying across the floor, nose twitching. Her eye was drawn to Jansen who had crossed the room and was hunkered down, looking intently at one of the wooden upright roof supports. He was examining the floor around it and the post.

'It looks as if a chain or something has been secured round this. You can see where it's dug into the wood as if someone or something was pulling at it.'

Gawn knew what he was thinking. She was thinking it too. Someone had been chained up here. Who would bother chaining up a dog or other animal upstairs? No, this had been for a human captive. She had never considered herself fanciful. She prided herself on being sensible and down-to-earth so she wouldn't have said to anyone that she felt a sense of evil here, but she did. She could smell it in the air as real to her now as the sour milk had been.

'What do you make of this?'

Jansen had moved across the room and was looking at papers strewn on the floor beside one of the armchairs. Someone had left in a hurry or perhaps they were expecting to be back to tidy up. He picked one sheet up and examined it.

'A lot of dates and times and names. It must mean something but what?'

Gawn took it from him and scanned it. Some of the names she recognised immediately. One was a well-known hotel and another a town in Donegal. Another page was part of a map, a map of Donegal and the north coast area.

'Jesus!' Jansen's sudden exclamation made her drop the page and swing round.

'What?'

'We've found Astrid's finger anyway.' He pointed to a bloodied mess on the floor. 'I think the rats have been at it but it's definitely been a finger at one time and there's a ring on it.'

She walked across and looked down where he was pointing. She felt her stomach lurch and was glad she had eaten little for breakfast.

'I better get the whole forensics team out here.' He drew his phone from his pocket and looked at the screen. 'I can't get a signal,' he said as he climbed down the stairs and headed out.

Left to herself, Gawn had another look at some of the pages. She turned one over and saw a doodle. It was a name, HOXT, or probably part of a name. Who or what or where was HOXT, she wondered. She was struggling to deal with all that had happened. Three people dead. Four, if you counted de Bek, and someone, probably Astrid, had been held here and tortured. What kind of people were they dealing with?

Jansen called from the bottom of the stairs. 'They've identified prints at Meyer's. It's just a small-time crook so it might be something to do with his death or it might not. They're bringing him in now and I want to be there to observe his interrogation. I've got the forensics team on its way here. We can leave this up to them.'

'Should I bring any of this paperwork?'

'Better leave it until they have catalogued it and fingerprinted it along with everything else. We'll need your fingerprints for elimination purposes.'

'Of course, no problem.'

'OK. Let's head back then. We'll probably pass the forensics team on their way here.'

She joined him outside. She was glad when she stepped back out into the air. Something evil had gone on here. She was sure of it, but what had it to do with her case?

Chapter 28

They left the farmhouse behind and headed back towards the city. Both detectives felt a sense of relief as the house diminished in the rear-view mirror although neither would have admitted it. The scene they were passing through now was quintessentially Dutch down to the white-sailed windmills in the distance and the canal which they were following along beside. Picture postcard perfect except for the weather and for the images they held in their minds. Gawn couldn't shake a sense that something terrible was going to happen as if the deaths which had already occurred were not terrible enough. It had just started raining heavily and a grey mist hung over the fields. The road looked wet and greasy after the prolonged period of dry weather. There was no other traffic and Jansen was driving just a little more quickly than Gawn was comfortable with. He was obviously as keen to get away as she was.

They didn't speak at first, both caught up in their own thoughts and speculations. It seemed this whole operation was bigger than they had originally suspected. Gawn already knew from the casual but ruthless way Astrid and her boyfriend had been disposed of when they had either outgrown their usefulness or posed a threat, that they were dealing with someone or some people who would stop at nothing to protect themselves.

The gloom was deepening not just an effect of the weather but also the onset of the afternoon. It mirrored the sense of gloom she was feeling. Lights were visible far in front of them. It wouldn't be too long until they were back on the main road. They had passed no other cars.

'What are you thinking?' she said.

Jansen took his eyes off the road long enough to glance at her face. She was sure he could read her concern.

'That we need to get back and find out what the hell is going on. People are dying.'

He had been aware for some time of two beams of light, the headlights of an approaching car, growing bigger in his rear-view mirror and wondered where it could have come from. He pulled tightly into the right-hand side of the narrow road, ready to let the other car go past, not wanting to hold them up with his little Fiat. Suddenly the interior of the car lit up. Powerful headlights seemed to be right on their bumper. The beams were turned up full, blinding them so that they couldn't make out what kind of vehicle it was.

'What the hell?' he said.

Jansen clutched the wheel more tightly and fought with it as the vehicle behind slammed into the back of their little car sending it lurching forward and veering across into the centre of the road. He managed to get it back under control and increased his speed to try to get away.

'That was no accident. Hold on tight, Gawn.' His voice was excited rather than fearful.

She felt the effect as his foot pressed down harder on the accelerator and their speed rose. She was pushed back into the passenger seat. A quick glance at the speedometer showed her they were now hurtling along at over one hundred kilometres an hour down a narrow road edged by stands of trees. Jansen seemed barely in control of the vehicle and Gawn wished she were driving herself in her own car which was speedier and more solid. She was aware of the lights behind them. They were still there and they were coming closer again. The little Italian city runabout was no match for whatever the vehicle was that was following them.

'We'll never outrun them. I'm going to try something. Hang on.'

Gawn held on tightly with both hands to the grab handle over the passenger door. Jansen threw the car across the road in a more or less controlled slide and slammed on the brakes hard, hoping the other vehicle would be forced to drive past, unable to stop in time without skidding itself. Either that or it would slam into them. Which is what it did. They were virtually stationary, a sitting duck when the collision happened.

She braced herself for what she knew was coming but even so its force surprised her. She felt the car lurch forward, seeming to take off into the air. And head towards the canal. A rusty metal gate loomed into sight and she knew they were going to hit it. At least it might stop them plunging into the water. She felt and heard the car scrape along the flaking material, setting her teeth on edge waiting for the jagged rusty metal to penetrate the window and skewer them like human kebabs. The airbags deployed and she was showered with powder. She felt it sting her eyes. Her vision was blocked and she felt a sharp pain in her knee as her body was jerked sideways. Looking across at Jansen, she watched as, almost in slow motion, his head was whipped backwards like that of a rag doll and his airbag deployed too, hiding him from her sight.

The car came to rest on its side half off the road at a crazy angle with the front at the edge of the canal. She was trapped by the seatbelt, hanging helplessly, looking down at the Dutchman. She realised she was still alive but how seriously injured she was, she didn't know. She could feel a stabbing pain in her leg and something wet and sticky at her knee. The airbags had deflated and she could see Jansen clearly now. His eyes were closed. She reached down and put her hand on his chest. Relief flooded through her as she felt the rise and fall of his breathing. At least he was still alive. Injured but alive. Then she suddenly realised they could still be in danger. She tried to look around to see what had happened to the other vehicle. Were they waiting? Should she expect a door to be flung open and someone to finish the job they had started? She could barely move her head. Then Jansen moaned and his eyes opened.

'What happened?' he asked.

'They hit us again. We crashed.'

'Are you alright?'

'I think so. What about you?'

'It hurts to breathe,' he wheezed.

She watched as he fumbled in his pocket. His hand emerged clutching a mobile phone.

'Get help.'

He reached the phone to her and she saw her hand was shaking as she took it. Her emergency call was answered quickly and, not for the first time in her life, she was glad that so many people spoke English. She had no difficulty in making herself understood although she was more uncertain about explaining exactly where they were. Her companion couldn't help her. He had lapsed back into unconsciousness.

She hung there, held in place almost hovering over the Dutch policeman and waited. It seemed to be forever. It couldn't have been that long really. Their own people – the forensics team on their way to the farm – had come across them first. When she finally heard the friendly voices and felt the doors opening, letting in the fresh evening air, she succumbed to the blissful escape of unconsciousness which she had been fighting.

* * *

The bright light blinded her. Was it them? Was another collision coming? If it was, there was nothing she could do about it. She could see nothing but the light. Then it slowly receded and she could see the man who had been holding the torch up to her eyes. His white coat, his gentle smile, and the sight of a blue-uniformed nurse standing behind him, gave her the clue as to where she was.

'Back with us?' His voice was rich and deep, the sort of voice which exuded confidence and made you feel safe.

'Where am I?' she heard herself ask, almost as if a stranger were speaking. 'You're in the University Hospital. You had an accident. Do you remember?' His voice sounded concerned.

'Yes. I remember.' Gawn moved her leg to try to get more comfortable and immediately let out a groan as a sharp pain shot through her kneecap.

'Try not to move. We've given you some morphine but it will take a little time to work. You've made a bit of a mess of your knee but it's nothing a few stitches won't put right, and rest, of course.'

She suddenly remembered Jansen. 'What about Hendrik?'

'Commissaris Jansen? He's going to be alright.' The doctor smiled, a reassuring smile. 'Now, we'll stitch you up and then nurse de Jong here will get you up to the ward. A good night's rest and you'll be sore in the morning but you should be fit to be discharged.'

Gawn thought of arguing but didn't have the energy for it. She could feel the effects of the morphine kicking in. She needed to sleep. She was safe here. She closed her eyes.

Chapter 29

She had had a fitful night's sleep. Waking or only half waking, imagining all sorts of things were happening around her in the ward. If she had been in a better place the night before, she would have told them, no morphine. She'd hated it after her injuries in Afghanistan and had had to be weaned off it. She wouldn't want to go through that again. The doctors were right. She had woken to a body which seemed to ache in places she didn't even know she had. At first even turning her head had been a struggle – the effects of the seatbelt or whiplash, she thought to herself. When they had helped her to the bathroom to wash, having insisted she could wash herself and wasn't going to be washed lying in bed like a baby, she saw the red marks on her face from the airbag. The nurse, who had insisted on staying with her in case she collapsed, was very reassuring that they would fade quickly.

'Good morning, Chief Inspector.' A younger doctor this morning, not her comforting older friend from last night in the emergency department. 'You'll be pleased to hear that your X-rays and tests are all clear and we are happy to discharge you this morning.' He beamed as if this was all his personal doing.

'Thank you. When can I see my colleague?'

'Commissaris Jansen? He's in the next ward. If you speak nicely to the sister here, she might let you slip along and visit him.' He was about to move onto his next patient when he turned back and looked at her with a serious expression on his face. 'You two were very lucky last night. You'll be sore and it will take time for your knee to heal. You will need to get it checked in about a week's time by your own doctor or at hospital. In the meantime, don't play the hero. If you need painkillers, take them. That's what they're there for.'

'Thank you, doctor.' She had no intention of taking any more medication than she absolutely had to.

* * *

Thirty minutes later, having spent nearly all that time struggling to dress herself, and very aware of the flapping material which had once been the leg of her trousers but which they had had to cut open to get at her knee last night, she shuffled along the corridor between her ward and the next. She felt like an octogenarian and thought she probably looked like one too. Her hair, normally tied back or held in a neat chignon, was hanging lankly over her shoulders. She wouldn't be winning any beauty contests today or any hundred-metre races.

As soon as she pushed open the swing doors to the ward, she spotted Jansen lying linked up to a drip. As she neared the bed, he opened his eyes and smiled weakly.

'Hi!' he said. 'You look like I feel.'

'Thanks.' At least he still had a sense of humour.

'They tell me you're being discharged.'

'Yes. I have a taxi booked to take me back to the hotel. I need to change out of the latest fashion look.' She pointed down to the gaping leg on her trousers, the material flapping open to reveal the bandage on her knee and cuts and scrapes extending down her leg.

'Nice look, but I don't think it'll catch on.'

They laughed and he clutched his chest. Obviously laughing was painful. Gawn found herself thinking that that was like something Seb would say. She suddenly realised he wouldn't know about the accident. Or would someone have informed him? If so, he would be frantic. It would be just like him to hop on a plane and appear at the hospital. And she wasn't sure she didn't want him to do just that. It would be good to see him, feel his arms around her.

'It hurts to laugh,' Jansen half-apologised. 'Two broken ribs and a collapsed lung.' She realised she had got off lightly. 'You'll be interested to hear that they've found the car, or rather the truck, that forced us off the road.'

'That was quick work.'

'We can be quick when we have to be.' He remembered her stinging comments about their lack of urgency when they had first met. Her criticism had probably been deserved although he would never have admitted that to her. A dead man on a plane in Belfast with no indication of foul play hadn't been very far up their list of priorities.

'It was a blue Ford Ranger. They found paint scrapings on our bumper which they were able to match to this type of vehicle and tyre tracks consistent with its wheel size. One was reported stolen yesterday morning and then a Ranger was found burned out on the outskirts of the city late last night. The VIN numbers matched so it's our truck. There were no cameras where they left it but they're working to try to retrace its route and pick up pictures of it elsewhere in the city and maybe see where it came from.'

Something clicked with Gawn.

'When we were visiting Meyer's, I noticed a blue truck sitting further along the road.' It was her old habit of scanning around, always being aware of her surroundings and potential dangers. 'I'm not sure exactly what a Ford Ranger looks like but I would be able to identify it if I saw a picture.'

'Great. So they had been following us for two days. If it was at Meyer's, they should be able to pick up images there and then track it though I suspect they will only end up tracking our route to Monnickendam if it was following us. I didn't notice it anywhere behind us, I'm afraid. ANPR should be able to locate it and hopefully we'll be able to get a clear image somewhere along the way of who was driving. Anyway, my bosses have already been here this morning. They take attacks on their officers very seriously and they're putting a lot of resources into finding out who did this. They want to speak to you down at headquarters. Do you feel up to it?'

She didn't really. She wanted to get back to the hotel and lie down and sleep, or actually she wanted to get back to the hotel and phone Seb. She wanted to hear his voice.

'Of course. I'll go back to the hotel and change.' She realized she would have to get another pair of trousers somewhere. She would have to factor in a shopping trip before heading to Police Headquarters. She certainly couldn't appear there looking like this. 'Maybe I could be there about' – she looked down at her watch and noticed for the first time that its face was broken, but at least it was still working – 'three o'clock?' That should give her plenty of time.

Chapter 30

The taxi driver had been most solicitous and insisted on helping her out of the car and into the foyer of the hotel. She had collected her room key card from reception, ignoring the curious glances she was getting from staff and other guests. She lent back against the wall in the elevator to ease the pressure on her knee. It was becoming more painful, probably a combination of using it more and the effects of the drugs wearing off. If she was going to get through the next few hours and her trip downtown to police headquarters she would have to take some more. Still, she was glad she had not accepted the hospital's offer of a wheelchair or crutches.

She had only just managed to hobble to the bed and was about to throw herself down onto it, when there was a knock on the door. She was going to ignore it but couldn't. Maybe it was an important message; some breakthrough in the case. Gritting her teeth, she was ready to bite the head off any hapless hotel staff member who might be standing there offering some clean towels or to restock the minibar. Just as she flung the door open, she realised she was so far gone she hadn't even bothered to look through the security spyhole. What if it were some of the gang coming to finish the job they had started yesterday? But it wasn't. It was Seb.

He took one step towards her, his face a picture of anguish, and she fell into his arms. She hadn't allowed herself to cry before so she made up for it now. Sobs caught her breath and she felt hot tears coursing down her face. He wiped her hair back so that he could look at her and then clutched her to him.

'He said you'd been in an accident. He didn't know how badly hurt you were. They wouldn't tell me anything at the hospital. Just because I wasn't a relative. I nearly lied and told them I was your husband but then I reckoned they'd already know you weren't married from your police records.' His words were coming out in a rush.

'Who told you?

'Your sergeant. Harris.'

She didn't know whether to be furious with him or if she should buy him a drink when she got back.

Then Seb looked down at her leg. 'My God, Gawn, it's like déjà vu.' He was referring to their very first evening together when she had been injured and he had tended to her leg.

'Only this time they did get me out of my trousers.' She laughed and it felt so good to have this connection; this shared life with him.

* * *

Seb had insisted she phone Jansen's bosses and tell them she wasn't up to talking to them today. She would be there at nine in the morning. She had already had an argument with him about it and expected the same from them but they accepted her decision without comment and wished her a speedy recovery. She had spent the entire day in bed with him sitting, reading in a chair, watching her intently as if she might disappear if he didn't keep her in sight. She had dozed at first but then fell into a deep sleep. She was surprised to wake to a night-time sky outside the window and no sign of Seb. For an instant she panicked. Then she wondered if she had imagined him, just an effect of the painkillers. Once or twice she had hallucinated after her life-saving surgery. Maybe it was that.

She heard the key card click in the lock and looked up to see him walk in carrying a flat cardboard box and a carrier bag. Spots of rain glistened on his coat and hair and as he crossed the room he carried with him the aroma of pizza.

'Back with us, Sleeping Beauty?' A smile spread across his face.

He set his packages down and perched beside her on the edge of the bed. Then he leaned over and kissed her gently on the forehead. Instead of responding as he had expected, she pushed him away. All she could think of was how near she had come to betraying him in this very room; how, even though it was only for a moment, she had enjoyed Jansen's advances; been flattered by his attention; and she wondered how easily she might have spent the night with him. Guilt swept over her.

'What did I do?' His face puckered into a frown of confusion.

'Nothing. You didn't do anything. I'm just still tired and upset and I don't want to be playing lovey-dovey with you tonight.'

'Is that what we're doing? Playing?' He was angry and hurt and it sounded in his voice. He had dropped everything and flown to the Netherlands, terrified that she was seriously injured or worse. 'All this isn't part of some game to me, Gawn. This isn't "shag-a-cop week for a hundred bonus points" or something. I thought you knew how I feel about you but I never know where I stand with you. One minute you're coming on to me like you can't get enough of me; other times I'm a nuisance. I just get in the way of the great detective. I'm a distraction.' Bitterness rang through every word although really, it was his fear talking. All the time on the flight over he had been imagining what he would do if she was seriously hurt; how he could cope if he lost her.

He didn't realise that with every word he spoke, he was making it harder and harder for her to tell him about Jansen. Is this what commitment means? she thought. Something, that in the bigger scheme of things was nothing – a kiss, an embrace, a momentary temptation. Playing with her head. She couldn't cope with this. Not today. Not after what had happened. Not with everything that was going on.

'No. You're not. I…' She trailed off. She couldn't explain how she felt without confessing to him how close she had come to cheating on him and she didn't know how he would react to that. They had never explicitly said they were exclusive and she knew Seb had had lots of girlfriends in the past, but she was pretty sure he hadn't been with anyone else since they met. At least she didn't think so. She certainly hadn't.

He stood up abruptly and walked across to the pizza.

'I got us something. I thought you might be hungry. And there's beer or I got you diet soda.'

He passed her a slice of pizza and opened a can of soda for her. Then he opened a beer from the six-pack and took a long drink of it. He sat down at the window without speaking, clutching the neck of the bottle tightly. It was obvious he was still angry and she wasn't sure what she could say that would make things better. She bit into the pizza and enjoyed the delicious flavour of pepperoni and anchovies. He had remembered to get her anchovies. Of course he had. He was thoughtful and she was a bitch. He was caring and she was selfish and self-centred and didn't appreciate how lucky she was to have him. She felt miserable. He stood up and walked over to her, and with a paper napkin, gently wiped the side of her mouth where she had a streak of tomato sauce. She swiped his hand away.

'I'm not a baby. You don't need to treat me like one.'

How could he be so kind when she was such a bitch? She didn't deserve to be loved like this. Then, before he could move away again, she reached out and took his hand and tried to pull him down onto the bed beside her, but he resisted.

'You need to get your rest. You're due at police HQ at 9am. I'll get a room. I'll meet you in the morning in reception at 8.30. By the way, I got you a new pair of jeans. They're in the bag.' He gave her no opportunity to argue with him. He kissed the top of her head and walked out letting the door close with a thud behind him.

Chapter 31

She had woken at seven and was glad she had. It had taken so long to shower and dress. The jeans fitted perfectly. She looked in the mirror as she applied some makeup. She didn't really like what she saw. She couldn't look herself in the eye so how could she face Seb? The marks from the airbag had faded, not completely, but enough that she could disguise them with some foundation and concealer. When she was ready, she began the trek to the elevator. Her knee was slightly less painful. She had taken some more of the hospital painkillers and that, plus time and rest, was helping. She hoped.

When the automatic doors slid open she was faced with a busy foyer. Some people were queued up at the reception desk obviously waiting to check out. A group of tourists stood in the middle of the space pouring over an open map, planning their day's sightseeing. There was no sign of Seb anywhere. It was only 8.20. Perhaps he wasn't down yet. His timekeeping was not as precise as hers which had sometimes caused the odd row between them.

Then she saw him entering from the street. He was carrying a walking stick.

'Where did you get that?'

'I bought it at the apotheek down the street. I thought you might need it to get around.'

'I'm not using that. I'll look like some decrepit old woman. I can't arrive at Police Headquarters on a walking stick.'

'Suit yourself.' She could tell from his tone of voice, he was annoyed. He was only trying to be helpful. 'I have a taxi booked for half past. I'll travel over with you but my flight leaves at two so I'll come back and check out. If you want, I can check you out as well and get another ticket. There was still room on the flight last time I checked.'

'I don't know how long I'll be.'

'Of course.' He wasn't going to push it. 'You're a big girl now. You can take care of yourself. You don't need me to organise your life for you.'

She couldn't think when she had ever heard him so bitter.

'York!' a voice called from the doorway. 'Taxi for York!'

* * *

The journey to Elandsgracht had been tense. They had exchanged only a few words. Suddenly, the taxi had to swerve to avoid another seemingly suicidal cyclist and she was thrown against him and winced as her knee hit against his.

'Alright?' Concern showed on his face.

'Yes. Fine.'

The traffic had been heavy but the journey was reasonably short and soon the car came to a halt outside the glass-fronted building. Seb got out and held the door open for her. She slid gingerly across the seat and stepped out, careful to use her good leg to take her weight as she stood up.

'I'll see you back in Belfast then.' She reached up and kissed him not too passionately, aware that she was on view to anyone watching out of the windows or passing on the street. 'Safe flight.'

His lips responded to hers and for a split second all seemed as it had been between them. Then he stood back. She was so used to seeing his cheeky grin, his face shining with happiness, that the serious-looking man in front of her was almost a stranger.

'Take care, Gawn. Goodbye.'

Again, no 'I love you' from either of them. As his taxi moved away and she waved, she wondered if this really was goodbye.

Chapter 32

Hoofdcommissaris Hoedemaker and Commissaris Jani Kuipers greeted her when she was escorted up to an office on the top floor. They had introduced themselves as Jansen's superior and the officer who had now taken over from him and was leading the investigation. They were extremely solicitous and thanked her so much for coming in to help them.

'How are you, Chief Inspector?'

'I think I was very lucky. More lucky than Hendrik.' Then she corrected herself. 'Commissaris Jansen. How is he?'

'He's making good progress. I rang the hospital this morning and they said he had a good night. Another couple of days and he'll be out.'

'I'm glad to hear that.'

Pleasantries over, the two men began to question her carefully about what had led her and Jansen to the old farmhouse and what they had seen there. Hoedemaker explained that when the forensics team had arrived at the farmhouse, the barn had been well ablaze. This was the first she had heard of this. The fire brigade had been quickly on the scene and had managed to put the fire out eventually, but a lot of evidence, most of it in fact, had been lost. They had found human blood and the charred finger but they would have to wait for DNA results. They had taken samples from de Bek's widow and children and anticipated a match.

If all the evidence at the barn had been destroyed then what she and Jansen had seen was all they had to go on. Kuipers probed to find what else she could remember. His questions were gentle but she was under no illusion that her answers were crucial. The earnest expression on both men's faces was evidence of that. Gawn explained about the papers. Why hadn't they taken them with them? She told them that they had felt it was better to leave them in place rather than start interfering with the crime scene. One time when sticking to protocol had worked against them.

She was surprised to learn they had spoken with Jansen again the previous night. No doubt they felt they could insist on speaking to him. He was after all a serving officer. But she was not and they had had to graciously allow her to wait until this morning. They must be so eager to hear what she had to say and yet they had been patient in their dealings with her. Jansen had been able to give them some indication about the papers but he had only taken a quick glance so he couldn't tell them too much. They already knew that they included a map of somewhere and some names and dates. Gawn wished she had taken the time to use the camera on her phone to take some pictures of them. They had thought the forensics experts would have plenty of time to go over everything in detail. They didn't expect to be attacked, didn't anticipate that everything would simply disappear up in smoke. They had been so busy with what they had found that they hadn't realized they were being watched. Their attackers must have been watching them and had followed them from the barn, forcing them off the road before going back to set it ablaze and destroy all the evidence of what had been going on and what was planned still to happen. All they had was what she could remember.

'The map was of an area in the north of Ireland.' She remembered that clearly. 'It covered Donegal and into County Londonderry,' she explained. Several places were circled in red or marked with Xs and some roads were marked as well. She thought she could remember some of them but wouldn't be able to recall them all. She would need to see a map of the area again. Could they get her one? Hoedemaker spoke to someone on the phone making an arrangement to get hold of a map.

'What about the other documents?'

'One was a list with dates and times.'

'Which dates? In the past or in the future?' Kuipers asked.

'Oh, in the future. Next week mostly, I think.'

They asked her to write down any dates she could remember and to recreate the page as closely as she could. She would need to think. It would take her some time and they had left her to it.

Sitting there in the office, Gawn found it all too easy to visualise the scene inside the barn. She could picture the wooden post and the chain where a human being, probably Astrid, had been held like an animal; the deep gouges where she had pulled at the chain trying to escape. She wondered what had gone through the girl's mind. She had probably been so relieved when she was released and was back with Rudy. She had thought her ordeal was over. Then Gawn focused her thoughts on the papers. She had held them in her hands. She closed her eyes and imagined they were there now. She could almost feel them in her fingers. First, the map. It was old. She could see and feel the rough edges where this section had been ripped from a bigger map or perhaps out of an atlas. This area must be important, specially selected for some reason. She saw the outline of the… for a moment she could not remember the name… but, glancing down at the map on the table in front of her which they had provided for her, she saw it was the Inishowen Peninsula. She didn't know this area well. Her father had always been wary of travelling to the Free State, as he called it – a throwback to a past time. For a RUC officer it had held dangers, whether real or imaginary. So, even though the Good Friday Agreement had brought relative peace, when she was a small child, they had spent holidays on the east coast, mostly in caravan parks under the majestic blanket of the Mourne Mountains.

She looked closely at the map the commissaris had provided for her. Derry was clearly marked and she circled it as it had been on the map in the barn. Strabane had been circled too, she remembered, another border region where people would come and go between the two jurisdictions every day, some for work, some for shopping or visiting friends. Nowhere were there any border controls. Police patrols were infrequent and anyone wanting to get something into or out of the country could easily find a way. The road from Strabane heading south had been drawn over with a blue line. She remembered that. On the barn map it had run off the bottom of the page. On this map she could see that it connected to the M1 straight to Dublin. She covered the area directly opposite Magilligan Point across Lough Foyle in red hatching as it had been in the original. She thought that was all she could remember from the map.

She decided to set it aside and think about the names and dates. She knew one of the dates was next Saturday. She remembered it especially because it had been her mother's birthday and she usually made a point of leaving flowers on her grave that day. She couldn't be sure of the others. At least two or three were before Saturday and one after, she thought. But the more she thought, the more she doubted herself and her memory. Then the names. She clearly remembered the Sperrin Valley Spa Resort. She had noticed an advertisement for it in the airport in Belfast before she left. It had a golf course and she knew it was very popular although she had never been there. Large letters 'HOXT' were written in red inside the red hatching, so whatever it referred to was in Donegal. Was there a place, a townland maybe that began with those letters? Or maybe it was the beginning of someone's name. She remembered the red so clearly because they had seen so much of it the previous day at the canal boat. She had no idea what any of it meant but maybe it would mean something to the Dutch police or the Garda for they would have to be informed as well.

When she was almost finished, the two Dutch detectives returned bringing a cup of coffee with them. Gawn handed Kuipers her notes. Although she had identified a general area for them and some dates, she didn't feel she'd been much help.

'We appreciate what you've been able to tell us,' Kuipers assured her.

She noticed a significant look pass between the two men.

'Do you have any idea what HOXT refers to? Might it be someone's name?' Hoedemaker asked.

'I've never heard of anyone with that name. There's an area in London called Hoxton, I think. Maybe it refers to that. Perhaps someone coming from there to Ireland?' she suggested.

'Our forensic people recovered a fingerprint from the barn. It was of a man we know only as the Fleischer,' Hoedemaker said and then waited for her reaction.

'The butcher?' She translated the word for herself and her brow furrowed.

'The name means nothing to you?' he asked.

'No. I've never heard of him.'

'That is what I would expect. Very few people have. You may have heard of Carlos the Jackal?' Hoedemaker paused and waited for her reply.

She shook her head.

'Before your time, Chief Inspector. He was – is – an assassin. He's still alive serving three life sentences in France for a string of murders and the wounding of over one hundred and fifty people. Or maybe you have seen the film *The Day of the Jackal* about an assassin in France?' He paused again.

This time Gawn nodded to show she had.

'Well, the reason you've never heard of the Fleischer is because he is so good at what he does and he is ruthless. He doesn't leave anything to chance. He covers his tracks and he gets rid of anyone who stands in his way or who could identify him. He works for the highest bidder. He's been associated with the murder of politicians and businessmen in several countries in Europe and in South America. No one knows what he looks like. He seems to be able to change his appearance so any pictures we have of him are practically useless. But, if he was in that barn and you saw a map of Ireland, it would seem to suggest he is heading your way.'

Gawn got the impression Hoedemaker was glad that it seemed the Fleischer was not going to be the Netherlands' problem.

'You think he's planning to kill someone in Ireland?'

'One or more than one. Who knows? But it is certainly what we suspect. We have already spoken with your Chief Constable and with the Garda Commissioner and I'm sure you will be in demand when you get back. They'll want to question you,' Hoedemaker added.

'I see. Yes, of course.'

'Our main priority is solving the murder of the two on the boat and Meyer. We will also be trying to find who attacked you and Jansen, of course, but I believe if we get the man, or more likely, men who did one, we'll have solved them all and I doubt any of them will be the Fleischer himself. He uses others – cheap muscle and guns for hire – to eliminate any problems for him. Then he carries out the contract killing he's being paid for himself.'

'Meyer was murdered?'

He nodded solemnly. 'Poisoned.'

'You think Astrid de Bek and Rudy and Meyer are all collateral damage for whatever this Fleischer is planning?'

It was hard for her to think of someone organising the killing of three people and the attempted murder of two police officers like that just to cover his tracks.

'Make no mistake about this man, Chief Inspector. He has managed to evade police all over the world. He has carried out assassinations all over the world and got away with it. We know he is a skilled marksman but he generally prefers to kill up close. He likes to be there; to watch the kill. He is meticulous in his preparations. And ruthless. He doesn't leave any loose ends.'

'Like a military campaign,' added Kuipers. 'Which is why it's thought he may have a military background. Perhaps Foreign Legion or Russian SSO or even your SAS.'

'No one even knows his nationality?'

'No. He is a shadow.'

'And he's heading our way?'

'Probably already there.' Hoedemaker stated. 'He has killed three times here and we shall continue to investigate those killings.'

Gawn realised just how lucky she and Jansen had been. They hadn't just been being warned off. The driver's intention had been to kill them because of what they might have seen. She felt a twinge of pain in her knee and almost welcomed it as proof that she was still alive.

'We have, of course, already passed over everything we know to the PSNI and also to An Garda Síochána and we'll forward what you've told us and drawn for us this morning. If you remember anything or think of anything which might help our investigation here, please get in touch.' Kuipers handed her his card.

Hoedemaker stood and held out his hand to her.

Gingerly Gawn stood up. She had been sitting for so long, she expected her knee to complain and make its presence felt. And it did. It almost gave way under her and she had to stifle a whimper of pain. She grabbed the arm of the chair for support. Kuipers stepped forward quickly and took her arm to help her.

'Sorry. I was just sitting too long. I'm fine.' She smiled to reassure them.

'Take care, Chief Inspector.' She didn't think Kuipers meant just about her knee.

Chapter 33

Gawn had debated whether or not to visit Jansen in hospital. When she rang the airline and found she couldn't get a flight back until early evening and would have several hours to spend just waiting around, she decided she would.

The familiar hospital smells brought back memories of waking in the emergency department. All around, as she waited for an elevator to the wards, she saw human life in all its variations. There were the young nurses giggling together, those same young women who, later today, would bring comfort to the ill and hold the hand of the dying, the serious-looking young doctors who seemed full of their own importance but who faced life and death decisions for others every day, and the nervous visitors not sure what would confront them when they reached the wards and saw their loved ones. In this place there was much suffering but also much hope, the best of humanity just as she had seen the worst of it in Monnickendam. Gawn smiled to herself. She was becoming philosophical in her old age, or maybe she was just becoming more human, more aware of how awful but also how wonderful people could be. And she couldn't help thinking of Seb. Why was she pushing him away? She thought she knew now. She didn't deserve to be loved, not by anyone. He deserved someone better than her who could love him, really love him, no matter what happened.

As she walked into the ward, she was surprised to see that Jansen already had a visitor. Why she should be surprised, she didn't know. He was sure to have lots of friends and colleagues.

'Gawn.' He looked a little flustered, pleased but also a little embarrassed to see her.

'Hendrik. I hope I'm not intruding. I'm flying home tonight and I just wanted to check in with you before I go. See how you're doing.'

His eyes moved to the pretty blonde sitting by the side of his bed.

'Trudi, this is Chief Inspector Gawn Girvin. I told you about her.' His eyes moved to Gawn. 'Gawn, this is my wife, Trudi.'

She thought she kept her face unchanged. She hoped she had. He might have told Trudi about her but he certainly hadn't told Gawn about Trudi. So Hendrik was married. He hadn't pledged undying love to her and nothing had really happened between them. One dinner and a slight spark. But it could have happened if she'd let it. She shouldn't be too surprised. Men were men. And it wasn't up to her to go interfering in his marriage. Trudi was obviously crazy about him from the way she sat looking at him, doe-eyed, and Gawn wasn't going to create some kind of scene.

She spent only a few minutes by the bedside. Enough time to wish him and his wife well and him a speedy recovery and thank him for his help with her case. As she walked out of the ward, she glanced back and noticed the two were already deep in conversation, heads close together and holding hands, in their own little world which she had no part in.

Chapter 34

The journey home had been tougher than she had expected. The walking and queueing at the airport, the steps up to the plane, standing waiting at immigration and customs too. By the time she had reached her car in the car park, the sweat was sitting on her brow with the effort she had had to exert. She had assumed, because her car was automatic, it would be relatively simple to drive, but even with the limited amount of movement as she changed between accelerator and brake pedal, by the time she was moving into her allotted space in the car park at her apartment building, she was exhausted.

She hobbled from the elevator to her front door and paused before going in not just to gather her strength but in preparation. Preparing for what? She didn't know whether she was preparing for Seb being there waiting for her or him not being there. And she couldn't make her mind up which would be worse.

The room was in darkness. No Seb, but a flashing light on her answering machine told her someone had phoned. She was almost too tired to pick it up. If he wanted to talk to her, she didn't think she could face it just now. If he was ending everything with her, she didn't want to hear that either. Instead, it was the gruff voice of Chief Superintendent Reid. He wanted to see her first thing in the morning even though it was Sunday. She realised she shouldn't be surprised. They would be in major panic mode. They needed to hear directly from her, not second hand from the Dutch. Tomorrow was going to be a tough day.

She headed straight for the bedroom, practically fell out of her clothes and into bed. The throbbing of her knee woke her at 4am and she couldn't get back to sleep. She lay, her mind racing, jumbled thoughts competing for her attention. If what they thought in Amsterdam was correct, there was an assassin on the loose. Someone was going to die. Maybe more than one someone. And it was going to happen next week. That should be her primary focus but she couldn't shake a sense of personal emptiness. She thought of Mrs de Bek, crushed under a burden of loss for her husband even though he sounded like a difficult man to live with; she thought of Astrid and Rudy building a life for themselves together. OK, it wasn't her idea of a wonderful life but they had chosen it for themselves and they were together sharing it. She even thought of Jansen who basked in the adoration of his wife even though he was a cheat. But who was she to judge? She had blown it with Seb. She knew she had. But she knew as well that she couldn't go back to the days before she knew him when her whole life had revolved around her work. With dark thoughts in her mind, she fell asleep only to wake to the sound of her alarm at 5.59 calling her to duty.

Chapter 35

She had a supply of tramadol which her doctor had prescribed for her last year but she had never taken. She had never bothered to get rid of them and now she was thankful to whatever god or luck or fate had made her keep them. This morning she took two and placed the rest of the packet into her bag. She needed to walk into the office looking as if nothing had happened or Reid would send her home on sick leave and she didn't want that. She was involved in this up to her neck and it was personal. She couldn't just leave it to others. Not just because she had seen the after-effects of the Fleischer's handiwork or that of his men but also because they had tried to kill her. She wasn't going to walk away and let someone else find him.

She braced herself as she opened the main door and greeted the desk sergeant. Before she had time to make it to the elevator, he responded.

'Chief Superintendent Reid wants to see you right away, ma'am.'

She wanted to see him too. She wanted him to see she was OK and didn't need to be stood down from duty and she wanted to convince him she should be allowed to continue her investigation.

'Come.' Reid's voice, even in just one word, sounded even more harried than usual.

'You wanted to see me, sir?' As she spoke, she became aware that Reid was not alone in the room awaiting her. Donald Fulton, Head of Specialist Operations Branch, was seated across the desk from him. Assistant Chief Constable Deirdre Mackie was standing at the window. All three turned and looked at her. Fulton didn't stand up but cast an appraising eye over her. She felt as if she were being X-rayed, laid bare before his stern gaze.

'Yes. Come in, Chief Inspector. Sit down.'

She noticed that Reid glanced at her knee as he spoke. He had obviously been fully briefed by the Dutch. She hoped he hadn't been told how messed up her knee was. His voice, when he spoke again was sympathetic, almost as if he felt some responsibility to protect her from what he knew she was going to have to endure.

'You know ACC Mackie, of course.'

'Ma'am.' Gawn nodded in acknowledgement.

'And this is Chief Superintendent Fulton.'

'Sir.'

Deirdre Mackie moved across from the window so she was standing directly in front of Gawn.

'Chief Inspector, the reports we've received from the Netherlands make rather disturbing reading. We need you to go through everything that happened and all you learned on your trip with the team from Specialist Operations. They'll be taking the lead in this case and liaising with An Garda Síochána.'

Gawn realised there would be no point in putting up an argument just now. Better to bide her time. Fulton stood up.

'Follow me.' Obviously a man of few words.

He walked her in silence along the corridor and down to an interview room. He was striding out and she found it difficult to keep up with him. When he opened the door and stood aside to let her walk in, she saw two plain-clothes detectives whom she had never seen before sitting at the table waiting for her. She was beginning to feel like one of the suspects she had interviewed in this very room. They introduced themselves as DCI McNeill and DS Forrester. They offered her tea or coffee or some water. All the time, all she could think of was the flashing light from the video camera high in the corner. Someone would be watching. Probably several someones. And one would almost certainly be from the Security Services, MI5, MI6, she didn't know which or maybe both. She had always managed to stay out of their way, until now.

The questioning began. They started right back on the Monday morning when she had got the call to City Airport. That seemed so long ago. So much had happened since then. The initial interviews, the PM results, their discovery about Smith/Clinton, what they had learned from Dr O'Dowd at the museum. They went through it all. Then they asked all about what had happened in the Netherlands. They were interested in the de Beks and Meyer and what had happened to Astrid and Rudy, but when she got to the part where she and Jansen had gone to the farmhouse at Monnickendam the door opened and another stranger walked in. He didn't introduce himself but stood behind her in the corner of the room. She was not under investigation. At least she thought not. But she had no doubt that the whole interview was being taped. She felt uncomfortable with this silent man behind her, not sure of what he was doing; not able to gauge his reactions to her responses.

It had taken over two hours to get through all their questions and then they offered her a break before they started all over again. Did they think she had deliberately left something out? She made a conscious decision to answer their questions using slightly different phraseology this second time through so that it didn't sound as if she had learned the answers off pat.

When they got to her final visit to Politie HQ, they produced copies of the lists and map she had given the Dutch police. They asked her to talk them through the places she had marked. They asked her to look closely at the map again and make sure she hadn't left anything out.

She was getting tired. She had been answering questions for nearly five hours. Her kneecap was throbbing and she didn't want to ask for a cup of water to take painkillers in front of them. Just as it seemed they were going to go through everything for a third time, ACC Mackie entered the room. She looked immaculate in her formal uniform. Gawn noted the gleam on her polished shoes. She felt grubby in comparison, aware that she had taken less trouble than usual with her own appearance.

'I think we've got about as much as we can. Thank you, Chief Inspector, for your cooperation.'

Gawn braced herself to stand up. She didn't want a repeat performance of what had happened to her at Politie HQ. By dint of holding on to the edge of the table and then steadying herself before she tried to move away, she thought they wouldn't have noticed anything.

Before she made it to the door, Fulton's voice brought her to a standstill. It was chilling in its intensity.

'Nothing that you saw, nothing that happened in Amsterdam, nothing you have discussed here is to be shared with anyone, Chief Inspector. Is that clear?'

'Yes, sir.'

'No one.'

'What about my team?'

'Especially your team. This stays between these four walls. It is need-to-know and they don't need to know. Clear, Chief Inspector?'

'Perfectly, sir.'

'And Chief Inspector,' ACC Mackey added, 'Chief Superintendent Reid would like a word with you before you leave.'

What was he going to say? Would this be a warning to stay clear?

She knocked and this time his voice sounded more welcoming.

'Gawn, you've survived your interrogation then.' She was surprised that he had called her by name and surprised too by the conspiratorial twinkle in his eye as he referred to her 'interrogation'.

'That's certainly what it felt like, sir.'

'It's a very serious situation. The British are concerned that some bigwig will be bumped off either on our patch or across the border and escape through the north. Either way it would be very embarrassing for everyone. They needed to get everything out of you they could.'

'Understood, sir.'

'Now, what are we going to do about you?'

She looked at him as if she had no idea what he could be talking about.

'You are to have nothing to do with any investigation regarding this Fleischer. Leave it up to Special Ops and others.' The way he pronounced the word 'others' signalled his distaste for their work. 'They have the intelligence sources and the resources to deal with it. If they get it right, we'll never hear anything more about it. That would be the best outcome we could hope for. You have your own investigation, Chief Inspector.'

She threw him a quizzical look.

'De Bek was smuggling something, his body was discovered here and the coroner requested an investigation. You found evidence of a crime. Not murder, but a crime. Follow it up.'

'But if that leads me to the Fleischer, what then?'

'You told us yourself that he uses others to carry out everything but the contract killing he's being paid for.' So Reid had been listening in on her interview too. 'We need to know what de Bek was smuggling and whether this route has been used before and stop it being used in the future. Let the others go after the big one, you concentrate on the minnows that do his bidding. You and your team concentrate on that. Understood?'

'Yes, sir.'

When she got out of his office, she lent back against the door. She was exhausted but also elated. Reid hadn't stood her down altogether. He hadn't made her take time off to recover. A good night's sleep and she could be back with her team tomorrow.

Chapter 36

She had slept really well. Thanks to the tramadol. But it was not dreamless. She was being interrogated but not by the two officers from Special Ops. No, it was Seb. He wasn't asking about the Fleischer or the bodies in Amsterdam. His questions were about Jansen. She could see herself sitting at the table, facing him, and she saw

Jansen's wife standing behind her listening to what she was saying. She was trying to convince them both she had done nothing wrong. When she woke it was with a sense of guilt hanging over her. She tried to convince herself too that she had done nothing wrong but then why did she feel like this, if that was so? She had made no promises to anyone. She had taken no vows.

A long hot shower and plenty of strong coffee later, she was ready to face the task of getting dressed. Her knee felt marginally stronger and less painful this morning. She would just need to stay off it as much as possible. She picked up the jeans she had discarded on the floor on Saturday night and stuffed them into a plastic bag. She would leave them for her cleaning lady to take to the dry cleaners. Sunday's clothes were also still lying in a heap over a chair. What was happening to her? She was becoming a slob. Next thing she would be wearing sweatpants all weekend and eating snack food in front of the TV because she had nothing better to do. Her life was disintegrating. She felt the four walls of her apartment closing in on her and recognised the early symptoms of a panic attack. She could feel her heart beginning to race. It had been so long since she had needed them that it took several minutes to find the medication her doctor had prescribed for her. It had been put away in a drawer with the tramadol. She had thought she would never need it again either.

She started to dress. She had a choice of three clean and pressed suits and went for a dark grey one. It always looked well with her pink shirt so she lifted it from the wardrobe and put it on. She selected a pair of flat-heeled boots. No high heels today. As she was brushing her hair, she wondered what it would be like to have it cut. She had always worn her hair long even when she was in the army; even when she was on deployment. Some of the other women had told her she was mad. They said how much easier it would be not to have to worry about keeping stray hairs in place, just to flick a quick brush through it and you were ready for anything. She thought it might change her image to have short hair and didn't know if she was ready for that. The chief inspector with the long red hair. That was her. Recognisable. Known. Was she questioning who she was? Was she unhappy with herself?

All the way into the city, as she battled the traffic on the Belfast Road and then the M2, she was preparing her thoughts. She needed to find out quickly what was new in the case. Secretly she feared the answer would be nothing. She hoped Harris had gone back to see Andrews and had turned something up or maybe they had an identity for the figure who had picked up the switched bag. That would be useful. She thought Clinton had probably told them as much as he knew. He was strictly small-time, she was sure. He could probably count himself lucky he had not found himself with his throat cut at the bottom of the canal, if he only knew.

Everything was as she had left it last night and yet it wasn't. Yesterday, Sunday, fewer officers had been about. Her own team was only working a skeleton crew. She hadn't made it near her office but there wouldn't have been anything to do there. Today it was all back to normal. She could hear loud laughter even before she opened the door. Someone, probably Logan, had cracked a joke or maybe Grant was bragging again about his girlfriends and the others were mocking him.

'Morning, boss,' Logan greeted her. He was walking across to his desk clutching the remains of a sausage roll. She could see the flakes of pastry down the front of his tie. In an instant she recollected how smart-looking he had always been when his wife Eileen had been around. Since the break-up she could see he had gone downhill. She was afraid the decline in his appearance might just be the tip of the iceberg and wondered in what other ways his life had changed and whether something similar might happen to her.

'No time for breakfast at home this morning, Billy?'

'That's breakfast number two, ma'am.' Jack Dee laughed.

'OK. Who's going to get me a cup of coffee so you can all bring me up to speed on what's gone on?' she asked of the room generally. But Harris had pre-empted her. He turned from the corner of the room where they kept a kettle, a jar of instant coffee and some tea bags with a plastic cup already poured and walked across.

'I know you like the proper stuff, ma'am. Will this do?'

'Better than nothing.' She was aware she risked sounding ungracious. She didn't often request anyone make coffee for her, even junior officers never mind her sergeant. She was usually happy to do it for herself, preferred to do it for herself, but she didn't want to be moving more than she needed to. 'Thank you, Michael.' She smiled at him. She perched on the edge of McKeown's desk and asked, 'Well, who's going to start? What progress have we made?'

She could see them exchanging glances and wondered who would be brave enough to speak. It was the girl sitting behind her who spoke up. Gawn had to swivel so she didn't have her back to McKeown.

'We showed the picture of our Victoria Man, as we've called him' – McKeown indicated the photograph of the man pinned on the board, the man from the shopping mall who had picked up the bag – 'to Clinton and he was definite that it was not the man who had given him the money to switch the bags. I think we can believe him. He was so scared of that man that he said he would never forget his face.'

'But, if he was so scared of him, would he be prepared to identify him? That's the question, Erin. Wouldn't it just be easier for him to deny all knowledge, not risk tangling with him again?' As Gawn spoke she stared at the photograph. It was taken from mall security footage. The man was quite a distance away. He was dressed in a long camel hair coat and had a heavy scarf wound across his face. His hair was covered by a black baseball cap which was pulled down over his eyes. It had been a cold day and no one would have paid any heed to a man hopped up against the weather. Gawn allowed herself to wonder if this could be the Fleischer himself but she could say nothing to the others.

'I watched him closely when he was looking. I showed him a range of photographs of roughly similar types and I watched his face. There was no flicker of recognition that I could see anyway.'

Gawn was still staring at the photograph. She was aware that there was something vaguely familiar about the man. Had she seen him somewhere? Where?

'We had a photofit drawn up of Clinton's thug.' McKeown walked over and pinned another photograph alongside the one of Victoria Man. Forgetting about her knee, Gawn stood up and walked across to the board to get a better look. 'We've started showing it around. The guys in the Drugs Squad say they don't recognize him.'

'Get a copy sent over to Amsterdam. They'll probably know him and might be able to make a connection. Anything else?'

There wasn't a lot. She hoped Special Ops were having better luck with their investigation. She knew she couldn't share any information about the assassin with her team.

'I went out to speak to Andrews again, as you suggested, ma'am,' Harris said.

She waited. 'And?'

'He wasn't there.'

'For a busy farmer, he does a lot of travelling. Was no one there?'

'His wife was. Mrs Andrews explained he had gone down to Dublin to visit their daughter for a couple of days.'

'Did she give any reason?'

'No.' He shook his head. 'Just a wee trip. A spur of the moment thing, she said. He hadn't seen her for a while. He and his daughter are very close apparently.'

And then it clicked.

'Do we have the name of the Andrews' son-in-law?'

Harris rifled through his notebook. 'Sean McGladdery.'

'Sean McGladdery. Get me a photo of him.'

'Where would we get that, ma'am?' asked Grant.

'He's a solicitor in Dublin. He must be on some website or other. I thought no one could do anything these days without it ending up on the internet,' she snapped.

'Here, ma'am.' McKeown had turned her monitor around so Gawn could see the image on the screen.

'Does he look familiar to you?' Gawn asked.

The girl's eyes flicked between her screen and the picture on the board and back again.

'It could be him. It's hard to tell. Victoria Man's face is obscured with his scarf and this picture's just head and shoulders. It would help if we could get a full-length photo of McGladdery to get an idea of his height and build.'

'Do that. See if you can get any film footage too.'

'Right, ma'am.'

'Meanwhile we need to dig deeper into Andrews. His travels, his finances and his family. Michael, get on to the Guards and see if they have anything on McGladdery. He's probably a divorce lawyer or something and they know nothing about him but wouldn't it be nice if he was a criminal lawyer with lots of drug connections as clients?'

She was aware that it was all very flimsy. Victoria Man could be any one of thousands of men. There was nothing outstanding about his appearance. And he might not necessarily even be Irish. Sean McGladdery could be a respectable solicitor with no criminal connections beyond his work and Mr Andrews could be the upstanding pillar of the community hard-working farmer he had seemed at the beginning of the investigation. Or not.

Chapter 37

Gawn had been glad to get into her own office, behind her own desk where she could rest her knee. She thought she had managed to pull things off quite well. The others didn't seem to have noticed anything or at least no one had commented.

'Excuse me, ma'am.' It was Harris. 'I was just wondering how you're doing.'

Of course, he knew about the accident. He was the one who had contacted Seb.

'I'm fine, Michael. Just a couple of stitches.'

'The Dutch made it sound a lot worse than that.'

'You were talking to the Dutch police?'

'Yes, ma'am. And the hospital. They phoned here to get your contact details.'

He seemed to be about to turn and go back to his desk when he stopped.

'I hope I did the right thing to phone your friend.' There was a minute pause before he used the word 'friend'. 'He was in your contact details in case of emergency.'

She looked up from the papers she was pretending to read.

'Yes. Of course. Thank you. He appreciated being informed.'

'He seemed very upset when I picked him up.'

'You picked him up?'

'Yes. He didn't have his own car. Someone had borrowed it or something so I dropped him down to the airport to get the plane. He was in quite a state.'

She didn't know what to say.

'He seems like a good bloke.'

He made his final comment and walked out of the room.

A good bloke. Yes. He was.

She was still thinking about Seb and wondering how things stood between them, when her phone rang.

'Girvin.'

'Gawn, how are you?' Jenny Norris sounded relieved to hear her voice. 'I didn't know whether you'd be back in the office or not yet. No one seemed to know how you were. Some people had you half dead.'

'Reports of my demise were obviously exaggerated.' Gawn laughed. She was glad to hear her new friend's voice. 'Are you just ringing or checking up on me? Which is OK, by the way. I appreciate your concern. Or is there something else?'

'Nope. If I was just doing a doctor's house call, I would have rung you on the mobile. No. I do have something else for you.'

Gawn heard that something in her voice that told her the pathologist thought she knew something that Gawn would want to hear.

'I got another tox result. I sent the rest of de Bek's clothing for testing.' Gawn rolled her eyes thinking of what McDowell would say about the extra expense. 'It showed up trace amounts of tetrodotoxin.'

'OK. I'm not playing the game. Don't blind me with another long medical term. What's tetrodotoxin? Is it some drug they might be trying to smuggle in?'

'You wouldn't want to sell this on the street or take it yourself, for sure. You'd be buying yourself a one-way ticket.'

'What is it?'

'It's usually found in the organs of puffer fish.' She paused, sure Gawn would make the connection.

'Puffer fish? You mean that stuff that poisons people in Japan?'

'Yes. It's found in the skin and organs of the puffer fish. If it's properly prepared, they're safe to eat so they have specially trained chefs and licensed restaurants that serve fugu. If you get it wrong, it's over a hundred, some people say, a thousand times more deadly than cyanide.'

Gawn was stunned into silence. 'A thousand times? And you think de Bek was eating puffer fish?'

'No. For a start it wasn't in his intestine. If he'd eaten it, it would have killed him. Full stop. No. I asked the guys to look at everything else and they picked up traces on the stitching around one of his shoes. It was really good work, Gawn.'

'So he walked on some of this stuff or had it dropped on his foot, but that doesn't necessarily mean he was bringing it into the country and why would he if it can't be sold on the streets?' Gawn was thinking aloud. 'If someone wanted it, couldn't they just put it in a bottle and pack it in a suitcase?'

'I don't know what the rules are about importing it but there was something special about this stuff.'

Gawn waited, sure Jenny was going to add to what she'd said.

'This particular tetrodotoxin was not your common or garden stuff,' she continued. 'I mean, you can have pet puffer fish, I think, so it would be possible to get your own stuff, I guess. But tetrodotoxin is regulated because it's used in research. And the stuff on de Bek's shoe had been modified to be more potent.'

'What do they use it for?'

'Well, basically a few of the big pharmaceutical companies are doing research into sodium ion channels. You don't need to know all about it – unless you want to, of course,' she added, mindful of the time she had told Gawn she would give her the dummy's version of her report, 'but basically, sodium channels are involved in almost every process within the human body, like cardiac function and muscle contraction, so they're a key part of developing new drugs including new painkillers.'

'And this more potent tetrodotoxin, why would anyone want it?'

'I can only guess but if eating a bit of bad puffer fish can kill you, a minute amount of this stuff certainly could. It could induce heart failure, or someone eating it could suffocate because their muscles aren't working to let them breathe. Normally, if you ingest tetrodotoxin you would expect to see symptoms maybe any time between thirty minutes and several hours later and there's the chance to get some treatment so it doesn't have to be fatal, but I would guess with this modified version it would all be speeded up and because of that there would be less time for any medical intervention. They probably wouldn't even know what had caused the reaction until the PM and even then it mightn't be picked up.'

'So, basically, you could use it to kill someone? And de Bek had been somewhere around this stuff or around someone with this stuff? Could it be what caused his heart attack?'

'No. I'm confident that it was natural causes with him. I was able to identify evidence of a previous myocardial infarction and he had an enlarged heart associated with heart failure. The man had probably been displaying symptoms for some time but ignoring them. But surely there are easier, more straightforward ways, to kill someone. Unless you're a paid assassin, in a Bond movie.' She laughed at the idea.

Gawn's mind was in overdrive. The Fleischer was an assassin who liked to kill up close; to see his victim die. Tetrodotoxin would be a perfect weapon for him. It could even be mistaken for death by natural causes, making it easy for him to make his escape after watching his victim die. And there was one place she knew for sure de Bek had been – the barn in Monnickendam.

'How long would this last on a shoe, say the sole of a shoe?'

'I don't know off-hand. I'd have to do some research.'

Gawn wondered if it was worth having her own shoes tested. She had been walking around in the barn. But she'd then been wearing the shoes the next day so it was unlikely anything would have survived if it had ever been there. Any traces on the floor would have been destroyed in the fire but if she had got some on her shoe they could establish another link in the chain. She could tell none of this to her friend or anyone else on her team but she needed to let Fulton know.

'Thanks, Jenny. Great work.'

'We'll have to get together soon for a drink.'

'Definitely.'

Gawn put the receiver down and picked it up again right away. 'Get me Chief Superintendent Fulton. It's urgent.'

Chapter 38

She hadn't expected quick results on Andrews' finances so she was amazed when Grant knocked on her door with a sheet of paper in his hand within thirty minutes of their briefing. He held it out to her. And smiled, pleased with himself.

'Andrews' finances, ma'am.'

'That was quick. How did you manage to get hold of them so quickly?'

'We already had them.' He smiled again and she was sure she must look puzzled.

'We had them?'

'Well, not us exactly. Organised Crime did. When I started to do some research I saw Andrews had already been flagged on our system.'

'Why didn't we know this?'

'He was only on the periphery of our case, ma'am, and of theirs. They hadn't got too far with him yet and we were only checking his details, not going in too deep.'

She realised he was covering for Dee who had done the first research and turned up nothing. She looked down at the page he had handed her.

'His farm's not doing too well,' he ventured.

'Well, it's a tough time for farmers all round, I think. What's this Bako Investments?' She tapped the paper.

'According to Organised Crimes it started off as a legit business but it was taken over by criminals. It's based in Dublin but run by a crime syndicate out of Eastern Europe. That's how they came across Andrews. It's Bako they and the Guards were looking into and Andrews was one of their minor investors they were checking.'

'He's put quite a bit of money into it.'

'Yes. Part of its activities is gambling. So it could be that, boss, or maybe he was really trying to make some money investing. And got hooked.'

'Does McGladdery or any of his associates have any connection to this Bako Investments?'

'Don't know yet, ma'am.'

'Good work. Keep on it, Jamie. Find out about McGladdery and more about Bako Investments. You have a friend in Organised Crimes, haven't you?' She knew he had. They had dated a few times but after the first night he had refused to say anything about her, so either she had knocked him back or he was serious about her.

'Yes, ma'am.'

'Take her out for a drink tonight. See what you can get out of her to help our case.'

He had barely closed the door behind him when her phone rang.

'Chief Inspector? Commissaris Kuipers here.'

'Yes, Commissaris. Good to hear from you.'

'I have some interesting information for you.'

She waited.

'We've identified your alley thug, as I think your officer called him, from the drawing you sent us. That's exactly what he is. A hired thug. Jurgen Meissner. Not too much brain and a lot of muscle.' He laughed. 'He will put the frighteners on someone for a remarkably small amount of money. We're looking for him now. Obviously we'll be questioning him to see if he has any connection to the murders here and we'll see what he has to say about Clinton.'

'Thank you.'

'All I hope is we don't find him floating in the Amstel, another loose end taken care of. We will do our best to get to him first.'

'Thank you, Commissaris.'

She was about to ask after Jansen and then finish the call when he continued.

'Our investigations have turned up something odd which I am sure you will find interesting.'

Again she waited in silence.

'When we checked into de Bek's flight booking to Belfast, we found it had been done through a travel agency. Apparently Meyer used this company for all his travel arrangements.'

'That's quite unusual nowadays. Most people tend to book directly with the airline to get the best prices but there are still some people who like to get it done for them with no trouble.'

'Yes. Of course. But this is a small agency, just one office on the outskirts of the city nowhere near Meyer's business, and when we checked names of other passengers, all your other witnesses showed up. They were all booked through the same place.'

Gawn sucked in her breath sharply in surprise.

'All of them? Clinton, Andrews and Vanhoeven?'

'Yes. All of them. All on the same day.'

'That couldn't be a coincidence or chance.'

'No. Definitely not. Bako Travel is a small concern. You would need to know it was there before you would bother going to it.'

She almost physically jumped in her seat. Bako was not a common name. It had to be part of the same organisation. It was a link. She didn't rush to share this with Kuipers. The Bako investigation was not hers. It was Organised Crimes' case and they wouldn't welcome her briefing outsiders without consulting them first. She kept her voice even as she continued the conversation.

'Have you made enquiries there yet?'

'Yes. Of course. The girl in the office – there's only one girl so you can see it's not exactly a big business – claims she doesn't know anything and, to be honest, I think I believe her. She takes the phone calls and makes the bookings.'

'So the bookings were made over the phone?'

'Yes.'

'And were they collected in person?'

'No. E-tickets were issued.'

'But they were all booked at the same time?'

'She says she can't remember but I would bet my pension they were. The business doesn't have a big turnover. She'll admit it eventually when she realizes how much trouble she could be in.'

'And how were they paid for?'

Gawn waited expectantly. This could be vitally important, a big breakthrough.

'All were on Meyer's account.'

She couldn't help slamming her hand down onto her desk in disappointment.

'He was up to his eyes in this, wasn't he? And we questioned him and got nothing.'

'When you and Commissaris Jansen spoke to him you knew nothing about all this. You were investigating the possibility of smuggling. We suspected Meyer was involved in fencing stolen property but I think we're all aware now it was much more than that. I have let your team investigating the Fleischer have all this info, of course, but I wanted to let you know too. You deserve that. If it hadn't been for your thoroughness we would know nothing of any of this. We'd be investigating separate murders.'

'And if Willem de Bek hadn't had his heart attack we'd all be none the wiser.' And if Jenny Norris hadn't been prepared to follow her instincts, she added to herself.

'Indeed.'

Chapter 39

When Harris walked over to Gawn's office and looked through the glass he saw her sitting at her desk, her head in her hands. He hesitated. Was it something to do with the case or was she upset about something personal? Or was she in pain? He didn't want to intrude but before he could move back out of her sight, she looked up and saw him. She waved for him to come in.

'Everything alright, ma'am?'

'With me, yes. With the case, no.'

He waited for her to explain her comment. She filled him in on what she had learned from Grant and then from Kuipers. She was careful to make no mention of the Fleischer.

'Bloody hell! They were all booked on the plane by the same person? We talked to Andrews in his own home. He seemed like an ordinary family man.'

'Funny you should say that, Michael. Astrid de Bek was abducted and held and her finger cut off, and I think that had to have been to get her father to cooperate with them. So maybe, bear with me, I'm thinking out loud here, maybe Andrews was being pressured to help too.'

Harris had been nodding in agreement while she was speaking. 'You think Dawn McGladdery might have been kidnapped too?'

'Let's get the Guards to call out at the house and check she's alright. Then we'll know for sure.'

Harris had a sudden thought. 'If they're investigating these Bako Investments people, McGladdery might be involved and they mightn't want to show up at his house and tip their hand.'

'Well, at least they could do a bit of surveillance and see if she puts in an appearance. We can but ask, Michael.' Gawn lifted the phone ready to contact the Garda Síochána liaison officer whose name she had been given, when she looked up at her sergeant as he prepared to leave the room.

'Have you looked at the CCTV stuff from the airport yet? Andrews told us his coat was stolen but we didn't know then he was up to his neck in something. We need to see what really happened to him.'

'I haven't had the time to look at it yet, ma'am.'

'Do it now, Michael, and let me know what it looks like. And, Michael, have someone take another look at Vanhoeven. He must be involved some way too, most likely through his drugs connection.'

'Will do, boss.'

Chapter 40

It took several calls before she eventually got through to Superintendent Darragh O'Haire.

'Superintendent, I'm Chief Inspector Gawn Girvin.'

He didn't let her finish but interrupted in his soft Irish brogue. 'Yes. I remember you. We met. At that Cross-Border Policing event last year in Mullingar. Ernie Reid introduced us. You probably don't remember me but I remember you.' He laughed. Obviously he remembered the occasion well. All she remembered was a lot of boring speeches, hot air and idealistic rhetoric taking them all away from the jobs they should have been doing that day.

'I'm afraid I don't, sir.'

'Oh well, not to worry. I suppose you're phoning about Bako Investments.'

'Yes.' Her voice displayed some surprise that he knew why she was ringing.

'Word travels fast, Chief Inspector. Your people making all sorts of queries about the company and their investors and then about Sean McGladdery, well you couldn't expect it not to come to my attention.'

'No. Of course not. We were wondering if you have any surveillance on McGladdery and his wife.'

'And why would you want to know that now?'

'We're investigating William Andrews in relation to smuggling activities. He's visiting his daughter apparently. That's what we've been told anyway and we wondered if that was correct. We're also a little concerned about Mrs McGladdery's safety.'

'Her safety?'

'Yes, sir. We believe the gang has already abducted and murdered a woman in the Netherlands in order to force her father to smuggle for them and we suspect the same thing may be happening with Andrews and his daughter.'

There was a pause while O'Haire was considering how to respond.

'We've had Sean McGladdery under surveillance but not his wife.'

She could hear paper rustling in the background and thought he must be looking through reports.

'I'm just checking here. The last time we have a sighting of Mrs McGladdery is on Friday. She left the house on that morning, just before lunchtime. Our men were watching her husband so they didn't follow her. Her father arrived down at the house later on Friday afternoon and as far as we know he's still there.'

'But she hasn't been seen?'

'There's no report of her coming home.'

'I take it you're not prepared to question McGladdery or Andrews about the missing woman?'

'We don't even know she's missing, Chief Inspector. She's maybe gone away to visit friends for the weekend and she'll be back tonight. If we rush in, they're going to know we were watching them. We've nearly got everything we need but not quite. We need to hold off for another couple of days.'

'Dawn McGladdery could be dead in a couple of days.' She had spoken more sharply than she'd intended. She couldn't help herself. She had seen these people's handiwork up close.

'From what you say about the woman in the Netherlands, she could be dead already.'

Gawn was trying to muster her arguments to convince him to do something but he spoke again before she could.

'The men behind Bako Investments have so many interests and they're responsible for so much misery. They're engaged in prostitution, people trafficking, drugs, even gunrunning. We want to nail the bastards and if I have to risk one life for the greater good, then I will.' His tone of voice left her in no doubt that he was not going to change his mind. 'The second we can close these people down, when I have the go-ahead to move on them, then I'll look for Mrs McGladdery. Not until then.'

For the sake of inter-force relations and to keep herself out of trouble, Gawn didn't argue back. She thanked the Superintendent and asked that she be kept informed when they were going to make arrests. He didn't promise that but said when they had made arrests, he would let her know and that she'd be welcome to travel down to Dublin and question whoever she wanted then.

When she had put the phone down, she sat for a minute. She was powerless. In an ideal world she'd head straight down to Wicklow and knock on the door and ask to speak to Dawn. No way could she do that. She didn't want to jeopardise An Garda Síochána's investigation. If they were going to be able to close this gang down that was great. She just wasn't happy that it might be at the cost of another young woman's life.

She was tired. She had managed to stay off her feet most of the day but her knee was throbbing now. Most of the others had already gone off duty. Only Michael Harris was still sitting hunched over his computer screen. No doubt watching the video footage from the airport.

'Go home, Michael. That'll wait till the morning. Start afresh then.'

He beamed. 'Thanks, ma'am. I have a date tonight. I was just wondering how I was going to break it to Chloe that I'd be late again.'

'She better get used to it, Michael, if you're serious about her and your job. That'll be her life.'

As she walked to her car, Harris passed her in the corridor. He was whistling. He had something to look forward to. She had nothing. Only another lonely night.

Chapter 41

As soon as she opened her front door, she knew he was there. The light was blazing but it couldn't be a break-in. She trusted her expensive state-of-the-art security system. He knew the codes, of course. But she should have got a notification when it was disarmed. She glanced down at her phone in her hand and saw she had a missed text. She'd been too busy to notice. So, where was he? There was no music playing, no TV blaring and nothing cooking in the kitchen. Just as she was about to call his name, Seb appeared from the bedroom, looking sheepish. He obviously hadn't expected her to be there and looked like a guilty schoolboy caught red-handed.

'What's with the monkey suit?' she asked.

He was dressed in his tux with a bright red bow tie fastened around the collar of his dress shirt. She couldn't help thinking he looked handsome and debonair in a James Bond sort of way. She had sometimes caught women looking at him admiringly when they were together. The fragrance of the very expensive aftershave she had bought for him wafted across the room. He must have plastered a lot on, she thought to herself.

'I didn't think you'd be here yet.'

'Obviously.' She waited pointedly for him to explain.

'I'm going to a big dinner tonight at Hillsborough Castle. A reception. It was only when I started to get ready I realised my gold cufflinks, you know the ones that belonged to my grandfather, well, I'd left them here.'

'I see.'

He took a step nearer to her.

'Important event, is it?'

'Yes.'

'Going alone?'

He hesitated before he answered her. 'No. There's a whole group of us going from the university.'

She fixed him with her best interviewing stare. He was hiding something, she knew. He knew, she knew.

'I didn't invite you because I didn't think you'd be interested.' He could have added, you never are, but didn't. They both just thought it.

'Right. Of course. I'm not interested in sitting making small talk with people I don't know and have nothing in common with. I've better things to do with my time.' Like sitting at home all night alone drinking wine, she thought to herself. 'Who is she?'

'Who?'

'Your plus one.' She managed to put a lot of meaning into those three little words.

'I don't have a plus one.'

She didn't say anything, just raised one eyebrow and waited.

'There's a new girl in the department. We thought it would be a nice gesture to include her so she's coming as my guest.' He had emphasised the word 'we'.

'We?'

'The other lecturers. My colleagues, you don't know; have never met,' he added. It was now his turn to make a point.

'Just like you haven't met my colleagues either.'

'Yes.'

Seb looked down and bit his lip. He seemed to suddenly remember something and, glancing at his watch, exclaimed, 'I'm gonna have to go. I'm meeting everyone at seven for a drink before we go in.'

'Have a lovely evening.' The sarcasm was thick in her voice.

He stepped forward until he was standing right in front of her. There were only inches between them and again she was aware of his aftershave.

'Gawn I...' But before he could get any further, she turned and opened the front door holding it open for him to leave.

He seemed to hesitate, torn between kissing her goodbye and simply walking away. His eyes met hers and he hoped she could see in them all the words he couldn't speak and she wouldn't listen to anyway.

Then he was gone. She slammed the door closed behind him.

Chapter 42

For two days it seemed as if they had been sitting on their hands, just waiting. An Garda Síochána hadn't come back to them with any update. The Dutch hadn't been in touch with any news.

Clinton had been interviewed again. He was still adamant that the man in the picture at Victoria Mall picking up the bag was not the same man who had threatened him. Gawn had watched McKeown re-interviewing him and she agreed with the girl that Clinton was telling the truth. The photograph the Dutch had sent of Meissner seemed to confirm that. The photograph of Victoria Man was so fuzzy it could have been almost anyone but probably not Meissner. Anyway, Gawn was convinced now that that man was Sean McGladdery.

Surveillance on Andrews' farm confirmed there was no sign of him there. Harris had trawled the CCTV footage from the airport car park and identified the moment when two men on a motorbike had ridden past Andrews, pushed him to the ground and grabbed his coat from the top of his suitcase. They had then sped off onto the Sydenham Bypass and then on to the M2. He had followed their trail on traffic cameras up the hill out of Belfast as they headed north until they had turned off at junction 6 onto the B95 towards Antrim. Then they had just disappeared down a back road. Harris assumed they had a van or some other vehicle waiting and were able to put the bike inside and drive off. The plates on the bike were false. They belonged to a 2002 BMW car which had been stolen and left burnt-out outside Muckamore near Antrim. The bike had not turned up. It could be back sitting in its owner's driveway with its original plates back on it and no one knowing it had been used for a little trip to Belfast.

Gawn would have liked to question Mrs Andrews. She must know where her husband was and what he was up to. She would be able to tell them about her daughter too. At first, McDowell had vetoed any contact with the woman. They were to stay well away. He didn't want to risk the joint investigation with An Garda Síochána and the chance of closing down Bako Investments and finding the Fleischer. But by Thursday morning he had agreed they could talk to her again under the pretence that they wanted a word with her husband about the theft of his coat, nothing else. Gawn and Harris were on their way out of the office to question her when Logan stopped them.

The other line of enquiry they were pursuing was Vanhoeven. He had seemed to be totally uninvolved when they had questioned him at the airport. A South African who only visited Europe intermittently, they had never thought he had any connection to de Bek other than the serendipity of sitting near him on the plane. Now, knowing that his plane ticket had been bought through Bako Travel too, it seemed he must be part of what was going on. Their initial enquiries about him had all seemed straightforward. He was a well-respected businessman with no known links to criminal activity. Logan had been told to contact the authorities in Pretoria again and he stopped Gawn as she was about to walk out the door.

'Ma'am. The South Africans got back to me… eventually. We've got ourselves another mystery man. Vanhoeven.'

'Erin checked him.'

'Right. She did. Paul Vanhoeven is one of the vice presidents of a big pharmaceutical company, Pharmatrax, right enough. All the information about him is on the company website. The police confirmed to her that he had no criminal record and the company confirmed he was in Europe for business and then visiting family in the Netherlands. She even talked with people at the university too and they confirmed he had been there checking on their joint research. It all fitted.'

'But?' She waited.

'He's dead, ma'am.'

'What! Another one. Was he murdered too?'

'No, ma'am. He was in an accident. The taxi he was travelling in was T-boned by a lorry in the Netherlands. The authorities in Pretoria have only just found out about it.'

'When did it happen?'

'Before he came here. I mean before the man we thought was Vanhoeven came here.'

'A very convenient accident,' Harris said.

'No, I checked, Sarge. The Dutch traffic boys are adamant it was an accident,' Logan said. 'The lorry driver was way over the drink-driving limit.'

'It was still very convenient, wasn't it?'

She was about to walk on when she turned back and, speaking over her shoulder, said, 'I suppose Erin's beating herself up about missing this.'

'Well, you know what she's like,' Logan said. 'She takes it all very seriously and very personally.'

'Nothing wrong with that, Billy.' Turning to Harris she added, 'Remind me to speak to her when we get back. In the meantime, Billy, tell her to get back on to the university and check why they told her some cock and bull story about Vanhoeven being there. They'd met the man before. They must have known it wasn't him.'

Gawn had a decision to make now. She knew she should update McDowell about this new information but she was fearful that he would use it as a reason to stop her speaking to Margaret Andrews. She decided to take a calculated risk. She had already arranged to report back to the super after her talk with the farmer's wife. She would tell him about the fake Vanhoeven then too.

Chapter 43

The farmyard looked just as it had the night they had visited. They could hear the sounds of men's voices from the cowsheds. Life seemed to be going on as usual but it was clear that was not the case for Margaret Andrews when she opened the door to them. Last week she had looked like a typical farmer's wife, like her husband, solid, hard-working, ruddy complexion, at home in the kitchen producing wholesome food, a proud wife and mother. The woman standing in front of them now looked as if she hadn't slept since the night they'd been there. Her eyes were red from crying. Her hair was a mess. She had a hankie in her hands which she was twisting into a ball.

'Mrs Andrews, I don't know if you remember us. We were here speaking to your husband. I'm DCI Girvin and...' She didn't finish her sentence. She wasn't sure the woman was taking any of it in. Her eyes were unfocused and Gawn wondered if she'd been drinking or maybe had taken something.

'May we come in, Mrs Andrews?' It was Harris who took the woman's arm and led her into her own house.

He directed her towards the kitchen and eased her down into a chair at the table. Gawn walked behind. Harris seemed to have the same human empathy that Maxwell had possessed. He seemed to be able to exude a sense of sympathy that made witnesses cooperate. It was a good characteristic for a policeman to have and one which she sometimes lacked.

'How about I put the kettle on?' Harris asked and Gawn nodded to let him know he should go ahead.

'Mrs Andrews... Margaret, is your husband here?'

Gawn tried to be as gentle as possible. She leaned forward and put her hand on the woman's forearm. This woman probably knew nothing about Bako Investments but she did know her husband and daughter were in trouble.

Suddenly she seemed to realise she had been asked a question. 'What? Yes. No. He's away.'

'Away where?'

'He's in Dublin visiting our...' She didn't finish the sentence. Instead, the tears streamed down her face.

Harris set a cup of steaming tea on the table in front of her.

'There you are.'

'Thank you.' Margaret Andrews automatically muttered her thanks, years of good manners kicking in.

'Margaret, we want to help. We *can* help you, but we need you to tell us what's going on.' Gawn sat back again and waited for the distraught woman to take a sip of the hot tea before speaking.

'I can't. Bill said I was to tell no one. They'd kill her.' She burst into sobs again.

'Kill Dawn?'

The woman nodded.

Harris had sat down at the table now too on the other side of the woman.

'Who's they?' he asked.

'I don't know any names. I just know they took Dawn and Billy has to help them.'

'Help them how?' he asked.

'He brought something back from Holland for them but he didn't give it to them. They want it.'

'Do you know what, Margaret?'

'No.'

'And he had to take it down to Dublin to them?'

'No. He said they'd already tried to take it from him in Belfast. He didn't trust them. He still has it. Then they took Dawn to get it from him.' She broke into sobs again unable to say anything more until she gathered herself together and took another sip of tea.

The two detectives exchanged a look. The bikers had not been an opportunistic attack. They knew what they were after.

'He thought if he brought it back, he'd be able to bargain with them. He's been a wheeler-dealer all his life, Chief Inspector. Then they phoned and said they had Dawn and they would' – she had to brace herself to continue – 'kill her if he didn't get the package to them. He thought he'd be able to get them to release Dawn and then he'd give them the package and that would be an end to it. He's down with Sean now waiting to hear the arrangements for the handover.'

Gawn didn't like to tell her they weren't the sort of men who made bargains and if they did you could be sure they wouldn't keep their end of it.

'Have you spoken to your husband?'

'Not today. He said something was happening on Saturday and I just had to wait until then. It would all be over by Sunday. But the waiting's killing me.'

Gawn thought of the dates she had seen on the paper in the barn. It all tied in. Saturday – just two days away – was the day. This was confirmation. She needed to let McDowell know so he could update Special Ops.

Gawn and Harris stayed at the farmhouse until a search team and a Family Liaison Officer arrived. She wanted Mrs Andrews watched and supported at all times until this was over one way or another. And she wanted the house and, if need be, the farm searched from top to bottom. The chances were there was nothing to find. Andrews probably had the package, whatever it contained, with him, although he had told his wife he had hidden it, so maybe it was still there. But there might be other evidence of Andrews' dealings with Bako to find; something which would provide a clue to what was going to happen on Saturday.

Chapter 44

As soon as she got back to Belfast, Gawn reported to Superintendent McDowell. She began with the revelations about Vanhoeven. McDowell looked as surprised as she had been when Billy told her.

She had then had to take a bit of time convincing him that they had not interfered when they talked to Mrs Andrews, that they had done nothing which would endanger the task force working to shut down Bako Investments; that the woman had needed to tell someone what was going on. Margaret Andrews was cracking up under the strain of it all. Gawn explained that the FLO would ensure that the woman did not contact her husband and that if he phoned her, she wouldn't reveal that the police had been in touch with her. They had convinced her that the only way she could be sure to see her daughter alive again was to trust them and to do what they said. Gawn only hoped this was true.

Meanwhile they were searching the house from top to bottom. She wasn't very hopeful that they would find anything useful. Andrews was a pawn. He'd been sucked in probably either through gambling or losing money on investments. Finding himself owing a lot of money to these men he'd agreed to work for them. Probably he thought doing something once would be all they would ask. But once in, with men like these, there was no way out. She would love to know what he had done for them and what they were asking of him now.

'I'm telling you this because you've been in this since the start, Chief Inspector, but it goes no further. Saturday is the day it's all going to kick off. They've had a tap on McGladdery's phone so they know he and his father-in-law have been told to go up to Donegal and check in to the Shoreland Hotel for the weekend. They're to wait there and they'll be contacted.'

That was exactly what Gawn would have expected. She vividly remembered that piece of paper in her hand in the barn with Saturday's date and the map.

'By Sunday, hopefully it'll all be over – well this first bit of it anyway. They've planned coordinated raids on a number of premises and homes owned by people they've identified who are involved. Then the real work begins of getting them convicted.'

Gawn was pleased to hear this but wondered how high up the list of priorities Dawn McGladdery was.

'What about Dawn McGladdery, sir?'

'They'll probably find her in one of the places they raid.'

'Probably?'

'Don't use that tone with me, Chief Inspector. You know we always have to prioritise. They'll get a lot of very violent and dangerous people off the streets, probably a lot of drugs and God knows what else. They know they're going to find a group of women from Ukraine who've been trafficked for prostitution. They've had to leave them for a couple of extra days where they are so that they don't jeopardise the whole plan. The greater good, Chief Inspector.'

Tell that to Dawn McGladdery, Gawn thought to herself but held her tongue. She knew she'd never win an argument with him.

'Go home, Gawn. You've done some exceptional work on this.' His voice softened and he looked her in the eye. 'Tie up any loose ends tomorrow and then enjoy your weekend. I don't want your team anywhere near this until Monday. Then you can take it up again and finish it off. Your part in first identifying all this will be noted. Actually, it already has been. ACC Mackie was very impressed with you. You've done yourself a power of good.'

'Thank you, sir.'

As she walked down the corridor back to her own office, she mulled over what the superintendent had said. She didn't care that she'd been noticed. That wasn't why she did what she did. She'd heard 'the greater good' used as an excuse for bombing towns where innocent families were just trying to live a simple life. She hadn't been convinced by it then and she wasn't now.

When she walked in, Harris was still there. She told him he'd be able to enjoy his weekend. They would finish off a few odds and ends tomorrow and then leave it until Monday. He said Chloe would be delighted. They'd be able to spend the whole weekend together.

'Are you planning anything nice, ma'am?'

'Nothing in particular.'

'You should make the most of it. If Andrews is back at home next week and we get more info on Vanhoeven, we'll be busy.'

Where was Vanhoeven? Who was the man who called himself Vanhoeven? She was sure now he was really the Fleischer although she hadn't told McDowell that. She had no proof but she remembered shaking hands with him at the airport and thanking him for his help. She remembered the disgruntled businessman act and being annoyed that he showed so little sympathy for de Bek's death. Of course, it had thrown all his plans awry. He must have been 'bricking it' as Logan was fond of saying but he showed no sign of it, only of annoyance at being held up. He was a consummate actor. She wondered what guise he had assumed now. Gawn couldn't get him out of her mind as she drove home.

Chapter 45

Her mobile phone started ringing as soon as she walked in her front door. It was as if someone had been watching and knew she could take the call. She looked at the screen and saw it was Seb. For one second she contemplated ignoring it or rejecting it. Her finger hovered over the reject button but she couldn't press it. He would know and she feared she might never hear from him again.

'Hello.' She tried to keep her voice as neutral as possible, neither angry nor eager.

'Hi. How are you?'

She knew him well enough to know he was under pressure. She could hear it in his voice.

'Fine. How did your evening at Hillsborough go?'

She could hear his sigh down the phone.

'Do you really want to go there? I didn't ring to discuss the past. I rang to discuss the future.'

Gawn's heart skipped a beat. She had never heard him sounding so serious before. No jokes. No smart quips.

'Is there anything to discuss?'

She waited for his response. The seconds seemed to lengthen into minutes before he spoke again.

'I hope there is. I think we need to sit down and talk, away from everything. Not in your place or mine. Away somewhere. I'm free this weekend. We could book a night away some place, any place. Two rooms if that's what you want.'

She'd been wondering what she would do with a whole free weekend. She thought she would probably spend most of it worrying about Dawn McGladdery and what was happening with the task force. Maybe now was the chance to decide once and for all what the future held for them. If it held anything at all. If they had a future.

'Where do you suggest?' she asked.

She could hear his breath as if he had been holding it waiting for her response and could now breathe again.

'I don't mind,' he said. 'Wherever you want.'

'What about the Sperrin Valley Spa Resort?'

'Yes. Fine. What made you think of that?'

'I saw an advert for it in the airport when I was going to Amsterdam.' This was half true. She had seen the poster but that wasn't why she had suggested the hotel. She knew she was playing with fire. The name of the hotel had been on the map. The Fleischer himself could be staying there for all she knew. She could have named any one of a number of lovely hotels on the east coast or in County Fermanagh but she had named this one.

'I saw that poster too.' He was beginning to sound a little more like himself. 'I'll phone them and make a booking. Are you free to go up tomorrow night?'

'Yes. But I'll meet you up there. I better take my own car in case…'

'You get called out,' he finished her sentence with a note of resignation, or was it bitterness creeping in? 'OK. I'll see you there about six?' There was a brief pause, then he added, 'One room or two?'

She hesitated. This was the big question. If she said two, would he think that she had already made up her mind to end it with him? But if she said one was it suggesting she was going to be a pushover and just fall into his arms?

'One.'

'I'll see you there. I love you, Gawn.'

It was the first time she had heard those words for what seemed like a long time but she wondered what he really meant. *I feel guilty because I was with another woman? I think I've got away with it and she still believes me even though I am selling my house and I haven't told her? I expect to be able to charm her into bed with me?*

'Goodnight.'

Chapter 46

McKeown asked to speak to her privately before she had even made it as far as her door. She could see the serious look on the girl's face.

'Close the door and take a seat.'

'I'd rather stand, ma'am.'

'What is it, Erin?'

'I really stuffed up with Vanhoeven.'

'In what way?'

'He was dead all the time, ma'am.'

'Yes, Erin, but how were you supposed to know? The South African police didn't know. His company didn't know. The university people didn't know though how on earth they didn't is hard to understand. They'd met him several times. You would have thought they'd have recognised it wasn't him.'

'I phoned the university this morning, ma'am. In fact, I'm just off the phone with them. They explained that he had contacted them before he came. He said that he specifically wanted to meet staff he hadn't met before, new people working on the research. He didn't expect or want to be meeting the same people again. He was very definite about it. He seemed to suggest it was very important for him to be able to assess the expertise of the new people involved. And as the partnership grant is worth a lot of money, they were happy to comply. Also, it was only a very short visit. The other times he came, he spent two or three days and most of the time with them. This time he only came to the university once and stayed less than an hour. He explained he'd been called back to South Africa urgently and apologised.'

'It was still a risk. He might have bumped into someone who he was supposed to have met before.' But then this man takes risks, she thought to herself. He probably gets off on taking risks, not stupid ones, but calculated ones. Gawn was convinced now that the man who had sat across the table from her, whose hand she had shaken, was the Fleischer. 'I'm as much to blame as you are. I met him. I interviewed him, for God's sake, and no alarm bells went off for me. Forget it and move on, Erin.'

Gawn opened her office door and called, 'Billy, get the CCTV footage from the airport, I want to watch Vanhoeven when he was getting off the plane and in the airport building.'

Half an hour later a group was watching the footage on a big screen in the squad room controlled from Logan's computer.

'He looks a bit nervous,' Dee suggested.

'I think that's hindsight or maybe wishful thinking. He kept complaining that he was missing his meeting. He wanted to be interviewed first. He seemed more annoyed than nervous but keen to get away,' Gawn explained.

Harris walked closer to the screen and looked at it intently.

'What's that?' He pointed to a mark on the man's wrist.

'Can you freeze that, Billy?'

The picture froze but Gawn said, 'Go back a frame or two where his jacket sleeve moves up a wee bit and you get a better view of his wrist. Yes, that's it. Now can you enlarge it?'

Logan clicked the mouse and the screen was filled by a close-up of the man's wrist.

'What is it?' asked Harris, pointing to the mark. 'A birthmark?'

'A scar?' Logan suggested.

'No. It's a burn mark.' Gawn remembered that she had read in a report about the Fleischer that she had managed to get sight of from a contact in Special Ops, that he had set a building on fire to make his escape when he had assassinated a politician in South America last year. She couldn't tell the others but she was sure this was a burn from that fire.

Harris had Vanhoeven's passport details in his hand. He scanned through the document.

'There's no mention of any birthmark so our mystery man didn't add it to his appearance to pass as Vanhoeven.'

'So now we know our man probably has some kind of mark on his right wrist. I don't know how that helps us at the minute but just something to look out for if we ever come across him again.'

Gawn knew she couldn't keep this to herself. Being able to identify the Fleischer could be the key to stopping whatever he had planned, to saving a life. She hurried back to her office and closed the door behind her. None of the others could hear what she was going to tell McDowell.

Chapter 47

They had spent the rest of Friday waiting. Still nothing from Dublin or Amsterdam. Only Gawn knew that things were happening but she couldn't share that knowledge with anyone. By late afternoon, she surprised the others when she appeared with her coat on and her bag in her hand.

'I'm off. I'm heading up to the north coast for the weekend.'

'Enjoy, boss. You deserve it.' Harris wondered if he sounded a bit sycophantic. He didn't want anyone to think he was trying to keep in her good books. He did think she deserved it. She worked harder and longer than anyone else and, when they had been at the Andrews' farm, he had noticed how much pain she seemed to be in.

* * *

The drive towards Limavady had taken just over an hour. She had followed the M2, noting the exit to Antrim taken by the two biker muggers. Then she had skirted Lough Neagh before meeting a bit of a bottleneck in Magherafelt and a heavy shower of rain too. After that, traffic had cleared and she drove through the gates of the hotel and leisure complex just after six o'clock. The driveway up to the hotel block wound through the golf course dissecting it and she passed a few hardy souls still out on the greens even though evening had descended. She had brought only an overnight case. She wheeled it behind her as she walked through the red brick archway to the courtyard, passing the leisure complex on the way. She hoped Seb hadn't planned for them to go swimming. The only holiday they had ever taken together was to New York around Christmas when there had been lots of sightseeing to do and they'd neither had the weather nor the inclination to swim. So she had never shared with him her reticence to wear a swimsuit in public because of her scarring.

As she approached the door, an older man, wearing the type of diamond-patterned jumper so favoured by golfers, stepped back and held it open for her.

'Nice evening. Up for a wee weekend break, are you, love?' he queried.

'Yes.'

'Playing golf?'

'No. I don't play. Just relaxing, having a few nice meals.'

'Well, I can recommend the restaurant here. Some lovely fish dishes, if you like fish.'

'Yes, I do. Thank you.'

'And if you're really into fish there's a brilliant fish restaurant just over the border near Moville. Mind you, you'd be very lucky to get in there on a Friday or Saturday night. It's usually booked out months in advance. They've had all sorts of famous people there – presidents and politicians and some Hollywood film stars too.'

He seemed to be keen to chat and neither went in nor out, standing with her at the door blocking her from getting any further. She caught sight of Seb sitting in the foyer which doubled as a lounge with comfortable-looking sofas dotted around the open space. He was reading a newspaper. She wished he would notice her and come to her rescue.

'I must get checked in. I see my friend over there waiting. Cheerio.'

'Bye now. Have a nice time, love, with your friend.'

She smiled at the man and moved forward, forcing him to stand aside. When she was within ten feet of Seb, he looked up.

'Hey, you. Looking good.' He smiled and her heart took a jump. He stood up and walked into the gap between them to kiss her on the cheek. No passion, just a friendly greeting.

'I like the jumper,' he said. 'Is it new?'

She had taken the time to call in at home and change out of her formal suit. Now she was dressed in jeans and, he was right, a new jumper in emerald green, a colour which everyone said suited her.

'Yes.'

'I've already checked in for us. We're in the St Andrews Suite. All the suites are named after famous golf courses,' he explained. He made to take her case but she held onto the handle. 'It's OK. I can manage.'

'Of course.' He managed to make that sound like a criticism, or maybe that was just how she was interpreting it.

He led the way across the foyer past a smiling girl standing at the reception desk who nodded at him in recognition. They took the elevator to the second floor which was also the top floor. This was not a high-rise hotel but linear with corridors stretching away as far as they could see to left and right. They hadn't spoken on their short journey upwards.

'This way.'

He turned to the left and began to stride along the brightly lit corridor past a soft drinks vending machine and another dispensing ice. The walls were decorated with sepia prints of the local area, farming and fishing scenes predominated. The St Andrews Suite was the very last one on the corridor. He inserted the key card and stood aside to let her walk in before him. She smiled at her first sight of the room. He had obviously chosen well and spared no expense. They had a small area with a dining table and four chairs if they wanted to eat in the room. There was a huge round-the-corner sofa which faced out to a Juliet balcony. She walked across to it and threw the balcony door open to let in some fresh air. The view was lovely. She would have been able to see for miles over the golf course and out over the open countryside which encircled the resort if darkness hadn't already fallen. Instead, low lights illuminated the trees all around, creating an almost magical effect of a wonderland beyond them. Through the open double doors she caught a glimpse of a huge king size bed with a cascade of soft colourful cushions strewn over it.

'You could almost live here.' She laughed.

'Apparently, according to the receptionist, American businessmen like to come here and play golf and do business so there's plenty of room to feed and entertain their guests. Who knows what multi-million-pound deals have been concluded over this table?'

Or in this bed, she couldn't help thinking to herself.

She set her bag down and turned to explore the rest of the suite. There was a bathroom with a double walk-in shower and a jacuzzi bath. Double hand basins too. She was looking at herself in the mirror above them when she saw Seb move in behind her. She thought how different he looked in mirror reflection, his features changed by the reverse image.

'Well, does it all meet with your approval, madam?' he asked with a bow.

'It's lovely. Thank you.'

He put his hand on her shoulders and made to turn her around to face him, but she resisted.

'I'm quite hungry. It must have been the drive up. It's given me an appetite. Can we get a meal here?'

'Of course, I'll ring down and get us a table.'

'And I'll get ready.'

He moved into the sitting area to use the in-house phone and she closed the door behind him.

Chapter 48

She thought it was the most excruciating two hours of her life. It was like a bad first date, only worse because at least on a first date you could make small talk about family or friends or work. They were long past that stage and yet they didn't seem to have anything to say to each other. Seb had made a few desultory attempts to tell funny anecdotes about work and his colleagues and students but when he began one which featured his evening at the Hillsborough reception, he hastily stopped and changed the subject. They were both glad when they had finished their last mouthful of dessert. The meal had been lovely but Gawn realised she could hardly remember what she'd eaten.

'Would you like to get a drink in the bar?' he asked.

What was the point in putting things off any longer? They needed to talk, really talk.

'No. Thank you.' That stranger politeness, a symptom of where they had come to in their relationship.

The journey up in the elevator and the walk along the corridor seemed to go on forever. Analogies to gallows walks came into her mind. Once the suite door was closed behind them, Gawn sat down on the sofa. She was aware that she was perching on the edge almost as if she was ready to jump up and run away; make her escape, she thought. Seb removed his jacket and sat down ponderously not beside her but diagonally across from her, keeping his distance. He sat forward and put his elbows on his knees interlocking his fingers. His head was down as if he was examining the floor. He looked pale and strained.

The silence stood between them like a physical entity. The double glazing ensured there were no outside noises to break it. Gawn thought she could hear her heart beating. Then Seb looked up and their eyes met.

'God, I love you so much, Gawn,'

She thought there were tears in his eyes. She saw his hands were shaking.

She wondered what he expected of her. Did he think he would say the three magic words and everything would be alright again? Just like that. They were only words and words were cheap and easy. They were spoken and then they dissipated like smoke on a windy day and the only evidence of their ever being spoken was either the hurt or the joy they left behind.

'Aren't you going to say something? Anything? Don't you care?'

'Of course I care,' she snapped at him, her eyes flashing.

She was on her feet now. She turned her back to him and composed herself before turning to face him again.

'I wish I could believe that, Seb. If you really loved me you would understand who I am, what I am, what I have to do. You would understand what my work means to me. I can't be what I'm not, even for you.'

Now he was on his feet too. They stood facing off like a couple of boxers before the start of their bout.

'Have I ever asked you to change? I love you no matter what. I've known what you are from the very first time we met.'

'You were such a supercilious bastard that day, so sure of yourself. *Doctor* York.'

'You are who you are. I don't want to change you. I just want to be part of your life. I can compromise. If I can only have a little part while you go off tilting at windmills and saving the world, so be it. I'll settle for that. But you've got to accept me too for what I am. You've got to be honest with me. I have to have a place in your life. Not be just some sort of appendage. Just a distraction which sometimes you want and sometimes you don't.'

He moved a little closer but still not within touching distance.

'I know I'm crazy, disorganised, infuriating. I even infuriate myself sometimes. But I'm crazy about you and that's not going to change. No matter what.' He moved a step closer to her. 'You've shared some of your past with me but I know there's a lot more you're still keeping from me. I know you've been hurt. I don't mean just physically. You've been let down. But I'm not that person. When I say I love you, I mean it. For keeps. No matter what.'

Now he was directly in front of her. She couldn't take her eyes off him. If it wasn't Seb, she might even have felt threatened. She would have if it had been Jansen. She thought she knew Seb well and yet in this moment she realised there was so much more to him. He wasn't just saying he loved her, he meant it.

'When I first saw this room online, I considered doing the whole Romeo and Juliet thing with you at the Juliet window but then I realised I'd probably end up breaking my neck. The hotel didn't provide a handy trellis like Mr Shakespeare did for Romeo. And I can't write some sonnet to sweep you off your feet. But I'm asking you to let me be part of your world for you are my world, Gawn.'

She saw that his breathing was so shallow she was aware of the rapid rise and fall of his chest. He was waiting for her response, just waiting. She'd never really known anyone else like him, maddening and infuriating and fantastic and wonderful all at the same time. She reached out and placed her hand on his chest. The sensation of his warm smooth skin beneath her fingers reminded her of leaning across and putting her hand on Jansen's chest to check if he was still alive. Seb was very much alive and she could feel him shaking and before she knew what was happening, they were in each other's arms. Later, thinking about it, she wasn't sure whether she had kissed him first or he had made the first move. It didn't matter. After that kiss, nothing else did. He picked her up and carried her into the bedroom with her unwilling now to let go of him. She had told Jenny Norris that Seb was a good lover but she had never experienced such a sense of being loved as she did that night. Neither of them would ever forget it.

Chapter 49

In the morning, as soon as they woke, they made love again. Being together seemed like the most natural thing in the world. They lay afterwards, her cuddled in his arms, and watched the birds in the trees outside their window. Buds were beginning to show on the branches, the promise of an early Spring. New life. New beginnings. That was what it felt like for them too.

'Do you fancy breakfast in bed? We could just stay here all day.' He ran his fingers along her arm.

'Seems a pity to waste such a nice day and all this lovely countryside. We spend so little waking time together, Seb, let's do something normal like take a little drive out and maybe get a pub lunch or something.'

'Sounds good to me, darling.'

They breakfasted in the hotel restaurant and collected a tourist map of the area from reception on the way past.

'Anywhere in particular you fancy going?' he asked as they sat, heads touching, looking over the map in the foyer, finishing off their breakfast coffee.

For a second Gawn was back in the barn in Monnickendam, the torn map in her hand. She pointed to Seb's tourist map.

'The Inishowen Peninsula's supposed to be lovely. Have you ever been?'

'No. Never. Inishowen Peninsula, it is then.' He folded the map very deliberately and reached across to kiss her.

* * *

They had gone in his car. She thought it would be a good gesture on her part to let him drive, to show she

207

didn't always want to be in control. His Porsche was even faster than her Audi but he seldom drove quickly. Like a lot of things about Seb, it was more for show, more to gel with his image than anything else. They headed first towards Ballykelly and then Eglinton before seeing the signs welcoming them to Londonderry or Derry, as the roadside signage proclaimed it, locals having blacked out the first part of the name. The approach over the Foyle Bridge gave a panoramic view of the city. The grey waters far below were still, the windsock on the bridge showed them that today it would be open for high-sided vehicles. They were being lucky with the weather.

At the Culmore Roundabout, they followed the sign for the A2 to Moville, a name Gawn instantly recognised. It was marked as the route for the Wild Atlantic Way, a famous tourist magnet. Shortly the dual carriageway narrowed to a two-way road. Large, detached houses lined it, obviously a prosperous part of the city. Gawn noticed a 'For Sale' sign on one of them and wondered when Seb was going to get around to telling her he was selling his house. Occasionally they would catch glimpses of the Foyle.

They stopped at a garage and filled up with petrol and bought two takeaway coffees. The houses lining the road now were older, smaller, more traditionally Irish in style. Mostly single storey. The waters of Lough Foyle, visible behind the scattered houses, were spoiled by the white smoke emanating from an industrial complex on the far bank. Eventually they entered the little village of Muff. There was a petrol filling station and a couple of Chinese restaurants or takeaways but no suitable pub that they could see. They suddenly realised they were in the Republic of Ireland without even knowing they had passed over an invisible border. The traffic was light. It was a bit early in the year for the tourists who flocked to Donegal. Instead, their main problem was tractors. As they headed past Quigley's Point and towards Redcastle, their view of the water was unobstructed. The sun was out, a weak sun but brightening the grey of departing winter as it headed into spring.

They were in a happy mood, almost like what Gawn imagined how honeymooners might feel. They were just approaching Moville when Seb spotted a sign for a hotel, the Shoreland. The building was not visible from the road.

'Are you prepared to risk it? I'm hungry,' he asked.

He meant risking if the food would be good. She knew she would be risking much more than that.

'I'm sure there's another nice hotel I remember reading about near here.'

This was the hotel where Andrews and his son-in-law had been told to wait. For all she knew they could still be here, waiting. What would happen if Andrews saw her or if whoever was watching them from the task force recognised her? She could jeopardise the whole investigation. She almost told Seb to turn around; that she didn't want to stop here but to do that she would have to explain why and she knew what his reaction would be if he realized she had brought them to this area because of her work. Everything she had said, everything they had done last night, she had meant but he would never believe that.

'I'm starving, Gawn. Please. I'm gonna collapse if I don't get something to eat soon.' He put on a plaintive face.

'Sure, why not?' She could think of lots of reasons but none she could share with him.

As they drove down to the car park in front of the L-shaped building, they were aware of the beautiful scenery. The hotel was perched on the side of the lough with its own private beach. Magilligan Point was in view across the water. They parked and walked into the reception area. A sign pointed to the bar and they decided to check it out. All the time Gawn was watching all around her. No one was sitting about in the easy chairs or sofas in the reception area. Next point of danger – were Andrews and

McGladdery in the Seafarer's Bar? When they pushed the door open and Seb let her walk through before him, she spotted a lone figure sitting in the corner facing the door. It was neither of those two men but it could be someone from the task force. That was where she would position herself if she was on a surveillance job; somewhere reasonably unobtrusive but where everyone coming and going was clearly visible. She chose a table out of the man's direct line of sight.

'What do you fancy, darling?' Seb was already pouring over the menu. He hadn't been joking when he said he was starving.

She had lost her appetite at the thought of what she was risking just being here. After a quick glance, she selected chowder with Guinness bread and lemon oil. He ordered a burger with bacon and cheese on a brioche bun and chips on the side.

'You'll not be able to eat anything for dinner if you eat all that.'

'I have to keep my strength up.' And he laughed, a suggestive laugh.

The order came quickly but it couldn't be quickly enough for Gawn. Every time the door opened she imagined Andrews walking through and recognising her or someone arriving at her side and forcefully removing her to be hauled before O'Haire or whoever was in charge of the stakeout. Every mouthful of food felt more and more difficult to swallow. All the time Seb was keeping up the chatter, suggesting places they could go.

'How about the Famine Village?'

She hadn't really been listening properly and only caught the end of his question as he sat and waited for her reply.

'Yes. That sounds good. Is it far?'

'I don't think so. We passed a poster and a rack of leaflets about it on the way in.'

She would have agreed to go anywhere if it meant they could leave soon. Fortunately, Seb was a fast eater and being hungry he had wolfed down the burger and chips as soon as they were placed before him.

He was being very good and had stuck to mineral water because he was driving. He told her they would have champagne tonight. He wanted it to be very special. He had the engagement ring he had bought for her months ago in his pocket ready to produce along with the bubbly.

Once back in the car, Gawn felt as if she had been holding her breath the whole time she had been inside the hotel. She had come out to the car while Seb paid the bill but she was surprised at how long it took until he joined her.

'Was there a problem?' she asked as he climbed in beside her.

'No. I've got us a very special treat.' He looked so pleased with himself. He had told the waiter that he was going to propose to his girlfriend tonight. 'There's a fish restaurant up the coast from here. O'Halloran's. I've heard people talking about it at work. Apparently, it's fabulous. I mean it has an international reputation. I didn't realise we were so near it. Anyway, I mentioned to the guy behind the bar when I was paying that I would have loved to go there this evening and, as luck would have it, his cousin is the manager. He phoned for me and hey presto he's got us a table for tonight. Someone cancelled. Lucky or what?'

His smile said it all. She only hoped her face didn't betray how she was feeling just so obviously. Suddenly she remembered the area on the map shaded in red with an outline of a fish inside it. How could she have forgotten that? Somewhere here was where the Fleischer was going to strike. She just knew it. How could she get word to the task force about a fish restaurant as one potential target without revealing where she was and essentially ending her own career?

* * *

They spent the afternoon at the Famine Village. Gawn had checked her mobile but had no signal. She would just have to keep trying to get through to McDowell but there were only so many times she could break away from the tour group where Seb wouldn't see her or excuse herself to go to the ladies.

They had arrived just in time to get onto the last guided tour of the day. It was interesting. The tour guide had his patter of amusing and heart-wrenching stories about life in times past. Seb, as an historian, found it fascinating and was able to add information about many of the events they were hearing about, but Gawn's mind was everywhere but there. Seb enjoyed the recreated shebeen and the free sample of poitín. She could enjoy none of it and she still hadn't been able to contact anyone.

'You seem a bit distracted. Are you feeling alright, darling?' he asked as they got back into the car.

This was her last chance. She could lie and say she wasn't feeling well, which wouldn't be too far from the truth. He would be disappointed about O'Halloran's but he would take her back to the hotel. Then she would be able to phone McDowell and tell him she'd remembered the fish drawing, it might be important and he could update the task force and she could stay well out of the way. But she couldn't do it. She didn't want to disappoint Seb but even more she realised she wanted to be there if she could when this, whatever it was, went down; when the Fleischer made his move and the task force took him down.

Chapter 50

The little fishing village was quiet and sleepy, most of the time. You could imagine that not much happened here. It was not the sort of place you expected to bump into a president or a Hollywood A-lister. The boats tied up in the harbour were not pleasure craft for the rich but working boats ready to head out again first thing in the morning to bring the fresh fish for markets and restaurants all over the north of Ireland. O'Halloran's would no doubt have first pick of the catch. The two-storey white-painted building sat on the main road directly opposite the seawall. Outside, bright lights illuminated a sign proclaiming it a 'Seafood Bar'. It was very ordinary-looking but the cars already filling all the spaces directly outside the front door showed how popular it was. Seb had to drive further along the road to find a space to park. As they walked back towards the restaurant, the noise grew. Light shone through a line of white-framed windows spilling out onto the roadway.

When they opened the door, the noise and heat of bodies packed into a relatively small space hit them. At first glance, Gawn thought they would never be able to fit anyone else in and perhaps they would be turned away. Part of her hoped that was so. But, she admitted to herself, she was feeling that anticipation she knew so well from raids in the past, the growing sense of excitement, the nerves, the thrill of the approaching crisis. Her pulse was beginning to race.

She was delighted when they were shown to a table right at the back of the room, near the entrance to the kitchen. Probably anyone else would have been disappointed to be in such an obscure position but it suited her well. She was more or less out of sight with her back turned to the room but she could see most of what was going on from the large gilded mirror behind Seb's head.

In spite of the number of customers, service was speedy. Seb had read her some reviews on TripAdvisor earlier and everyone had mentioned the pleasant and efficient staff. It seemed like they had no sooner sat down than they were being greeted by a friendly face, the little candle in the centre of their table lit and a menu held out for their perusal.

'Look, they have local oysters in the starters. A wee aphrodisiac,' Seb suggested.

'Like you need an aphrodisiac. No, I think I'll have the calamari and then the roasted turbot.' She had no appetite for food.

'Good choice.'

Seb made his selection and when the waiter came he ordered for both of them. He ordered a bottle of white wine and some water too. He would get a bottle of champagne with dessert. He had to drive back to the hotel and didn't want to fall foul of any Garda traffic patrol. With such a reputation, he was sure they kept a watchful eye on the patrons to catch anyone drinking and driving after a meal.

'Boy, wait till I tell them all on Monday, we had a meal at Harry O's.'

'What did you call it? I thought this was called O'Halloran's.' Her heart seemed to have stopped. She held her breath.

'It is but the guy who opened it, fifty years ago, was called Harry O'Halloran and it became Harry O's to the locals and the name stuck.' Then suddenly Seb said, excitedly, 'Don't look round, Gawn, but Xavier Tain and some friend has just come in.'

'Who?'

'Darling, do you not follow any news or social media? You're a media dinosaur, aren't you?' He sounded exasperated. 'Everyone's heard of Tain. Even my mother, for goodness sake. He's one of the three richest men in the world. I don't know who the other guy with him is, though. Probably some Far Eastern millionaire. They've probably just bought Ireland!' He smiled at his own joke.

Gawn's stomach did a somersault. The HO on the map could be, must be Harry O's. And XT must be Xavier Tain. And they were right here in the middle of it. She tried to look round surreptitiously to see if she could spot any undercover police but of course she couldn't. They wouldn't be very good at their job if she could. She just hoped to God they were really good at their job.

Gawn risked a quick look to see who Seb was talking about. She spotted Tain and his companion, an Asian man. Both were dressed rather formally, not as if they were enjoying a casual holiday together. Most people were trying very pointedly not to look at him but there was some whispering and nudging going on. Obviously Seb was not the only one who had recognised him. What he hadn't recognised but Gawn's years of experience showed her was that the two men who had walked in behind him were his bodyguards. From her perspective they might as well have been wearing uniforms or signs on their foreheads. She expected they would probably be armed. She could feel her senses start to sharpen. Her stomach fluttered as it had before big raids or operations in the past. It was the awareness that something was about to happen. She scanned the room but still couldn't see any sign of a police presence.

While she couldn't be one hundred percent sure, it seemed most likely that Tain was the Fleischer's target. XT. She looked around at the other diners. No one stood out. If they were rich or famous or powerful she had no way of knowing but the fact that the third richest man in the world was in the room must be significant. She was sure he must have enemies or business rivals. And someone who was his rival would have the money to pay the kind of figure the Fleischer was used to receiving for his services. But was the Fleisher sitting at one of the other tables? Some of the diners she could discount, but not many.

'Does Tain have a lot of enemies?'

'That's a weird sort of question. I don't know. I suppose so. Somebody who's successful usually does, I guess.' His face creased in a frown. 'Is something wrong? What's going on, Gawn?'

'Nothing.'

Gawn couldn't remember ever feeling as tense and alone as she did right now. She had given the task force the area and the initials. They had all assumed that HO was the name of the target. She just had to hope that they had worked out that it referred to O'Halloran's or that they were still following Andrews and McGladdery and the Fleischer had summoned them here. Otherwise she was on her own if anything happened. But with a certainty she couldn't have explained, she knew it wasn't *if* anything happened, but when.

'You're very quiet, Gawn. Are you feeling a bit off? We can go, you know. I want you to enjoy the evening.'

'No. I'm fine. Just a bit tired. You did keep me awake quite late, you know.' She smiled at him. What was she getting him into? she wondered. If all hell broke loose, she couldn't protect him. She tried to keep up a conversation but only half her mind was on it. All the time she was observing in the mirror. Every time someone stood up to leave or every time the door to the street swung open, she tensed. When one table of six who were obviously out celebrating together suddenly burst out into raucous laughter, she jumped.

'Are you sure you're OK?'

'Yes. I'm fine. How many times are you going to ask me?' she snapped at him. She saw his hurt reaction and suddenly thought, if anything happens to us, I don't want our last words to be angry. She reached across and put her hand on top of his. 'I'm fine. Honestly and I'm having a great time… with you,' she added and smiled at him. She could feel his foot touch her ankle under the table and his eyes twinkled.

'Let's get you some more water. Keep you hydrated.' He swivelled in his seat and called to a passing waiter, 'Could we have another carafe of water, please?'

'Of course, sir.'

It was not the waiter who had been serving them but he seemed happy to oblige and next time he passed carrying two bottles of water he set one down on their table.

'Thank you.' Seb's voice sounded from very far away. Gawn's mind was in a spin. The waiter's sleeve had risen up his arm as he had stretched across to place the carafe of water in the centre of their table. That arm had a mark on the wrist, a burn scar. She knew it, recognised it immediately and was in no doubt that this was the Fleischer. She didn't think she had made any move but something about her had alerted him. He turned quickly and moved towards Tain's table. God, don't let there be a shootout, she thought. Or a bomb. He wouldn't have explosives, would he? There were so many people in the room, some children too. It would be a bloodbath. She had to do something.

Gawn sprung up and shouted, 'Vanhoeven!'

It was the first word that came to her mind. He would know she had recognised him. Maybe he would be so focused on getting away, expecting that there would be other police here too, that he would simply turn and run. She lurched forward to grab him but she never got there. The two burly bodyguards intervened, blocking her way. One grabbed her by the arm. When she kicked out and tried to punch him, he twisted her arm violently and she felt a searing pain shoot up through her shoulder. She thought her arm was dislocated. All around was shouting and screaming. Tables were overturned as patrons tried to get out of the way. At one point she caught a glimpse of Seb rushing towards the man holding her. But before he could reach her, her captor had turned and slammed him in the face. One punch and he went down. His head bounced off the edge of a table and then hit the floor hard and she could see his eyes immediately glaze over.

In the confusion Vanhoeven or whatever he was calling himself now got away. Garda had materialised from nowhere, and for a second she thought they had had the whole place under surveillance and she had blown it for them, but from their demeanour it was soon obvious these were Traffic Branch who had been looking out for over-the-limit drivers not international assassins. Their presence, however, was enough to bring some semblance of order to the chaos. One organised the diners into a conservatory at the back of the building where they could be held until reinforcements arrived. Tain, his fellow diner and his goons were nowhere to be seen. They had made a speedy exit. One of the younger guards was on his knees beside Seb working with him. Even more quickly than she had dared to hope, other black-attired and heavily armed guards arrived. They had obviously been somewhere nearby as part of the Bako raids. Their leader wanted to question Gawn but the paramedics who had now also arrived insisted that she needed hospital treatment. She was packed into an ambulance with an armed officer travelling with her, whether to protect or arrest her, she wasn't sure. She tried to argue with them, refuse to go, but they wouldn't listen to her. They were still working on Seb as the ambulance doors closed and hid him from her sight.

Chapter 51

A&E at Letterkenny Hospital was busy. It was probably a typical Saturday night and they had their usual share of car accidents and drunks. Being wheeled in with an armed escort ensured she was seen right away. It didn't take the doctor more than a perfunctory look at her shoulder to diagnose a potential dislocation. They put an ice pack on it and ordered a scan to see the extent of any damage or tearing. That had taken what seemed like an age with Gawn all the time begging her guard for news of Seb. Eventually she was wheeled back into the cubicle.

'This is going to be a bit painful but we'll make it as quick as we can. I'm going to inject something that will relax the muscles and then I'm going to try to pop your arm back fully into its socket.' The doctor was young and seemed a bit intimidated by the guard standing at the cubicle curtain, sub-machine gun at his hip.

He had said it was going to be painful and it was. They gave her gas and air to suck on as well as a muscle relaxant. She had seen pregnant women on TV giving birth and using something similar.

'That's done the job, I think.'

She wished he sounded more confident.

'We're going to give you a sling for your arm. It's important to keep the arm immobile for a week or two to prevent future problems.'

She wondered what sort of future problems he was referring to. Just now she had more pressing present problems to worry about. She still had heard nothing about Seb's condition and the guard refused to even discuss anything about Bako Investments or the Fleischer.

***

When she was discharged, clutching yet more hospital-prescribed painkillers, she was taken to the Garda Station in Letterkenny. Superintendent O'Haire was waiting for her.

'My God, you look awful. Sit down before you fall down, woman.'

Gawn was sure she did look terrible. She had glimpsed herself reflected in the glass doors as she walked in and had noted her dishevelled clothes and untidy hair, her arm in a sling and even a slight limp from the car accident. She knew what Seb would say – she was going for the *Die Hard* look. She felt the tears pricking at the back of her eyes as she thought of him.

'Now what the hell were you playing at?' His voice was not unkind.

She wondered if he was just going easy on her because of her injury or if he had bad news to impart.

'Please, sir, before I answer any questions, I need to know about my friend.' She was surprised her voice sounded so controlled and reasonable. It wasn't how she was feeling.

'You mean Dr York?'

'Yes.'

'I thought he might be more than a friend.'

Friend, boyfriend, lover, partner. What did it matter what she called him?

'How is he, sir?'

O'Haire took pity on her.

'He was taken to Altnagelvin. I've no update on his condition.'

'Can you find out?' She waited. 'Please.'

He moved around his desk, sat down and picked up the telephone.

'Get me Altnagelvin Hospital.' He waited then spoke again. 'This is Superintendent O'Haire from An Garda Síochána in Letterkenny. I'm checking the condition of a patient you have there. My officers would have brought him in. Sebastian York. He was admitted a couple of hours ago after an incident in Moville.' She watched his face closely, fearing he would hear bad news. 'I see. Thank you.' His expression was inscrutable. He set the receiver down. How much more slowly could he move? She wanted to scream at him. 'He's regained consciousness and they've got him in ICU but I got the impression that's more a precaution than anything else. Now can we get onto the Fleischer and Tain?'

She answered all his questions. She didn't offer excuses about any of it. When they had finished, it was already dawn and Gawn was exhausted. All she wanted to do was see Seb. O'Haire arranged for a car to take her as far as the hospital.

Chapter 52

Gawn recognised the woman as soon as she saw her even though they had never met. Seb had suggested a few times taking her to meet his mother but somehow the timing had never been right; it seemed there was always a good reason.

When she entered the ICU she saw Seb's mother sitting by his bedside, his hand sandwiched between her two. She was stroking the back of his hand tenderly. She was talking to him but Gawn was too far away to hear what she was saying. While she watched, the woman stood up, lent over her son and kissed him on the forehead. She saw him raise his hand slightly off the bed to wave to her as she turned and walked out.

When she stepped into the corridor, the two came face to face.

'Mrs York, I'm—'

'You're Gawn. I recognise you. Seb showed me photos of the two of you.'

'I'm so sorry about what happened. How is he?'

'He's going to be alright. I know because when they told him his brain scan had come back normal, he told them there must be something wrong, he was never normal before.'

It seemed she was going to laugh. Instead she started to cry. Not loudly. Just gentle sobbing.

'I'm really really sorry.'

Gawn reached out and patted the older woman's arm. Mrs York took a handkerchief from her pocket and blew her nose. She used the time it took to look Gawn up and down.

'You don't look so great yourself.' She nodded at Gawn's arm held rigidly to her side by the sling.

'I'm OK.' She hesitated before asking, 'Is it alright if I speak to him?'

'I don't know if he'll want to see you. But go ahead.'

Gawn was walking past her when the woman added, 'He was crazy about you, you know. He wanted to marry you.' Gawn noticed the past tense.

She walked towards his bed. His eyes were closed and she thought he was asleep. She hesitated, torn between turning and leaving or sitting down in the seat vacated by his mother. Before she had come to any decision, he opened his eyes. His expression didn't change.

She took one step nearer the bed.

'Seb, I'm so sorry.' She seemed to be spending all her time apologising.

'Fuck you, Gawn.'

His words and the vehemence with which he spoke shocked her.

'I didn't mean for this to happen.'

'Didn't you? You used me. It was all for your investigation, your case. Your bloody work always comes first. I'm just a poor second. Useful for a bit of sex but you don't really want to share your life with me. I don't want to be some kind of a friend with benefits. I'm finished with it. I'm finished with you.'

'Seb, please.' But she didn't get any further.

'Just go.' He had become agitated and was speaking so loudly now a frowning nurse scurried across and whispered authoritatively, 'I think Mr York needs some rest now. You have to leave.'

She had no alternative but to turn and walk away.

Chapter 53

The day had started badly and it was all downhill from there. She woke to a scream and a crash as her cleaning lady, Martha, discovered her slumped half on and half off the sofa, still fully dressed. Stooping down to pick up the contents of a bag of groceries she had brought to restock Gawn's fridge, which were now scattered all over the floor, she scolded, 'Dear God, Gawn. You scared the life out of me. What happened to you?'

'Sorry, Martha.' She seemed to have spent most of yesterday apologising and now here she was, starting again already. 'I'm OK. Or rather I will be. Don't worry. It looks worse than it is. What time is it?'

'Ten o'clock.'

'Ten o'clock!' How had she slept so late? She hadn't got back from Derry until late on Sunday afternoon by the time a car and driver had been arranged to ferry her home. At first, she had wanted to go back to the hotel and pick up her own car and then realised she was in no condition to drive. She would be a danger to herself and others on the road.

'You look terrible. I'm going to make you a nice cup of tea and then I'm going to call the doctor.'

A nice cup of tea was Martha's answer to every problem.

'I'm OK. I don't need to see a doctor. I saw one at the hospital.'

Martha liked to mother her, she knew. Her own daughters lived abroad and she had once told Gawn she would come even if she wasn't being paid. It made her feel needed. That got Gawn thinking now. Who did she need? And she knew there was only one answer to that.

'I have to get to work.'

'Have a bit of sense. You're not going anywhere.' The woman was helping her to her feet and guiding her towards the bedroom. 'Where's that man of yours? He should be here looking after you.'

Gawn knew Martha and Seb shared gossip and coffee after she left for work on mornings when he had stayed over. She treated him like a naughty schoolboy; like the son she had never had. He had bought her a beautiful bouquet on her birthday and given her a plane ticket to visit her daughter in Paris as a Christmas present. Thoughtful, personal gifts. In her eyes he could do no wrong. Gawn wondered how she would react when she heard they'd split up.

Getting showered and dressed took a long time and a lot of effort. She had never realised how many little things you needed two hands for. She eventually discarded the sling, flinging it away disdainfully into a corner and determined just to be careful with her arm, but not before she had had to resort to asking Martha to help her with her bra when she hadn't been able to manage the hooks by herself. She had phoned Harris and, without explaining any details, had asked him to get Logan to come and fetch her and to send Dee and Grant to collect her car from the hotel. Her spare car keys were in her desk drawer. She wondered who would drive it back. Probably Dee would pull seniority.

By the time she was dressed and sitting over a second cup of coffee with Martha, the phone rang and Harris announced he was waiting outside. He had come himself. With a final word of thanks to her cleaner and a final check in the mirror to see she looked more or less like her normal self, she had gone down to meet him.

'Morning, ma'am.' He was waiting outside the car, leaning against the wing and held the door open for her to get in.

She just smiled and nodded to him. They passed the first part of the journey in silence and it wasn't until they were on the motorway that she spoke.

'What have you heard?'

'About you or about the case?'

'Let's start with the case.'

'They raided houses and industrial buildings across the country. Most were down south and I haven't heard too many details about them yet. Just that a large amount of drugs was discovered in a factory complex outside Dublin city and some people, mostly women, were found in Galway.'

So they had got the trafficked women. Good.

'They got some trucks and stuff in Tyrone that they think are linked to it all. Our boys are going over them.'

'What about Donegal?'

'Oh, it made the headlines. Apparently, there was some kind of incident involving a very famous American but the press hasn't named him. Whether they haven't been able to discover who it was or they're being gagged, I don't know.'

'And what about me?'

'You're the talk of the place.' He looked across at her and smiled.

She didn't smile back.

'Word is, you single-handedly saved some VIP but nobody knows who and from what. Sorcha down in the canteen has a friend who lives near Moville and she was talking to her on the phone last night. Apparently, you tackled two men who were going to attack someone. It was all a bit garbled and there's all kinds of speculation in the press about who it could have been. They say an American ex-president was over playing golf and it was him. So, what's the true story, boss?'

She wondered how much she should tell him. Unless they got the Fleischer and were putting him on trial, she imagined they wouldn't want word of him to get out. Some sort of cover story would be cobbled together and she just hoped it didn't involve her having to lie too much and become some sort of police pin-up to mask what had really nearly happened.

She chose not to answer his question, instead asking another of her own.

'What about our case? Any progress? Have we got Dawn McGladdery or her father yet?'

'We can't find anything about the man who was posing as Vanhoeven. He's a ghost. There's no sign of him leaving the country, not as Vanhoeven anyway, so he could still be here.' He was putting off telling her the bad news.

'And?'

'We haven't found either of them, ma'am.' He saw her expression and hurried on. 'We're still watching the house.'

'And the FLO's still there with Margaret?'

'Yes.'

'Good. This isn't over yet.'

Chapter 54

She wasn't sure if it was an inquisition or a celebration that she was still alive. She had been called to the top floor. She assumed it would be to McDowell's office but she was re-directed to the conference room. There she was confronted by the Superintendent, plus DCS Reid, ACC Mackie and Chief Superintendent Fulton from Special Ops. One other figure was there and she was pleased to recognise ACC Norman Smyth, her godfather.

'I'm amazed to see you still walking about, Chief Inspector. You seem to make a habit of getting yourself bashed about, one way or another,' Mackie stated, with a wry smile on her face.

'Nice to see you more or less in one piece, Gawn.' It was Smyth.

'Thank you, sir.'

When they were all seated around the long mahogany table, all except Fulton who remained standing by the window, Gawn was invited to sit too.

'The Fleischer has managed to evade both our colleagues across the border and possibly also ourselves,' began Chief Superintendent Reid.

'Possibly, sir?'

'Well, let's be frank within these four walls. We have no idea where he disappeared off to. He could have headed south or east from Donegal. He might have crossed the border and be God knows where. He could be halfway to South America by now. He must have contacts all over the world. We're sure he would have had a contingency plan, probably more than one.'

'Good to be sure of something, sir.'

Reid raised an eyebrow at her but didn't respond to her comment.

'Is there anything you can tell us either about what happened in Donegal or anything from your own investigation that could suggest where he might head; anywhere he might hide up if he didn't get out of the country?'

All eyes were turned on her and she would have loved to produce some magic suggestion but the truth was she had no idea at all. Apart from that one short interview with the man at the airport when he was posing as Vanhoeven and then her brief identification of him in the restaurant, she knew little about him.

'I haven't been briefed about the Fleischer. Anything I know about him came from conversations with the Dutch and at that time they didn't know for sure he was heading to Ireland. They told me a little about how he operated but not much. Surely you've had a lot more information from other sources?' She looked around the table as she spoke, including them all in her comments.

'How did you recognise him? He's supposed to be a master of disguise,' Reid continued.

Gawn took a deep breath. 'I told Superintendent McDowell on Friday we identified a burn scar on Vanhoeven's wrist when we looked at the footage from the airport. But in the restaurant I think it was just instinct. He recognised me and I picked up something in his manner. He's very good at changing his appearance and blending into whatever character he's supposed to be. At the airport we would never have queried he was what he said he was. He was very convincing, how he looked, how he sounded, his attitude, everything. When I saw him again he was totally different-looking. He'd lost the paunch which I presume must have been padding. His skin tone was much lighter, his hair was different, he wasn't wearing glasses and his whole stance was changed so that he appeared taller. At the airport he had sort of hunched himself over and given the impression of being a small man. But I saw a scar on his wrist when he reached across our table.'

'You could have been wrong,' McDowell said.

'Yes. When I stood up and shouted his name, I could have been wrong. He would have ignored it and I would have looked a fool. I was prepared for that to happen. But he didn't. He recognised the name and reacted. He turned and looked at me and then made for Tain's table. I was sure then.'

'We heard about the bodyguards and what happened.'

'They were just doing what they're paid to do. There wasn't time to start explaining why I was yelling and running towards their boss. I must have looked threatening. They reacted. I should have taken more evasive action but at least it was enough of a distraction to let Tain get safely away.'

'And unfortunately the Fleischer too.'

'Yes, sir.'

'If you're sure there's nothing else you can tell us…' Reid left the sentence unfinished.

'Am I allowed to ask how de Bek and Vanhoeven and the Bako people all fit together? And Clinton. I can't understand what his role was in the whole plan.'

The men and woman around the table exchanged looks. It was Smyth who spoke eventually.

'I think you've done enough to deserve that,' he said. 'But anything you hear must not go any further. This is for your ears only.'

She nodded her understanding.

'Some of the minor figures who have been arrested are singing their heads off trying to save themselves. The guards have pieced most of it together. Bako Investments has been operating in Ireland for some time. Vanhoeven, or the Fleischer, linked up with them. We presume whoever was paying him to kill Tain is one of the top men running Bako. Take your pick from half a dozen oligarchs who all have had disputes with Tain. Meyer had been working with Bako for years and de Bek had been smuggling for them. Not drugs. Mostly antiques and artifacts through his museum contacts. Except he was going to draw a line at getting involved in murder. Apparently they grabbed him off the street, injected him with some anaesthetic to subdue him and then showed him his daughter held hostage to get his cooperation. But they still didn't trust him They used Clinton as insurance in case de Bek took cold feet and didn't deliver the goods.'

'And Andrews?' Gawn asked.

'Andrews had got himself in deep with them. He owes them a lot of money and getting him to smuggle for them was his way out. The presumption is de Bek was bringing in the…' Smyth paused and looked down at a notepad in front of him.

'Tetrodotoxin?' Gawn suggested.

Smyth looked up. He was surprised that she already knew about the drug. 'Yes. And the Dutch authorities have proof Andrews was smuggling diamonds which was going to be how Vanhoeven was to be paid for killing Tain. They reckon he would have been carrying over ten million's worth.'

Gawn couldn't help her face showing her reaction to the figure.

'Are we sure how he intended to kill Tain? I didn't see a gun or knife. Was it the tetrodotoxin?'

'We've only just got the latest forensics report through from our Garda colleagues. Yes. It seems he was going to poison him. Quick, efficient. Natural-looking and giving himself lots of time to simply slip away.'

Gawn nodded. It was what she had expected to hear. 'Dr Norris found traces of it on de Bek's shoe.'

'Did she now? Well, apparently, the real Vanhoeven's company is developing its use, and taking over Vanhoeven's persona not only gave him an identity but also access to the drugs he needed. We've asked the Dutch to go over Vanhoeven's car accident again as it just seems too convenient.'

'We were lucky. Tain brought his meeting forward unexpectedly and that meant they were rushing their preparations. The Fleischer is meticulous in his preparations with every contingency covered but this time he had to rush; had to improvise. I don't expect under normal circumstances in his original plan he would ever have travelled together with the smugglers. Or even that de Bek and Andrews would have been on the same flight. The flight booking was a bit sloppy of Bako. But it worked for us.'

He paused for a moment, then added, 'You should know that the tetrodotoxin was in the bottle of water he had put on your table too. He obviously recognised you and was taking the opportunity to get rid of you.'

The colour drained from Gawn's face as she realised how easily she and Seb could have been poisoned if she hadn't noticed the mark on the waiter's arm. She pulled herself together and asked, 'What about Bill Andrews and his daughter and son-in-law, sir? They are still part of my investigation.'

It was ACC Mackie who spoke.

'Unfortunately, knowing what we do about the Fleischer and how he likes to tidy up loose ends, it seems likely they're all dead. Their bodies may never be found.'

'But I can still have my team look for them?'

'No. The special task force will deal with everything to do with Bako and the Fleischer.'

'That's right. I have a meeting in Dublin in the morning and we'll move on from there,' Fulton added.

'So, that's it for you and your team. No more is to be said about this matter. Your team doesn't know about the Fleischer?' Smyth asked.

'No, sir.'

'Good. That's how it stays. I'm sure Mr Tain or his people will be in touch with you privately. He's already spoken to the Chief Constable and the Taoiseach. His meeting in Donegal was crucial for the interests of both the Irish and British governments. Everyone is very grateful to you, Gawn. If Tain and his associate had been murdered on Irish soil there could have been serious repercussions.' After a momentary pause he added, 'By the way, how's your friend?'

'I don't know, sir. I haven't spoken to him.'

'He doesn't know anything?'

'No, sir. He was in the dark about what was going on.'

'Good.'

She stood up. 'Thank you, sirs, ma'am.' She looked around the room. They were prepared to just write off three people. The task force would have other priorities. Andrews and the McGladderys would be forgotten, but she couldn't forget she had promised Margaret Andrews she would get her daughter back safely. And she wasn't prepared to give up just yet.

Chapter 55

She was fuming by the time she got back to the squad room. The others could read her mood and stayed out of her way. In her office, she sat trying to figure out how she could trace the missing three. They had nothing to go on.

'Ma'am.'

Harris stood in the doorway.

'Andrews has just phoned his wife.'

So they were still alive.

'I thought Special Ops had taken the trace off and withdrawn.'

'They did withdraw, ma'am, and the FLO's gone too but the trace was still active. They mustn't have got around to calling it off and Erin was monitoring it for our case.'

She didn't tell him they didn't have a case anymore. Instead she jumped up from her seat and followed him over to McKeown's desk.

'Can you play it for us?'

The girl clicked on her computer and a man's breathy voice sounded.

'Margaret?'

'Bill? Where are you? Bill, are you all–' But he didn't let her finish.

'Have the police been?'

'Yes, but they're all away now.'

'Are you sure?'

'Yes. Are you alright? Where's Dawn?'

'We're alright. We'll be there tonight after dark. Make sure the security lights are switched off. We're coming in over the back fields from the Muckie Burn. I need you to make sure there's nothing blocking the field where I put the football pitch for the kids. If there's any machinery you'll have to get it moved. Understand? This is very important.'

'Yes. I'll do it. Yes.'

The phone line went dead and they heard Margaret Andrews calling her husband's name but he wasn't there anymore.

'Can you get a fix where he was speaking from?' Gawn asked.

'It was a mobile, ma'am, and it's been turned off now,' McKeown said.

'OK. It won't be dark for about five hours. That'll give them time to get people into place. We'll have to let Special Ops know.' She was thinking aloud and when she saw the look of consternation on her sergeant's face she added, 'it'll all be part of the Bako operation so they need to be involved, plus these people are armed and not afraid to use their weapons.'

'Do you think Andrews is one of their bosses behind all this?' asked McKeown.

'Did you not hear his voice? He's terrified. No. He's acting under duress and we can only hope they keep him and his family alive until ARU can get to them.'

'Who are they, boss? Did they not get them in the raids?'

She hesitated. The task force probably had got a lot of the top men at a local level but the really top bosses would be thousands of miles away in Eastern Europe keeping their hands nice and clean or maybe sitting in a penthouse apartment in Dublin. It was the Fleischer who was still here like a wounded animal trying to make his escape but not before he got the payment owed to him and Andrews was the key to that. She knew the Fleischer didn't like loose ends. And wounded animals were always the most dangerous. Once he got the diamonds, all the Andrews would be a liability. But she couldn't tell them any of this without revealing the Fleischer's existence and what had been going on. She made an instant decision.

'We'll stay well out of it. Let our armed response team deal with it.'

It didn't really sit well with her to order them to stand down but to do anything else would be putting them in danger.

She rushed into her office and spoke to McDowell, briefing him on what they had learned.

'OK. Let the glory boys take over now. There's plenty of time for them to get into place and be waiting to give the target a nice surprise. Good work, Gawn. Tell your team.'

He rang off.

Chapter 56

Gawn and Harris were in the car. She was driving and they were headed to a meeting with Jenny Norris at her office about a hit and run death the pathologist had been reviewing. Gawn had needed to be doing something. She couldn't just sit around doing nothing. The task force should be in place within the next couple of hours in plenty of time before darkness fell to cover the Fleischer's arrival. She and Harris were on the Westlink when the phone call had come through to her mobile just after two o'clock. She had it on handsfree speaker so he could hear too.

At first they couldn't make out what was being said. The caller was whispering and the voice was quivery. Eventually, by dint of telling them to slow down, they recognised Margaret Andrews' frightened voice.

'They're here. He's going to kill us all. I can't–' And then the phone went dead.

The two looked at each other.

'Shit. Our boys won't be in position yet. It's far too early, boss.'

'Call McDowell. Now!' she shouted, as Harris hesitated.

He dialled the number and Gawn was put straight through. As briefly as possible she told him what Margaret Andrews had said. She had already speeded up and joined the motorway as she was speaking, ignoring the speed limit.

'We're just at the start of the M1. I'm going to head on down there and see what we can see. Check it out.'

'Stay well back. They'll be armed. You've played the hero enough recently. You've probably used up your nine lives, Chief Inspector. I'll get the task force and ARU there as soon as possible.'

'Right, sir. Understood.' She nodded to Harris to indicate he should end the call.

'But you wouldn't stay well back, would you, ma'am, if someone's life was in danger?'

She didn't disagree with him.

* * *

Their journey was probably the fastest he had ever travelled except in a plane. Their speed never went below eighty and at some points was over one hundred. He was expecting to hear the siren and see the flashing blue lights of Traffic Branch but none appeared. It wouldn't have mattered anyway. She wasn't for stopping.

Just a little over fifteen minutes later she had slowed and parked down a laneway. They got out of the car and looked over the fields towards the farmhouse and its outbuildings.

'I need to get a bit nearer so I can see what's going on. You stay here, Michael. On no account go anywhere near these people.' She saw his reaction. 'There's no point in both of us going. The cavalry will be here soon.' She smiled at him. 'I just want to get an idea of where they're being held in the house and how many there are. Then I can update our boys when they arrive so they're not charging in blind. You watch out for Tactical Support and give them an update.'

She got out of the car and opened the boot. She took off her jacket and donned a Kevlar vest and on top she put the old black sweatshirt she kept in the car for when she got the urge to go running.

'Good luck, ma'am,' Harris said as she moved off, keeping her head below the level of the roadside hedges.

* * *

It had taken her longer than she expected to reach the house. She found a break in the hedge where she could force her way through. The twigs caught at her clothes and one dug into her knee causing her to wince. She advanced as far as a tractor sitting all alone in front of the house which offered her some cover. She paused and gathered her breath. Her heart was pounding, not from the exertion but from the adrenaline rush. How many times had she been in situations like this? Many. But never without a gun in her hand.

She sneaked a look around the end of the tractor past its engine housing. She could see no one. There was no movement at any of the windows. Then a flash of colour and movement caught her peripheral vision. It was a figure behind the cowshed. She could hear the cows and wondered if it was one of the farm labourers who was busy at his work unaware of any drama unfolding. Then she heard the thudding drone of a helicopter overhead. Bloody hell. Nothing like announcing your arrival, guys, she thought as she assumed it must be the PSNI helicopter. But it wasn't. She looked up and saw a flash of red on its side. This was a private helicopter and it was coming in to land. It could only be here for one reason – to pick up the Fleischer. And if he was ready to leave, then the Andrews were about to die, if they weren't already dead. Realising she would be visible to anyone watching out the windows and to the pilot of the helicopter, she ran across to the house anyway and flattened herself against the front wall in line with the door.

The shot, when it came, was loud even though it was coming from inside the building. Before she had time to react, the front door was flung open and a man ran out heading towards the cowshed. His hands were tied and she registered that it was McGladdery and he was wounded. She could see blood seeping through and staining the back of his shirt just at his shoulder. Then another man appeared. He had a gun. She didn't see his face but she knew this must be the Fleischer. He took two steps outside and then stopped and took aim at the fleeing figure. She made to move and he must have sensed her being there for he swung around and she found herself facing him. Now the gun was trained on her. His eyes were sparkling with the excitement of the kill. She knew that look. She had seen it before. In a split second she saw her life before her. She realised she was going to die and she wasn't afraid; only sad at lost possibilities.

'Police! Stop! Drop the gun!'

It was Harris. What was he doing? He shouldn't even be here. She had told him to wait by the car. She heard the shot and then another in rapid succession. Then it seemed time stood still. Black-clad masked figures seemed to be everywhere. One grabbed her and pulled her face down on the ground.

'All clear. Target neutralised.'

She became aware of the noise of the helicopter receding as the pilot made his escape. A hand helped her to her feet. She looked across and saw her sergeant still lying on the ground. Why wasn't someone helping him up too? She watched as one of the Tactical Support team knelt down beside him and then turned and shook his head.

'No!' She heard a woman screaming and realised it was her. She tried to run across to Harris but hands prevented her, holding her back and then manhandling her roughly into a waiting SUV. Her last sight before they turned out of the laneway was of Margaret Andrews and her daughter being led out of the front door while one of the men covered the prone figure with a jacket.

Chapter 57

The sat-nav had been a blessing. Without it they could have driven around in the dark trying to find the right street and the right house for ages. The estate was like a rabbit warren of cul-de-sacs with row upon row of near-identical houses, thrown up quickly after the war to house returning heroes and resettled evacuees from the bombing in Belfast and later to accommodate the move out of the city because of the Troubles. Now young families were adding their own features in a bid to personalise their homes and mimic the TV property shows which promised profits or at least a more glamorous lifestyle. Double glazing, conservatories and front porch extensions abounded. One or two of the houses featured decorative stone cladding.

There was nothing different about this particular house; nothing to make it stand out. It was a solid red-brick semi-detached house like its neighbours. It had no pretensions to grandeur. Gawn noted the neat pathway leading past the pocket handkerchief-sized garden. She could have imagined that in earlier times it would have been scrubbed down like the red steps on the houses her mother had grown up in on a main road in Belfast. She remembered her granny talking about red-leading the front step and had wondered why anyone would be bothered, not realising the sense of pride those working class women had taken in their homes. For that was obviously what this was. It was not a show house. It was a home, someone's pride and joy. The lawn was pristine, its edges razor sharp. She could imagine Mr Harris and his son working there on a summer's evening.

When they got up to the front door, she could see her own face reflected back at her in the glass panel. A strained, almost unrecognisable face. In the army she had had to write more condolence letters than she liked to remember, but that had been at a distance. She had not been there when they fell through the letterbox and landed with a dull heavy thud announcing their ominous contents. She had not had to be there when the knock came to their door and the life-changing words were spoken. She glanced across at the Family Liaison Officer beside her and was surprised to see a look of encouragement on her face. She was the senior officer. She should have been the one prepared for what lay ahead but this young woman was fully in control of herself and the situation. She stood back respectfully to let Gawn knock the door.

She knocked. Not too loudly. They waited. She felt the wait go on forever. Part of her hoped the family was not at home. Perhaps they were out late-night shopping or were visiting friends. But that would be cowardly. This had to be done and she should be the one to do it. That is what she had argued. She was his direct superior officer. It should not be some stranger who barely knew him. The porch light came on. Then she saw the outline of a man's figure approaching. The door opened and Mr Harris stood there, not quite an older replica of his son but the similarities were all there – the rugby player's build, the thick head of hair, the bright eyes, the open smile. There was no mistaking their relationship.

'Can I help you?' The voice was a little guarded. Like all police families, strangers coming to the door especially after dark were viewed with a certain amount of suspicion. Even if they didn't pose a threat, they could be trying to sell something or hoping to scam the elderly.

'Mr Harris, my name's Gawn Girvin.'

Before she could say anything else, he opened the door wider and his face broke out in a smile.

'Chief Inspector. Michael talks about you all the time.' Then it was as if a curtain had fallen down across his face. She could read what he was thinking. The man had realised that there could be no good reason why she would be visiting at their home at this time of night.

'Is it bad news?' There was a tremor in his voice.

'Could we come inside, sir? It would be better to talk inside than out here.'

Gawn was relieved that the sergeant had made the suggestion.

'This is Sergeant Lisa Kennedy.'

The man glanced across and smiled in a show of courtesy which came naturally to him. He already seemed to have shrunk even though they had not actually given him the news yet, not put it into hard, cold words. He turned and led the two women into a narrow hallway. Gawn noticed the ubiquitous print of a Chinese lady which she had seen hanging in so many homes. He led them into a front room and Gawn immediately thought of her visit with her sergeant to the Andrews home where they had been shown into just such a room set aside for visitors and special occasions.

'I'll get my wife.'

Left alone, Gawn and Kennedy didn't speak. They stood listening acutely for sounds coming from elsewhere in the house. For a minute, there was nothing but the ticking of a clock on the mantelpiece. Then they heard a woman sobbing.

'Do they always know?' Gawn asked.

'Mostly.'

Mr Harris appeared in the doorway pushing a woman in a wheelchair in front of him. She was clutching a handkerchief tightly to her face. It was already soaked with tears but she had regained her composure and it was the woman who spoke first.

'What happened? Is he…' She couldn't bring herself to finish the question.

Gawn knelt down in front of the wheelchair so that she was in the woman's direct eyeline rather than towering over her. She didn't even register the pain in her knee. She reached out and took the older woman's hand in hers. Her own action surprised her. She just felt a compulsion to do it; to offer the touch of a human hand in comfort.

'There's no easy way to tell you, Mrs Harris, Michael's dead.'

The woman gasped. She had known, of course, but to hear the words made it real, meant she could not pretend it was a mistake, a nightmare from which she would wake. Michael's father laid his hand on his wife's shoulder. Gawn could see it was shaking.

'How about I make us a wee cup of tea?' Gawn knew all about the healing properties of tea, copious amounts of it drunk after her father's funeral, then again when her mother died. It was part of the process. Part of the ritual which would help everyone get through this.

Lisa Kennedy, the Family Liaison Officer, would no doubt make lots of tea over the next few days. She would be the one staying with the family, helping them through the ordeal. She knew what they would need to do to register the death. She would arrange for them to see their son's body and accompany them to the mortuary. She would help them with the funeral arrangements. That would be more tricky this time when it wasn't an ordinary death. Of course, there was no such thing, but Kennedy knew that the funeral of a serving police officer killed in the line of duty would mean additional planning and she would have to negotiate between the PSNI hierarchy and the parents who might well have different ideas about what they wanted done.

Gawn stayed long enough to share a cup of tea. It was hot but she couldn't have told you anything else about it or about what was said in that room. Her attention was focused on this elderly couple whose lives had been changed utterly. She felt so sad for them. They were so gracious towards her. Michael had spoken of her often, they told her. He had been so pleased when he began to work on her team. When she eventually left, she made sure to leave her card and wrote her personal mobile number on the back.

'If there's anything I can do for you, anything at all, please get in touch. Michael was a fine police officer and a good man. I was proud to serve alongside him. I am so sorry for your loss.'

Her own words were still ringing in her ears as Kennedy walked her to the front door.

'Don't worry, ma'am. They'll be alright. Two minutes after you've gone, they'll start arriving. Word travels fast, especially bad news. The boiled cake and sandwich brigade will be here and I'll just sink into the background and let them reminisce and celebrate their son's life.'

'Is that how it works?'

'Usually. They'll get through it, ma'am.'

Kennedy closed the door behind her and Gawn noticed the curtains twitching in the next-door house. She was sure the FLO was right. If it brought them comfort, then so be it. She knew when she had lost Max she had just wanted to curl up into a ball and not speak to anyone but that was just her. Everyone was different. Whatever got them through.

Chapter 58

She didn't know who else she could tell. She considered ringing Jenny but she didn't know her well enough. They were building a friendship but it wasn't yet one where she could share her life like that with her. There was really only one person. Seb. She tried to pluck up the courage to ring him three times before she could bring herself to hit the call button. It went to voicemail. She wondered if he had blocked her; if he was going to sit and listen to what she had to say and then delete it or if he genuinely couldn't take her call. It had been nearly a week since their night at O'Halloran's. She knew he had been released from hospital three days ago.

'Seb, I don't know if you're there listening to this or if you're out or you're busy. I know you're probably still angry with me and I understand why. I just needed to tell you how sorry I am for what happened. I never intended for any of it. I did want just to be with you. I did want to talk about our future. I got caught up when you took us to the Shoreland for lunch. I didn't plan that. It was you who took us there. Then when you booked us a table at O'Halloran's, I still didn't know what was going to happen. I'm not making excuses. I was the one who suggested going to Sperrin Valley. I suppose it was all somewhere in the back of my mind but I never thought you would get hurt. When I saw you and I didn't know whether you were dead or alive, I realised how important you are in my life. I need you. I love you. I want to be with you. I need you in my life. I just can't think of life without you.'

Her voice was fading to barely louder than a whisper. Then she gathered herself and spoke again. 'I can't seem to help hurting the people around me. Michael's dead and that's my fault too. He wanted to impress me. I told him not to move; but he couldn't just stand by and do nothing. He said I wouldn't just stand by. It's his funeral on Monday. After that I don't know what will happen to me. I guess I could lose my job. But that wouldn't be as bad as losing you. I need you. I've never begged for anything in my life but I'm begging you to forgive me.'

She couldn't get another word out.

Chapter 59

Graveyards are always cold. No matter the time of year. No matter the weather. At least that's what Gawn thought. Even the guided tour she had taken to the First World War battlefields in France and Belgium in the height of summer when the temperatures were soaring was a cold experience for her. The things she remembered most about her visit to the Thiepval Tower and the Menin Gate were, yes, the rows of names of the young men commemorated there, row after row of them in long chiselled lists, but overwhelmingly a sense of coldness, of emptiness at such loss, such a deluge of sorrow.

The funeral service at St Anne's Cathedral had been suitably formal. Although it was meant to be all about Michael Harris, in reality it had been the PSNI on parade, their communal suffering on public view for the press and cameras. Not that that was done deliberately. Everything had been planned with military precision. Harris' family had been considered and consulted at every turn. She just wondered how much they had actually taken in as the whirlwind of events swirled around them, carrying them along in its wake.

The young uniformed officers, some of whom might have known Harris personally, were suitably serious and solemn-looking as they lined the steps up to the oversized front doors of the cathedral. The coffin bearers, all officers from the division where Harris had served, looked immaculate in uniforms which had never been so stiff and pristine before, as they concentrated on getting the coffin safely up the flight of steps without a fumble. The dean had spoken sympathetically, with compassion to the family, both the actual family and the police family, and seemed in his eulogy to have taken the time to find out about the young man lying cold in his Union Jack draped coffin at the front of the nave. The Chief Constable's booming voice had filled the cavernous space, hardly requiring use of any microphone. He had spoken well too, managing that precarious balancing act between what was essentially a sad personal occasion and the opportunity for political pronouncements about the dangers his officers faced every day doing their duty serving the public.

Gawn had dressed even more carefully this morning – if that were possible. She had had plenty of time to prepare; nearly a week of sitting at home with nothing to do but think and resist the temptation to open another bottle of wine. Her starched collar dug into her throat, her tie was so tight it threatened to cut off her air supply. Her shoes shone as they had in her army days. She had spent over an hour polishing them the previous evening, pouring her anger and grief into the repetitive action of the brush moving vigorously backwards and forwards across the leather. That was after she had come back from the funeral home.

Mr and Mrs Harris had been so gracious when she had asked their permission to visit Michael and told them what she wanted to do although she couldn't explain to them why. She had looked down on the young man lying so peacefully in his coffin and had placed her military medal on his chest. He had saved her life but the chances were no one would ever know. The newspapers were already reporting the incident at the farm as a shooting with Sean McGladdery sustaining a non-life-threatening wound and a police officer being fatally injured when a legally held firearm had been discharged in a struggle with a robber who had escaped and was being sought by police on both sides of the border.

There was no mention of the Fleischer. Just as he had lived in the shadows, an invisible figure who came and went, leaving a trail of death in his wake, so he had died. Her godfather Norman Smyth had visited her and explained that as far as everyone was concerned the Fleischer case was closed. In fact it had never been opened. The task force was working at bringing the Bako organisation to justice. Andrews and McGladdery were cooperating with the investigation and would be placed in witness protection after giving their evidence. They would simply disappear to begin a new life somewhere else in the world and the diamonds that Andrews had smuggled back for them in a bag of sweets had been recovered hidden in a water tank on the farm. She remembered the farmer tucking into his bag of sweets at the airport. If only they had searched them all that day, none of this might have happened and Michael would still be alive.

The last hymn *Amazing Grace* rang out bouncing off the old stone walls, the acoustics swelling the volume already provided by the PSNI choir and the vigorous singing of the congregation. Cynically Gawn wondered if the enthusiasm was for the sentiments of the hymn or in thankfulness that the ordeal was coming towards an end. She walked out down the central aisle following her superior officers. She tried not to look to right or left but her eyes met McKeown's as she passed her. The girl looked strange in uniform. Even in that brief single glance Gawn saw the tears swelling up in her eyes and felt a prickle behind her own in response. She glimpsed Jenny Norris in the crowd sitting near the back of the packed church, but thankfully the pathologist didn't seem to notice her. She was sure Paul Maxwell would be somewhere nearby but she was glad not to see him. That would be too much.

Outside, the noise of cameras whirring was almost overwhelming in the nearly silent street, drowning out the sound of distant traffic coming from Royal Avenue and the shuffling of feet and coughs of the onlookers trying to keep warm. It had been a cold stand. Applause broke out in the crowd as the coffin was manoeuvred back down the steps and slid into the waiting hearse. The six men marched off, no doubt relieved to have their part in the proceedings safely over, and the procession formed behind the sleek black undertaker's vehicle taking Harris on his last journey.

Mr Harris looked stooped and wizened as he and the other male members of his immediate family fell into place behind the hearse. The Chief Constable and the hierarchy of the PSNI formed into their allocated places behind with Gawn finding her spot beside the other chief inspectors and inspectors from local divisions. They set off at a slow pace just as a light flurry of snow began to fall. It had been threatening since last night and the weather forecasters had foretold its arrival but somehow it seemed appropriate that it should begin just now as if the sky was shedding its tears too, joining with those of Mrs Harris. Gawn had recognised her slumped inconsolably in the funeral car as she had passed it, the Family Liaison Officer sitting on one side of her with her arm around the older woman's shoulder. A younger woman, whom Gawn took to be Chloe, Harris' beloved girlfriend, sat dry-eyed on the other side. She stared straight ahead almost in a trance. Gawn had seen it before – the effects of the tablets provided by concerned doctors to 'get her through' the funeral.

They walked slowly past the John Hewitt and Gawn thought of her meeting with Jenny Norris there. She had had no idea as they sat over their meal that night of what lay ahead. The doors were closed today. No lights shone from inside. Later it would be open as usual with life going on as it always did for everyone else but the bereaved. An elderly man stood paused on the pavement near the front door and took his cloth cap off his head in a show of respect as the cortège passed. Her meeting there seemed so long ago now. So much had happened since then.

When they reached the end of Donegall Street the procession came to a halt. The family made their way to the following funeral cars. The Chief Constable, accompanied by ACC Smyth, walked over to his official car and, once inside, it moved slowly away towards High Street. The crowd started to break up. Some stepped onto the pavement in groups to wait until the hearse and funeral cars had moved away. One or two walked briskly away, keen to get out of sight to be able to light up their cigarettes while dressed in uniform.

Gawn turned without a word and made her way back the same way they had just walked. She passed the front of the cathedral where the doors were already closed and most of the crowd had dispersed back to their usual activities. She made her way to the cathedral's private car park and got into her car. Only then did she allow herself to take a deep breath. It seemed as if she had almost been holding her breath throughout the service. She clutched the steering wheel with both hands, tightening her grip until her knuckles turned white. She could feel herself beginning to shake. She clenched her teeth. She would not give in to the almost overwhelming sense of sadness she was feeling. She had been here before. She had buried young men before, men of Harris' age and younger. She had watched the grief of their loved ones, the attempts to assuage a sense of utter devastation with a sense of pride of what their son, husband, father, brother, had done and been. She became aware of other uniformed people, mostly men, moving past her car making their way to their own vehicles. One or two of them glanced in at her sitting there. She ran the back of her hand across her eyes and turned the key in the ignition. What had gone before was easier than what was to come. Mrs Harris had phoned and invited her to attend the private family burial at Roselawn Cemetery. So that was where she was headed now.

Chapter 60

She was glad of the heavy black serge coat she had brought to wear over her uniform. Its mid-calf length kept out some of the biting wind which swirled around her legs and the pulled-up collar saved her from the worst of the flurries of snow which were getting heavier. She was glad it covered her uniform. She wasn't here as a policewoman or even as Harris' boss, she hoped. She was here as his friend; as someone who mourned his loss too; as someone who owed her very life to him. She was not so self-consumed that she couldn't recognise that any sense of loss she might be feeling was nothing when compared with what his parents and Chloe were experiencing. Their futures had been stolen from them. Their lives would never be the same again. Nor was she so lacking in self-awareness that she didn't recognise some element of guilt in her feelings about his loss even though she had not ordered him to do what he did. She thought he might have been trying to impress her and that made her incredibly sad. She couldn't help but think of her own daughter too. Max had wanted to impress her just like Harris. She had joined the army to be like her, to make her proud. But she had already been proud of the young woman. Losing Max had left an emptiness in her heart. She knew how Mr and Mrs Harris were feeling.

There were only a few people who had made the journey out of Belfast to the cemetery on the edge of the city up the Castlereagh Hills. Most were men, none were police officers. There was a short eulogy, thankfully short in the biting wind. Now the vicar was reading from the 23rd psalm, the familiar words washing over her. '*Yea, though I walk through the valley of the shadow of death, I will fear no evil.'* She had walked through that valley. She had faced evil and goodness had won. This time. But she wondered how much longer she could go on when the world seemed such a dark place.

She became aware of someone moving in beside her and wondered who felt they needed to be so close; to invade her personal space. She turned her head to look and saw Sebastian York standing there, eyes staring straight ahead, not looking at her. Just being there. She noticed the scar on his temple, still red and livid from their night at the restaurant. She felt his hand touch against hers, his fingers warm while hers were icy cold. She allowed their fingers to intertwine. He squeezed her hand then, still without looking directly at her.

As the final prayer was intoned and the crowd began to move away from the open grave, Gawn turned away too. Now wasn't the time to speak to Mr and Mrs Harris. She would do that later in private when all the fuss was over and the sense of their loss had finally had time to sink in. She walked away from the grave and towards the car park at the top of the hill, disappointed when Seb withdrew his hand from hers. Then she felt the strength of his arm across her back, his hand resting lightly on her shoulder. He leaned his head close to hers and whispered into her ear. In the bleakness of the scene all around her and of the occasion, there was nothing he could have said that would have meant more to her.

'No matter what, Gawn.'

If you enjoyed this book, please let others know by leaving a quick review on Amazon. Also, if you spot anything untoward in the paperback, get in touch. We strive for the best quality and appreciate reader feedback.

editor@thebookfolks.com

MORE IN THIS SERIES

THE PERFUME KILLER (Book 1)

Stumped in a multiple murder investigation, with the only clue being a perfume bottle top left at a crime scene, DCI Gawn Girvin must wait for a serial killer to make a wrong move. Unless she puts herself in the firing line...

A FORCE TO BE RECKONED WITH (Book 3)

Investigating a cold case about a missing person, DCI Gawn Girvin stumbles upon another unsolved crime. A murder. But that is just the start of her problems. The clues point to powerful people who will stop at nothing to protect themselves, and some look like they're dangerously close to home.

KILLING THE VIBE (Book 4)

After a man's body is found with strange markings on his back, DCI Girvin and her team try to establish his identity. Convinced they are dealing with a personally motivated crime, the trail leads them to a group of people involved in a pop band during their youth. Will the killer face the music or get off scot-free?

THAT MUCH SHE KNEW (Book 5)

A woman is found murdered. The same night, state pathologist Jenny Norris goes missing. Worried that her colleague might be implicated, DCI Gawn Girvin in secret investigates the connection between the women. But Jenny has left few clues to go on, and before long Girvin's solo tactics risk muddling the murder investigation and putting her in danger.

MURDER ON THE TABLE (Book 6)

A charity dinner event should be a light-hearted affair, but two people dying as the result of one is certainly likely to put a damper on proceedings. DCI Gawn Girvin is actually an attendee, and ready at the scene to help establish if murder was on the table. But the bigger question is why, and if Gawn can catch a wily killer.

NOTHING BUT SMILES (Book 7)

A serial stalker is terrorising women on the streets of Belfast. The victims wake up with no recollection of the night before, but with a smiley-face calling card daubed on their bodies. DCI Gawn Girvin takes on the case although before long she herself is targeted. She must catch the sick creep before matters escalate.

All available free with Kindle Unlimited and in paperback!

www.thebookfolks.com

Printed in Great Britain
by Amazon

44881012R00148